TO KILL AN
EMPEROR

Like time-travel?

Check out the Turning Points series
at jodielane.com

The Siege of Masada
Transylvanian Knight
To Kill An Emperor
Renaissance Woman
Heart and Stomach of a Queen

Turning Points Short Stories:

Siege of the Heart
The Time-Traveller's Date
A Soldier's Love

TO KILL AN EMPEROR

JODIE LANE

To Kill An Emperor
Copyright © 2023 Jodie Lane

ISBN: 978-0-6487683-3-3

First published 2017 by Jodie Lane
www.jodielane.com

To Cazi and Nick.

ACKNOWLEDGMENTS

Once again, thank you to my family and friends for demanding the next book. You saw how my writing had improved between Masada and Knight, and told me so—as always, your encouragement is invaluable.

To my beta readers: Carolyn, Kate, Zane, Rebecca, Alicia, Jess, David—I love your feedback, criticism and encouragement. Anything that makes me think critically about my writing strengthens it, so thank you. My proof-readers: Mum, Barb and Tracey—you cleaned up my typos and punctuation, all those things my creative genius simply ignores (at least that's my story and I'm sticking to it).

To Dee, my mentor and friend. Once again you shredded my manuscript with good humour and an eagle eye, ridding it of fluff words and giving me just enough praise before your mocked my bad writing habits. I love it.

One

PRESENT DAY

Betrayed. Gwyn felt betrayed.

Why had she thought it was a good idea to tell her mother and sister about her time travel? She had arrived back from Transylvania battered, heartsick and injured and the pressure had been too much. Now they were treating her like she was crazy. She could hear the whispers between her parents as they hastily discussed potential psychologists here in Rome.

"What about Dr Rose Tran? Wasn't she having a sabbatical in the south of France? We could detour on our way to Spain." *Typical dad, trying not to upset the family holiday too much.*

"Stephen, she needs to see someone *now*. I don't know if she actually believes all this or if it's just a cry for attention, but it's serious. She's been starving herself, I'm sure, and engaging in self-harm."

Gwyn clenched her jaw but remained quiet as she listened at the door. She had lost weight but her body had toughened into muscle. Horse riding and walking every day—not to mention a far more restricted diet—would do that to a girl. But the self-harm comment upset her—her cuts, bruises, scrapes and wounds were proof of what she'd endured. Or so she had thought.

"Psst! Gwyn!"

Gwyn startled at being caught eavesdropping but then frowned. "Go away," she hissed at her sister.

"I just want to talk to you." Naomi's whisper was urgent. Gwyn ignored the pleading, flapping her hand, trying to dismiss her sister. The younger girl refused. Gwyn stalked back to the bedroom she shared with

1

her siblings, Naomi trailing behind her. Justin was asleep but the lamp beside his bed was still on, so the poky hotel room was lit in a warm orange glow.

"Please, Gwyn—"

Gwyn cut her sister off with a furious glare. "I don't want to talk to you. Go to sleep. We're going to be walking all day tomorrow." She flopped onto her makeshift bed—blankets and pillow on the faded carpet—and shut her eyes.

* * *

That was another thing, Gwyn realized with grim satisfaction as they trekked up and down the streets of Rome, she was fitter than she'd ever been. The cloudless blue sky offered a spectacular backdrop to the Spanish Steps and the Trevi Fountain, but by mid-afternoon the sun beat down and her parents called for a gelato break. Her brother and sister fanned themselves gratefully with paper serviettes. Gwyn slid into a hard plastic chair simply because it was in the shade. She could have kept walking, following the cheerful tour guide up and down the crowded streets of the Italian capital, losing herself in tales of history.

The gelato *was* good, if ridiculously overpriced. She shouted her family, wanting to make sure they hung around for the next tour. She didn't want to go back to the cheap hotel near Termini and she knew they wouldn't let her stay out by herself. *Huh. I've faced far worse than a bit of street harassment and risk of pickpocketing.* Her parents had been treating her like glass ever since they had left Romania a week ago.

"Well," her father said brightly, "isn't all this history interesting, Gwyn? Justin, Naomi—thank your sister for the ice cream."

The twins mumbled thanks through lemon sorbet and double chocolate and Gwyn's anger threatened to bubble out. Her parents were scientists, skeptical of wild tales, and rightly so. But the evidence she'd shown them—the stab wound in her shoulder, still healing, and the pocket-watch itself fused into her hand—should have been enough to make them believe her. *This stupid pocket-watch only works when it wants to!* She ground her teeth. She'd broken her word to the Time-Agent Michelle, telling her family, and this was her reward.

Gwyn found her anger directed at Michelle. *Interfering, arrogant cow! And where is she when I need her?* Gwyn had brought herself back to her own time without the help of the Time-Space Agent but she expected the woman to show up and… fix things?

Instead she was trying to act normal when her family thought she was nuts. This was supposed to be a holiday to escape her boring life back home. She needed time alone to think, to sort through everything that had happened to her, to exorcise the demons of her nightmares: Joshua and Vlad.

"The Turner family?"

They all looked up. A fashionably-dressed Italian woman with a lanyard and name tag proclaiming her to be Maria Sinardi, Official Tour Guide, smiled at the Australians. Gwyn snorted as her father inhaled the last of his gelato and, coughing slightly, held out a sweaty hand to shake.

"That's us! You're taking the Colosseum and Palace Hill tour?" he asked.

Gwyn rolled her eyes, "Palatine Hill, Dad."

"Yes, I am." Maria smiled, her makeup immaculate despite the heat and her Gucci sunglasses balanced on her elegant curls. For a second Gwyn was reminded of Alina but Maria was taller and slimmer. Gwyn scooped the last of her gelato into her mouth to suppress the dart of pain that struck her chest then fussed with her bag.

"Let's go, kids." Gwyn's mother encouraged them out of the café and the tour began.

* * *

"Actually known as the Flavian Amphitheatre, this arena was a grand attempt by Vespasian and his sons to ensure their popularity in Roma." Maria spoke smoothly, her Italian accent not marring her clarity. "The Flavian Emperors were a new dynasty that established themselves after the chaos of the Year of the Four Emperors. They knew that keeping the people of Roma entertained with gladiator fights and races in the Circus Maximus meant fewer plots to overthrow the Emperor."

"Where did the gladiators come out?" Justin had been bored on the earlier tour, but the prospect of blood and death caught his interest.

"And the lions?" Naomi seemed to be competing with her twin for morbidity. "What did they do with all the bodies—feed them to the lions?"

Their guide fielded their questions with an indulgent look, seemingly unsurprised by the typical tourist area of interest. Gwyn wandered down steps and closed her eyes, imagining how it must have looked in its hey-day: sparkling marble, large shade-sails over the seats rising up behind her, crowds bustling and the shouts of gladiators and other entertainers in the arena below.

A bump from a careless American tourist jolted Gwyn out of her daydream. She shot a furious glare at the American's oblivious back and thumped her fist on the railing, then saw her mother watching her worriedly. Gwyn scowled in the other direction.

"If you'd like to follow me?" Maria herded her charges through the crowded Colosseum, giving interesting facts and tidbits of information, before leading them out past the costumed centurions towards the Arch of Constantine. The twins sniggered at the centurions heckling other tourists but Gwyn just glared at any who dared cross her path. One persisted and told Gwyn to smile.

"Fuck off," she snarled. *I'm not here to light up your day, buddy—smiling is not a bloody obligation.*

"Gwyn!"

"Sorry, Mum." She didn't sound sorry but she didn't care. Accelerating past the last of the impersonators, she reached the Arch of Constantine first.

"We're doing all these tours to keep you happy, you know." Naomi was hard on her heels. "You don't have to be such a bitch to everyone."

Gwyn's response was fortunately cut off by Maria joining them. The rest of the Turners trailed her and the tour on the Palatine began.

"While an imperial house was built here by Tiberius, it is best known for being Domitian's palace. He was the third Flavian Emperor, and was assassinated by his servants and his wife. He was so paranoid he had the walls polished so he could see the reflections, so nobody could sneak up on him. He was also infamous for stabbing flies with his writing pen."

"Like a nasty little boy who never grew up," Gwyn's mum commented.

"He was not a nice person," Maria agreed. "He took his niece, Julia, for a mistress, but when she became pregnant he forced her to have an abortion and she died. He was heartbroken—Julia was his true love and after he was assassinated his old nurse mixed his ashes with that of his niece so they could be together forever." Maria gestured for them to follow her and pointed out features of the palace, like the gardens and the banquet hall.

Gwyn reflected that this is why people took tours on these ancient sites; crumbled stone walls and grassy steps hid the significance of the site. *Maybe I'll go on to study archaeology so I can actually interpret sites like these.*

At least there was a breeze up here. "The Ancient Romans were quite sophisticated when it came to heating and air conditioning their palaces," Maria told them as they walked on. "Tunnels under the floors carried cool breezes through in summer, and in winter fires were banked at the entrances of those tunnels and slaves fanned the warm air along."

"Clever." Gwyn's dad was impressed. Gwyn herself wasn't feeling so well. The breeze wasn't doing enough to cool her and her stomach turned over. A noise like waves on a beach filled her ears but they were nowhere near the sea. Her eyes blurred and a spine-tingling sensation washed through her. When her vision cleared she saw her mother peering in concern.

"What's wrong? Are you about to faint?"

Gwyn waved feebly and sat down hard, feeling sick. Orange blossoms peeked out from the grass edging the ruins. She focused on the petals until her breathing slowed.

"Is she alright?" A bearded man crouched beside Gwyn. "You might need some water," he offered.

Gwyn stared at him. She knew she'd never seen him before but his name tag pronounced him to be Mario Sinardi, Official Tour Guide.

"What happened to Maria?" she exclaimed.

Her parents exchanged puzzled glances with the guide. "Who's Maria?" her father asked.

Nausea retreated and Gwyn hauled herself to her feet. "I… I just felt a bit sick for a second. Sorry." She tried not to freak out at the fact that her father's hair was much shorter than it normally was—had he had it cut and she hadn't noticed? No, other things were different. Her mother wore a blue shirt, not the floral blouse she'd had on earlier. The twins were dressed differently too and when she gazed back down the hill to the Colosseum she gasped to see a massive tower on the far side which had not existed when they had walked around the ruin not half an hour past.

Don't panic. Something has changed. You just need to work out what. Her mind leapt to that awful, impossible, obvious conclusion. Only she had felt that sensation, and only she noticed a difference in the world.

History had changed.

Two

PRESENT DAY

What should she do? Panic lurked in Gwyn's chest. This was far more serious than she could handle alone. She wasn't qualified! She needed Michelle.

If only she'd given me some way to contact her! There was nothing for it. She was going to have to jump forward into Michelle's time and try to get in touch somehow. Her mind reached for the timepiece. Except... if she jumped forward from now, what kind of future would she find? Would Michelle even exist? The paradox had her trembling and uncertainty gnawed at her stomach. In her brain, the timeline stretched out in front of her as a haze of fine threads. The past was firm and solid but the future was as diaphanous as a cord of mist.

"Gwyn, you need a doctor, you're not well." Her mother clutched Gwyn's arm.

"I'm really sorry, Mario, but we're going to have to cut the tour short," her father doled out Euros as a tip, apologizing profusely to their guide. Mario accepted the money graciously and advised them he could arrange a taxi to take them to the English speaking doctors near Circo Massimo.

"No!" Gwyn protested. "I'm fine. Please can we finish the tour?" *I have to find out what went wrong. I have to find out what's different.*

"I'm sorry, dear," her mother began but Gwyn cut her off.

"I'm fine, Mum! Please! I'll see a doctor as soon as we're done. I'll see a shrink if you like! Please can we just finish the tour?"

The whole family stared at her pleading face in silence.

Mario suggested, "Perhaps we have a little rest, five minutes, no?

7

Drink water, sit." He gestured with both hands.

It broke the tension. Gwyn stood and marched to a rock, sitting down firmly and crossing her arms. The twins milled about and their parents conferred while Mario distanced himself enough to make an animated phone call in Italian. Justin and Naomi came over to Gwyn and sat down on the ground facing her. She eyed them warily, wishing they would buzz off so she could think about what to do.

"Naomi told me what's going on with you." Justin spoke, surprising Gwyn. She had expected their sister to talk.

"And?" she replied acidly. "She tell you I'm nuts?"

"Yeah but we knew that anyway," Justin rolled his eyes, and despite herself, Gwyn gave a half-hearted chuckle.

"Look, sis," Naomi shot a glance at their parents, who had moved away to argue quietly. "I'm sorry I took Mum's side before, when you first told us. It seemed crazy. But I do believe you. About the time travel and stuff."

"What?"

"Even I can see you're different," Justin chipped in. "And Nau was sharing a room with you—she can tell you've changed since we went to Israel. Mum and Dad haven't been around so they think something must've been going on back home before we came over, but you were your plain, boring self until we went to Masada."

"And there's your weird tattoo thing. Like I wouldn't have noticed you get that!"

Gwyn stared at her brother and sister. She felt nothing from the pocket-watch—no persuasion was in play here. "You... do believe me?" Her anger and panic subsided somewhat.

"Well," the twins exchanged looks as Justin spoke. "Can you prove it?"

The fury bubbled up again but Naomi put out a hand and touched Gwyn's arm. "Don't get pissed off. You've told us all this stuff but if it's really real, which we believe it is, it shouldn't be a problem to show us. Like, how does it work? Do you just disappear or something?"

Tempting. "I have to concentrate," Gwyn ground out. "And it takes a lot of energy." That was one thing she'd learned the hard way from her forays into Transylvania and Wallachia. Multiple jumps in short succession burnt her out. "But I can show you later. We have to finish this tour." Why later? Why not show her parents too? She could jump a minute into the future and they'd get the shock of their lives when she reappeared.

But wouldn't they just drag you to a physicist instead of a psychologist? Her parents' quest for knowledge was wonderful but Gwyn had no desire to become some sort of lab pet. If what she felt when she connected to the timepiece was correct, jumping into the future was fraught with uncertainty. To make the knowledge of time travel public in this time would probably mess up the time-space continuum even more.

Which spun her mind back to the current dilemma. Something was wrong and she had to find out what. "Look," she said, "I can't muck around showing you right now. But I will later, I promise." *After I've fixed things.* She waved them away as she stood and advanced on the tour guide.

Mario smiled and finished his phone call. "Feeling better?"

"Si, grazie." Gwyn heard the Italian trip out of her mouth and realized she'd instinctively spoken in his language. She concentrated on speaking English. "Can you tell me again what you said just before we came up here? I don't remember, sorry." She ignored her parents and siblings gathering behind her.

"Of course," Mario smiled. "I said how this palace was so sophisticated that tunnels under the floor acted as air conditioners or heaters depending on whether slaves fanned cool air or lit fires to heat the place. It was quite ingenious."

Gwyn nodded, but that fact didn't help. It was the same as what Maria had said. "And where was Domitian assassinated?" she asked.

Mario's smile was puzzled, but he answered kindly. "You must be thinking of another Emperor. Nero perhaps? His botched suicide was the end to a despicable and debaucherous life, but that took place at a villa outside Roma."

Gwyn frowned. "No one killed Domitian?"

"One man, Stephanus, came very close to assassinating Domitian, but the Emperor fought him off and killed him. Domitian's niece and wife were found guilty of treason for plotting with his freedmen, and executed. The Emperor never married again." He shrugged. "Some said he was too cynical after the treachery of his wife, but others claimed he was heartbroken by the death of his niece Julia, who was his mistress and died while pregnant with his child."

Gwyn didn't hear the rest. This was wrong. *Domitian was assassinated. Nerva became Emperor. Crap. This is all wrong.*

But what could she do? She didn't dare jump ahead into an uncertain future to search for a Michelle who might not even be there. And if she jumped back in time… well, was she just going to kill Domitian herself? *Like I could manage that.*

"Gwyn, this really is silly." It was her mother again. "You've zoned out again, I think you need to see a doctor right away."

"She is acting strange," Justin muttered to Naomi.

Gwyn hadn't moved but her family stood in a circle around her. Mario hovered uncertainly, hand clutching his phone. She frowned at them all. *I'm not crazy!* she wanted to shout. *Can't you see how important this is?*

They couldn't see—of course they couldn't—and it would take too long to explain and convince and persuade. Even if her parents believed her they would never let her rush off to a highly dangerous mission to murder someone. Who was she kidding? It was crazy.

That made her angrier. Her mother stepped towards her with an outstretched hand so Gwyn looked at the guide, Mario, instead. She used him as a focal point and slowed her breathing, closing her eyes.

She saw and felt the timeline in her mind's eye, using the pocket watch to reach back along it, searching for the moment she needed. When had it gone wrong? The timeline blurred past as her thoughts blew along it into the past.

There. A zig-zag was the best description she could give. Somewhere, here in Rome, something had not gone the way it should have. She would have to find out what and override it, ensuring the plot against the Emperor succeeded. She'd have to stay in the background— shadowy, so her own presence there wouldn't derail history even more.

She focused on the moments just before the zig-zag. Perhaps it was as simple as preventing Domitian from fighting off his attacker. Maybe all she had to do was create a distraction so the killer could do his job.

They'll freak out! She thought of the panic that would ensue when she vanished in front of her family. *No, you are fixing the timeline! It will never have happened.* She would make things right. No one would treat her like a child then.

Her concentration was broken by her mother grabbing her arm. "Gwyn!"

Gwyn shook her off and clutched after the moment. *Ancient Rome!* She had it, but the thought of Ancient Rome brought another face to light in her memory. A sunny smile, a carefree air.

Her mind slipped.

Flick!

Three

96 AD

Blue haze faded. Lovely, multi-colored marble lay under her feet. It was shiny, though not as shiny as the white marble walls, which contrasted brilliantly with the floor and showed the reflection of an anxious girl staring back at her. Other figures crowded the shine of the marble, but Gwyn barely registered them.

Stupid! You were thinking of Gaius so you messed up the times! You need to jump forward now! She was so angry but knew she needed to find a quiet corner to compose herself before jumping again. Her head was all scrambled. She didn't feel sick but her stomach clenched.

She backed up, desperate to find an quiet nook or alcove, and bumped into an elegant double-handled vase on a plinth. It teetered for a moment then crashed down onto the floor, drawing the attention of everyone in the chamber.

Gwyn froze.

"Who are you?" an indignant scribe demanded. "What business do you have in here?" He glared up from his elegantly carved desk, ink dripping from his stylus. People in the room stared at Gwyn. Young men and women in white tunics paused in their tasks of sweeping, carrying documents and serving trays of tidbits and drinks. Other people, well dressed, halted their conversations and gaped at her. Her clothes were nothing like theirs. She was sweaty and shaken, in this elegant room of palatial business. She didn't belong, and they knew it.

"Somebody seize her."

Gwyn didn't know who said it.

Panic set in. Her mind was not calm and as such the timepiece was

12

not in reach. Gwyn did the only logical thing with two slaves reaching towards her.

She ran.

* * *

Gwyn burst out of the chamber and pelted across a colonnade. A large courtyard lay before her, elegantly centered on a beautiful fountain. She dodged slaves and several stern-faced old men in togas who populated the peristyle. Exclamations of annoyance turned to shouts of dismay as her pursuers barreled after her. Gwyn concentrated on escape, not squashed toes.

One day I have to learn to be calm enough to time-jump when I'm being chased! She ducked under the outstretched arm of a burly man and almost went flying when she tripped on the foot of a man carrying a pile of scrolls. By some fluke she staggered but stayed upright while his scrolls went flying.

Gwyn dashed through a doorway and hurtled through room after room, desperate to find an exit. Another giant courtyard featuring a pool with a tiny island confronted her. This courtyard was emptier. Fewer obstacles meant she could speed up, but so could the slaves chasing her. A peek backwards showed two Praetorian guards had joined them. She thought about finding a corner or cupboard to hide in but dismissed the idea immediately. They'd find her before she had a chance to focus and jump.

She changed tack, zig-zagging through tall columns and back through a small chamber. This part of the palace was less ostentatious—it seemed to be for those in service; slaves and freedmen alike. The Roman tendency to build adjoining rooms kept her going through doorway after doorway. She prayed she wouldn't hit a dead end.

Sunlight! Another colonnade, much longer, stretching out left and right. A moment's hesitation then she made left, aiming for the arch that fed a steady stream of people in and out of the palace on a narrow paved road.

Two Praetorian guards stood at the arch, but their attention was on those entering the palace. The guards behind her had almost caught up when Gwyn launched herself up the stepped base of one of the grand columns.

Step, step, jump! She was lighter than the guards in their armor but still landed hard on the stones. She cried out in pain from her jarred knee but kept her momentum going. She flew across the courtyard and through the arch.

"Stop her!" She heard one guard yell as he attempted to duplicate her feat. She flashed a look behind as an almighty crash sounded and a flurry of curses stung Gwyn's ears. The other guard shoved through the people lingering at the base of the columns, but she had her lead now. The guards on the gate were too busy staring in confusion at the spectacle of her enraged pursuers.

Gwyn limped away from the arch and down the hill. She turned left onto a busy street. The Forum was ahead. The crowd provided only a moment's cover before an angry shout behind her spurred her into a run. She had been spotted.

Where can I go? Her heart pounded. The burning in her lungs was matched only by the pain in her knee, but the thought of what those guards might do to her kept her legs moving.

The street became busier as she lurched downhill. *More people means more cover? Or more witnesses?* She risked a glance around. The Praetorians hadn't given up, but her stunt over the column pedestal meant she had a bigger lead. They were shoving and hitting anyone slow enough to get in their way. Nobody was fool enough to put up a fight. "Move!" the guards screamed.

People scattered. "Look out!" a man cried, pulling a friend to safety. Gwyn wove between slaves, citizens and animals in the street. She dodged behind a food stall and half-ran, half-limped down the alleyway behind it. Shaded entrances and loitering dogs were all she saw. She considered hiding in the alley itself but the heavy footsteps of the guards told her that her attempt to lose them had failed.

Why do they have to be so bloody persistent! She leapt over a sleeping mutt and emerged from the alley into bright sunlight. *Where now?*

This street was less affluent than those near the palace, though still rich enough to have solid walls and gates. Gwyn couldn't keep running, so she ducked into a gateway set into a wall. She heaved great breaths.

"What is you doing?" a voice demanded and Gwyn jerked in fright. The gateway had a shuttered window in the wall beside her so the doorkeeper could look out. That little window was open now, and the face frowning at her belonged to a young African man with close-cropped black hair and a terrible scar clawing its way across his right cheek and eye.

"Please!" Gwyn whispered forcefully, still pressed against the wall. "Don't say anything." She willed him to cooperate.

His face disappeared for a moment and she heard a shutter open then close on the other side of his tiny gatehouse. Then swearing erupted and the young man rattled a cudgel against Gwyn's window.

"Get out! Those be palace guards. My master is crucifying me if you is bringing the Emperor's eye onto this house. Go on, go!"

He was so fierce that Gwyn gulped tears of desperation and fright and lurched forth again. Her brief respite had given her just enough time to catch her breath and she was grateful she was so much fitter than she used to be. She forced herself to ignore the pain in her legs and put on more speed, cutting through two more alleyways. She was running out of downhill. She knew at some point other guards would step in—it was a miracle none had already—or the Praetorians would catch up.

She'd managed to gain a lead but they were dogged. Changing tactics, Gwyn dashed up a stairway. If she could hide somewhere long enough to calm down and exude a sense of blankness, they might pass over her. She was out of puff.

The doorway at the top of the stairs opened into an unoccupied room. The furniture was plain wood—worn from use but not dilapidated. Gwyn fell through the second doorway, flailing past a beaded curtain that served as a privacy screen, and startled two astonished women. One was heavily pregnant and the other middle aged. The room had no other exits, save a window.

Shit! Tears fell freely now as she begged the women for help. "Hide me! Please!" *It's no good—why would they hide you against guards that everyone is terrified of?*

An eternity passed in a second and the older woman pointed to the wooden bed in the room. "Under there. Quick!"

Gwyn didn't wait. She dived under and rolled on her side to see blankets fall across her field of vision.

"Get on the bed, Maria," the older woman ordered. "Pretend the babe is come early. Be loud."

The wood creaked above Gwyn's head as the pregnant woman, Maria, heaved herself onto the bed and began to groan theatrically.

"Louder!" the older woman hissed, then called, "Breathe, Maria! The baby comes!"

Footsteps thumped up the stairs and a man's voice shouted, "In the Emperor's name!"

Maria half-groaned, half-shrieked, and the footsteps halted just inside the room. Gwyn dared not move.

"How can we be of service to our great and wise Master and God?" Gwyn heard the older woman say. She had an accent that sounded familiar, but Gwyn couldn't place it. She concentrated on being invisible.

"We're chasing a thief and a spy, woman, a girl. She came in here!" The guard sounded out of breath and Gwyn wondered if she'd almost outrun them. But then the other guard spoke and she dismissed that thought. He sounded fresh, and annoyed.

"I heard someone come into the other room and run into the kitchen." The older woman was deferential, but calm. "But I could not leave Maria, here—she is at her time."

As if to emphasize the point, Maria groaned and shifted. The bed creaked again. Gwyn realized her breathing had gone shallow and deepened it, projecting dullness. *Go away*, she prayed. *You don't want to be here in this room with a woman in labor. How icky! You're uncomfortable. You want to leave and look elsewhere.*

As if to answer her prayers, she heard one guard grunt in disgust or discomfort. Maria screamed and thumped the bed. Gwyn twitched at the creak of the wooden bed frame every time Maria's fists connected with the thin straw mattress.

"There's no girl here, Sextus. The only females here are either too old or too gravid to give us a merry chase. Those stupid slaves should never have let her get out of the room."

"Forgive me, Domine," the woman begged. "Please search the house if you seek a criminal. We house none here who dare speak or act against our lord and master."

What? She's selling you out! Gwyn panicked for only a second before common sense overtook her. The woman was trying to show she had nothing to hide in the hope that they'd not bother to look.

"Go back to your women's business." The one called Sextus sounded as if he was sneering. On cue, Maria groaned. The footsteps faded away and Gwyn almost grinned, but pain and exhaustion caught up with her and she slumped flat on the floor in relief instead. She heard whispers, then Maria said loudly.

"The pains have passed, mother, I think it was a false alarm."

"Very good. Fetch some things, my dear—I think you should come stay with your father and I until your time comes." The older woman bent down to peer under the bed. "You can come out now."

Gwyn crawled out from her hiding place and looked at the women. "Thank you so much. You saved me. I'm not a thief or a spy; I was just in the wrong place at the wrong time."

Maria's mother looked at her, dark eyes unfathomable, then said, "Your things, Maria—we'll send a slave for the rest and to tell your husband."

"Aye, mother, though I think you worry too much." Maria answered slightly sardonically. She appeared several years older than Gwyn but the other woman didn't look old enough to be her mother. *Maybe she's adopted.*

"Let me worry about who worries," Maria's mother snapped back. "What if those guards decide to come back and search the house? I don't want you here then. Fetch your things!"

Maria huffed and waddled out of the room, clattering into the kitchen. Gwyn wiped a dust-smudged hand across her forehead and cringed at the grit she smeared there.

"You need something to eat," Maria's mother said, looking every bit the Roman matron but with a hint of the exotic. Dark eyes, with twists of grey hair winding through black braids into a severe looking bun.

"I do, but –" She halted. Her brain told her one thing, but her ears told her another. *That wasn't Latin. That sounded like… Hebrew.*

Maria's mother stepped forward and gripped Gwyn's chin, tilting it gently upwards and peering into her face. "Gwyna?" she whispered, eyes widening in disbelief. She mispronounced it, stumbling over the "g" to say "Guh-winna" but Gwyn knew her all the same. Amazement pricked tears into Gwyn's eyes.

"Adi."

Her friend enfolded Gwyn in an immense hug.

Four

96 AD

Gwyn was full of questions but had to wait. They disguised her in an old green dress of Maria's and braided her hair, covering it with a shawl. Progress through the busy Roman streets was slow. The pregnant Maria waddled and complained, even after Gwyn offered to carry her bundle. Gwyn herself dared not whinge—she'd brought this trouble on them— but as they trekked up yet another of Rome's hills, she thought she would scream in impatience. The smell of sweat, food and animals in the late summer heat assaulted her and she longed for a cool drink.

"Here." Adi gestured them into a ground floor tenement. She welcomed them in and Maria made straight for an inner room. "Sit down, Gwyn," Adi sank onto a wide wooden chair, padded with cushions. Gwyn copied her and looked about. The room was simple and tidy, with few ornaments or pieces of furniture. The rugs that lay across the stone couches were rich in color, matching the cushions on the chairs. A half-furled scroll lay on a table, fruit sat in a bowl.

Adi called out, "Antonia!" but got no answer. Frowning, she got back up and raised a palm for Gwyn to stay put. She disappeared momentarily and Gwyn fidgeted, hearing a girl's voice—not Maria's— arguing. Then Adi returned with a jug of water and poured for herself and Gwyn.

"My daughter, Antonia, is bringing us something to eat," she said. An awkward silence fell, which Gwyn didn't know how to break. She gulped her water instead. A sulky teenager entered the room bearing a tray with a bowl of olives, bread and oil. Simple food, but good.

"Thank you, my dear. You may go help Maria, if you wish."

"Who is this, mother?" Antonia looked Gwyn over, unimpressed. "You're not one of mother's friends. I've never seen you before."

Gwyn wasn't sure how to respond. Adi saved her by waving her daughter away. "She is a distant cousin of mine, from Judea. Go help your sister, please."

Antonia flounced out. Gwyn was glad. She had so much she wanted to ask!

"Adi," she tried at the same time as her friend said,

"Gwyn—how is it you are here, and that you look still as you do? I— is it magic? Have you been sent by God to warn or punish us?" Her voice trembled and Gwyn realized her friend was afraid.

Well, look at what happened last time you appeared. Invasion, siege, mass suicide. Gwyn broke the pause and shook her head. "No, it's just me. Um, I mean, it is a kind of magic. I had no idea you'd be here, in Rome! I'm so glad you are okay! I–" She choked up, overwhelmed with relief and guilt. She knelt in front of Adi and clasped her hand. "I'm so sorry I abandoned you there, at Masada. I wondered and wondered if you would be alright." Tears welled in her eyes.

Adi stared at her, looking confused. "Don't cry, Gwyn. You saved me, remember, from Joshua and the Romans. If it weren't for you..." she trailed off.

"And Sarah?" Gwyn sniffed. "And the children who were there with you?"

"Sarah died on the voyage here." Adi's eyes became distant. "It broke her heart to leave her land, but the rest of us had to survive. We turned our backs on our home, and became Romans." She blinked and smiled crookedly. "As you see Maria is alive and well. Young though I was, I adopted her as my child. The Angel of Death took the others, her brother and my nephew Joel, before they reached manhood. It was a fever. They are blessed to be safe in the arms of God."

Despite Adi's words, Gwyn could feel the sadness that lay on her friend's heart, and she squeezed Adi's hands before retreating to her own chair. "You came to Rome," she said gently. "Did–"

"Adi?" A man's voice called out from the entryway. "I won't be here to dine tonight, my dear. Silva wants me as part of his retinue while he entertains some other senators." Gwyn heard a man walk into the room.

He stopped and paled as Gwyn turned to look at him.

She clutched the arms of her chair. Twenty years older and still handsome despite the grey creeping into his fair hair.

It was Gaius.

* * *

Well, this is awkward. Gwyn cracked her knuckles nervously as she looked at the two people from Masada she cared about the most. "You two… got *married.*" Her voice squeaked slightly. Never had she dreamt it. All her fears and thoughts about Adi and Gaius had focused on the time immediately after Masada. Logically she knew that was foolish. If they lived they still would have died almost two thousand years before she was born. Anything could have happened in that time. The guilt she felt over abandoning them was fast dissipating into embarrassment and a sensation of stupidity. She'd sent Gaius to look for Adi and the others, to protect them. How had it come to this? *He was mine!* She flushed jealously.

"Gwyn." Gaius stared at her. He crossed the room slowly to stand behind Adi, resting his hand on her shoulder. This simple gesture of solidarity punched Gwyn in the gut, and the tears she'd only just contained threatened to spill over again.

"She has magic, my love. Just like you told me when we first met." Adi covered her husband's hand with her own and suddenly Gwyn wanted to look anywhere but at them. She forced herself to speak.

"I'm so glad you are both alright. This is so weird. It's been only a few months for me. Since I saw you. That's why I don't look any older. Because I'm not."

"It's been more than twenty years!" Gaius made the declaration against the evidence of his own eyes. "I… I think I need a drink."

"Don't you have to be at Silva's villa?" Despite the bizarreness of the situation, Adi sounded just like the calm wife jogging her husband's memory. *She's a lot more settled than I remember.* Gwyn bit her lip. Of course Adi was calmer. She didn't live in a war zone now. She had grown up. They all had. Everyone but Gwyn.

"I'm not expected just yet. I'll make some excuse." Gaius leaned forward to grab a handful of olives and made for the kitchen, returning with another cup and a small jug of red wine.

"The Falerian, my dear." He poured and raised his cup. "To old friends." He spoke the toast quietly and took a long draft of his wine before topping up his cup and sitting on one of the couches.

Gwyn sipped her own wine and fidgeted. "You are both awfully calm about this." *Why aren't they freaking out? Oh yeah, the pocket watch.*

"It is... strange, that is certain." Gaius rubbed his forehead with the back of his hand. "Adi and I talked about it many times, but only to each other. Magic is illegal, of course—neither of us wanted to be accused of anything, especially now."

"I doubt anyone else would believe us, but that's not the point, given how the Emperor is about these things," Adi chimed quietly. "And I had no one except Gaius and the children when I first came here."

"Even Junilla–" Gaius cut himself off. Gwyn searched her memory for that name.

"Your sister?" she asked, then took a sip of wine. It was good. She took another. Her time in Transylvania and Wallachia had given her a taste for red wine. *Focus, you idiot,* she scolded herself. *You can't get drunk!* She kind of wanted to, though, just to rid herself of tension.

"Yes." Gaius glanced at Adi. "My sister." He said nothing more, and from the tight-lipped expression on his wife's face Gwyn wondered if the two women didn't get along. That confused her—when she had met Gaius, back in Masada, he had talked about his intelligent and independent sister, and Gwyn had wanted to meet the woman who was such a positive influence on her admirer's life.

There it was. Gaius had admired Gwyn, been attracted to her and she to him. He had been kind and considerate and respectful of her will and boundaries and she had carried the memory of him like a torch that lit her way through time. The thought of him had been a balm to her sore heart after letting go of her infatuation with Alina, but her daydreams of reuniting with him had not been like this! Not with the banality of a quiet Roman apartment, its domestic atmosphere intruded upon only by street noise outside the thick walls. Not with a pregnant adopted daughter and disgruntled teenager several rooms away.

None of it was as she had imagined.

"I won't impose on you," she heard herself saying. "I've business here, and I don't want to cause trouble." She met Adi's eyes then, trying to convey her double meaning.

"You must stay tonight at least. She must stay tonight," Gaius repeated to Adi. He frowned and stood, downing the rest of his wine then placing the cup on the wooden table with a click. "I must go. I'll be back late, no doubt, but Silva will send a slave with me to make sure I get home." He stooped to kiss his wife and then hesitated. He nodded formally to Gwyn and called out, "Antonia!"

"Papa?" The teenager was at the door to the kitchen. Her face lit when she saw Gaius and she practically skipped over to hug him. Gwyn's heart twisted and she frowned down at her wine.

"Be good for your mother," Gaius said. "We've a guest here to stay with us."

Antonia looked over at Gwyn and scowled. "But Maria is here and she can't do much. I need to help her."

"Why is Maria staying here? Is she alright?" Gaius questioned, puzzled.

"She's fine. I'll explain later," Adi rose and shooed him towards the door. "You'll be late. Try not to get too drunk or I'll tell the slave to dump you in the courtyard."

Forcing a laugh, Gaius allowed himself to be chivvied out, and the room fell silent. Gwyn looked up to see Antonia frowning at her, then the young Roman girl whirled in a flurry of skirts and disappeared into another room. Gwyn stood, clutching her empty wine cup. She put it down, then wished she'd hung onto it because it had given her something to do with her hands. She now clenched and unclenched her fists until she shoved them into the pockets of her skirts.

"I don't want to be trouble," she told Adi again. *Did Gaius tell her that he and I were once... involved? What is she thinking?*

Something akin to pity appeared in Adi's dark eyes and Gwyn flushed. "Hospitality to a friend is never trouble, Gwyn. I'll never forget the debt I owe you." She smiled ruefully. "Let me find somewhere for you to sleep and organize these girls into preparing some dinner. I'd best put the wine away or the slaves will sneak it. Are you still as useful at kitchen chores as I once was?"

Gwyn smiled at the joke. "Pretty much, but I'll have a go. I'm trying to be more useful these days." She'd picked up a few things in her time travels.

Like how to kill a man? She shivered and remembered why she had come back to this time in the first place. To kill Emperor Domitian.

Five

2623 AD

"Why didn't you wake me and tell me Owen had been kidnapped?" Michelle shouted. She slammed her palm down on the table, glaring at the others. Brrrys and Hanli gave her shocked looks, while the Rilan programmer sludged unhappily in her tub. Dirk, the handsome, black-skinned human director looked disappointed. Only Colsa the Shanista was implacable, its multi-faceted eyes reflecting light rather than Michelle's own irate form.

Michelle sighed and sat back down, trying to get herself under control. "I apologize, Citizens," she said formally, albeit through gritted teeth. "There is no excuse for my behaviour." No one responded so she grimaced and went on. "Please forgive my rudeness and unprofessional manner."

"We've been through a lot," Brrrys patted her hand with his blue furry tail. He needed his own hands to steady himself as he leaned on the table; he was still weak. "We were lucky to escape from Australia to Aotearoa."

"Agent Michelle's stress levels and exhaustion were taken into account." Colsa's tone was clipped and interspersed with clicks that signaled emphasis as it addressed the group. "That is why we elected to let her continue sleeping on arrival in Berlin. A tired mind is not a rational one. But she is a highly trained individual who knows better than to let her emotional state overwhelm her logic and manners."

Michelle was shamed. She had never been given such a dressing down in all her adult life. She felt like a child at the orphanage again, being disciplined for fighting.

"Citizen Colsa is correct. I have not been operating at optimum levels for some time." Michelle decided honesty was going to be her only saving grace. "I believe I need counselling. But a meeting to inform me that my friend and colleague Owen has been kidnapped, is not just a nicety. I respect Owen, and value him, but you would not have dragged Brrrys and me out of witness protection if you didn't need us."

The human, Dirk, glanced at Colsa before nodding at the amphibious Rilan, who spoke through a translating device. "The situation is worse than it appears. More than half of the time travel programmers on Vivaldis were arrested for being a part of ex-Commissioner Hera's subversive organization. Owen Chang filled a vital gap which enabled us to continue work in identifying and localizing turning points and wormholes." She sloshed anxiously and water spilt over the edge of her tub. *She must be old to need to be in water most of the time,* Michelle observed. Most Rilans could handle a few hours of dry-time before their skin was affected.

"So how do you know he was kidnapped? Owen's pretty reclusive, even if the University incident is off his record."

"Part of the condition of wiping his record was that he work for the Agency," Dirk's deep voice matched his somber appearance. "It was a mutually beneficial arrangement. A programmer and technician of his brilliance in the field of time travel is unprecedented outside Shanista circles." He nodded towards Colsa, whose wings fluttered like a pair of restless dragonflies.

"And Owen would be happy getting to work in the place he'd always dreamed of," Michelle finished. "With all the latest toys and bits of tech. Okay, but what happened?"

The Rilan spoke again. "He never arrived at the Agency two days ago. We attempted to locate him using his tracker." She squelched and scrunched up her piggy little eyes in embarrassment.

"Only Agents get trackers–" Michelle said deliberately. The reason for that was obvious. The fact that she didn't have one at the moment was due to her cutting it out of her skin. It had been used against her by Hera to try to steal her chronokinetor.

Colsa answered without a hint of ire, despite Michelle's antagonistic tone. "Owen Chang agreed to bide by our safety measures. We did not implant him with a tracking device without his consent."

Michelle couldn't argue. Everyone knew how particular the Shanista were about ethics. It was unlikely they'd broken with that just to tag Owen, though by the sound of it his value to the Agency was immense.

"So…" She was getting impatient again.

"He's not in the present," the Rilan said miserably. "We tracked his signature to Earth—that's why I'm here. I'm the next most senior programmer. We think he's in London. But he's in the past."

Ah. It was all falling into place. This was why they needed her. Not to mention there might be repercussions from the violent way she'd extracted evidence from Jaysen Fitz, the pretty playboy who'd messed Brrrys up so badly.

Still, she wanted them to say it. Michelle looked at Colsa. The insectile scientist stared back at her, implacable. It was Dirk who spoke.

"We need you to recover him, Agent Michelle." He spoke as calmly as he normally did. On previous missions he'd directed her back in time on Earth to rescue other Agents. Even, twice, to retrieve their bodies.

"Do you know when?" she asked. "And do you know from whom I am rescuing him?"

"We do not know." Colsa clicked in frustration. Michelle realized with a shock that it was the first sign of annoyance from the usually serene alien. *They don't show emotion usually. Maybe I should give Colsa more credit—this Agency exists because of them and their advances in time-space technology. They were the ones who discovered that the Shift was coming, and the danger we face if the Allied Planets fall apart. We'll all be vulnerable. We'll all be wiped out.*

"What we have developed is a mobile device that will enable you to search Owen Chang's time and location," Dirk said. "It will take a lot of time-jumps. You'll need to go back to search, then come forward again if necessary to move geographically if transport is not easily accessible."

The impact of that statement floored Michelle for a moment. "You think they—his kidnappers—have taken Owen back to a pre-industrial time?"

"We don't know."

Michelle searched the faces around her, then focused on Brrrys. He was in no condition to go anywhere through time with her, even if he had been human and able to blend in. But she valued his thoughts all the same. "What do you think?" she asked him.

His tail patted her again, then stabbed its point on the table. "First you have to ask why they took him. Let's work with what we know, then find out what we don't."

"Okay," Michelle took a deep breath. "Tell me everything you do know about Owen's work, movements and behaviour over the last week. Let's map it out, and go from there."

1995 AD

Flick! Flick! Flick!

Michelle paused her time jumps and looked about. Dark buildings loomed all around her, but the bitumen road was empty of people. Beside her, a thick metal pole was graffitied and damaged. The fluorescent light at the top valiantly attempted to penetrate the shadows. It only succeeded in casting more. Michelle ducked into one of those shadows and put her back against the bricks.

OK, computer, do your thing. She raised her right hand. Her wrist was circled by a chain of tiny crystals, fused end to end with flexible nanofibers. They cast a blue-white glow and sent a burst of light out in a small sphere. Michelle waited and kept one eye on the street while she watched the space above her upward facing palm. After several minutes the crystals flashed again and a holographic image formed on her hand.

It showed a diamond-shaped tracker. Michelle used her other hand to manipulate the image and zoom out. A leg, then a body appeared, ghosting into view around the tracker. Michelle kept going, even as numbers ticked in the space below the hologram. The images around Owen solidified as a bed and chair, but the more Michelle zoomed out the hazier the picture became.

Getting closer! She sighed, frustrated, then checked the numbers displayed. *I'm within a hundred years of him at least. Time to keep jumping.* She stepped forward.

"Orright missus, 'and over the bracelet an' any udda bi' o' bling, an' you won't get 'urt." The voice came from the shadow to Michelle's right. She almost rolled her eyes.

"Do you know how many people have tried to rob me before?" she asked conversationally, snapping her hand shut and extinguishing the hologram with its light.

"Doesn' ma'a," another voice slid into her ears just as the hand with the knife snaked around her throat. "We is the ones robbin' you now."

The decoy barely had time to chuckle at his mate's wit before Michelle yanked the knife hand down and elbowed her attacker's ribs. She activated the computer crystals on her wrist so they sent out a blinding flash of light, seen by her through closed eyelids. She turned and crouched, launching the knife man over her shoulder. He cannoned into the other robber. Michelle kicked them both hard for good measure and time-hopped away.

She wondered if she should have finished them off as several years flashed past. *Flick. Flick. Flick.* "I guess I can't go killing everyone who gets in my way," she muttered, congratulating herself on her restraint.

She stopped and had the crystals run their search again. The image of Owen and his surroundings grew clearer. Michelle quietened her mind and tried to feel along the timeline for an aberration that marked a body out of time. Finding nothing she scowled, jumping another few years to search again.

This time the tracking numbers on the hologram were much lower— she was getting there! She smiled when she checked the date and cracked her neck. She needed a rest and some food, so she'd be prepared when she reached the year Owen was in. She went in search of the bank with the long-term anonymous account for Agents, and waited for the dawn.

Six

1982 AD

Graffiti slashed itself across the political posters that covered the wall. Michelle glanced at the photo of a stern woman, backed by the British flag, and frowned. She wasn't aware of any major conflicts involving England in this year, but the theme of the poster looked distinctly nationalistic and military. The red spray paint defacing the poster seemed to concur with this: *war-mongering bitch* snarled hatred against the subject of the poster.

Michelle shrugged. If she stayed long she'd brush up on her history of the area for this time. But as she ran her search for Owen she saw she needed to move on.

1941 AD

Instead of the quiet Michelle expected as she materialized into the London night, a horrible mechanical wail assaulted her ears. Throwing her hands up to cover them, she was jolted enough to lose connection with the timepiece.

"'Ere, watch out!" A dark shape barreled into her, knocking her to the ground.

Michelle rolled and sprang upright but the man who'd crashed into her was tugging at her arm and yelling, "'Urry! 'Urry! Jerry's almost 'ere!"

The urgency in his voice stopped Michelle from fighting back. She allowed herself to be hustled into the gaping black maw of a tube station, bewildered as to who, or what, Jerry was. Her assailant steadied her as they hurtled down steep steps. The awful sound of the siren chased them underground. On the edge of her hearing Michelle thought she could hear something else; a low rumble, almost a drone, then a muffled boom.

1941. London. The Blitz. Shit, that could have gone badly!

The tube station was anything but quiet, though a hush quivered across platforms and into the tunnels. Hundreds of people huddled down there. Michelle saw flashes of torchlight stretch away around the curve of the tracks. She couldn't see the other end of the platform in the dim light, but she imagined it was the same that way too.

"Eddie, you cut it too close," a man's voice scolded. "What the 'ell were you doin' up there?"

Michelle's rescuer heaved a big sigh and fumbled in his coat pocket for something—tobacco, Michelle realized and wrinkled her nose. "This 'ere lady was just standin' in the street, 'Arry! I couldn't well just leave 'er there. Oi was all set to come down when Oi turned and there she was!"

Harry snatched up a lantern and tweaked the cover to permit more than just a sliver of light to shine out. He examined Michelle's face. She blinked away from the sudden light. "'Ere, love, didn't you 'ear the sirens? Where are you stayin'? Oi ain't never seen you 'ere before."

There was a nervous shuffling from those crowded nearby. Michelle offered a tentative smile. "I was looking for my friend—I'm staying with her. Mrs Smith, do you know her?" She peered past him into the darkness.

"Oi know several Mrs Smiffs, love," Harry declared. "Which one?"

"M-margaret Smith," Michelle coughed as a massive boom far above them shuddered dust into the air. Wide-eyed, she heard prayers and cries of distress, then voices hushing the fearful ones.

"Our Lord, who Art in Heaven," a woman's shaky voice began. "Hallowed be Thy name."

"Though I walk through the valley of the shadow of death, I shall fear no evil, for Thou Art with me," a man further away intoned.

Michelle could smell the paralyzing terror. She had no gods to pray to. What was considered supernatural in this time was merely fakery or yet to be proved by science. But she could have used some external comfort as another boom-shudder made the train platform tremble.

"Harry, you blithering idiot, get down here right now!" a caustic female voice laced with worry stung her questioner into action. He leapt down onto the rails and held a hand up to Michelle. She ignored it and jumped down, Eddie right behind her. They hunkered down near the tunnel entrance, listening for an eternity as the Luftwaffe strafed London.

Michelle sat with her knees pulled up and clenched her jaw. She could have time-jumped out of there—why didn't she? Partly because she didn't want to risk getting wiped out by a train if she jumped right there on the tracks, and partly because there was a strange sense of community in the tube station that night. Frightened, yes, but neighbors comforted each other and strangers sang quiet songs. Even after the sound of bombing died away, nobody stirred much, waiting for that all important siren that would signal the end of the ordeal.

Michelle yawned. She fought to keep her eyes open. Her head lolled to the side. Eddie made no complaint as her head drooped to rest on his shoulder. He tugged his thick woolen scarf off and tossed it one-handed to drape over her shoulders. When the siren sounded the end of the raid Michelle jerked upright and found herself tangled in tobacco-scented wool. Her hands flew up, trying to shrug the scarf off and ready to protect herself as she leapt to her feet.

"Easy, easy, love!" Eddie disentangled her and patted her shoulder. All around them people were rising and shuffling past—emerging from the tunnels, speaking in quiet voices caked with relief. Electric lights flickered on. Michelle stared and coughed to hide her embarrassment. How could she have fallen asleep?

"Excuse me." She nodded curt thanks and pushed herself up onto the platform in one athletic motion. With any luck she could lose herself in the crowd and run her computer search for Owen.

"Just a minute, ere, love," a heavy hand landed on her shoulder. "Where did you say you were stayin?"

Michelle turned innocent eyes to meet Harry's suspicious ones. "With Margaret Smith," she lied blandly, offering him nothing more.

His eyebrows raised. "And where do you live normally, madam? Or is it Miss?" He cast an eye down to her left hand, seeing bare fingers.

None of your business. In her own time, titles that denoted partnership status were unheard of. Occupations, such as her own "Agent", or more commonly "Citizen" were used. Michelle kept a wedding band as part of her time travel kit but hadn't bothered to wear it because she was jumping through the night on this mission. She could tell her attire was drawing some curious looks—utilitarian pants, boots and her all-weather jacket, so she sighed. She could break Harry's hold and his hand if she wanted to, but she wasn't after a fuss. She just needed to get away and find somewhere private to continue her search for Owen. "It's Miss. May I go now? I want to find Mrs Smith."

"Miss? Or Fraulein?" someone muttered. Harry's eyes hardened. Several people had stopped to listen, either reluctant to venture out into what might be a rubble-filled landscape, or curious about the woman being questioned by Old 'Arry.

"Oi don't think you're from round 'ere," Harry said slowly. His fingers tightened on Michelle's shoulder.

"Ow, you're hurting me!" she protested. A tear squeezed from her eye.

"'Ey, 'Arry, ease up!" That was Eddie, pulling himself over the edge of the platform and reaching for Harry and Michelle with a worried expression. "Bein' a tad rough there."

"What was she doin' up on the street, Eddie? All the folk were well below. Oi wouldn't put it past Jerry to send women as spies. Look at 'er! She don't look like an English gal."

This had gone far enough. Michelle mustered her best British accent and put the full weight of her will into her timepiece. "I am not a German spy. You're going to let me go and I will be on my way." All those things were true, if not exactly in the context Michelle wanted him to believe.

Unfortunately it seemed that Harry's mind was one of the rare ones that were not susceptible to the influence of the chronokinetor. He reached into his trouser pocket and drew out a small pistol, cocking it with his thumb. "Oi think you'd better come with me to the police and tell 'em your story, love. Something about you is just not right!"

Onlookers gasped at the sight of the gun. Michelle grabbed Harry's hand, pointing the pistol at the ceiling. It went off, the report echoing through the tube station and sending people screaming in every direction. "Idiot!" she snarled as she chopped Harry's arm. He released the pistol. "You could have killed someone!"

He had let go of her shoulder to try to recover the gun but she flipped it, cocked it and had the barrel in his face in a flash. "Be quiet!" she roared. The people nearest her froze, eyes fixated on the gun. People further away still pushed and shoved to escape. *Shit.* She hadn't wanted to start a stampede.

"They'll bring the police," Harry was sweating despite the chilly underground air. "You'll never escape."

At least she wasn't on the train tracks anymore, she reflected. She looked at the terrified faces around her. Their fear annoyed her. The bombs that forced them to cower down there in the dark annoyed her. The war and the stupidity of humans to fight over the differences in their beliefs... For a second she wanted to kill them all and put them out of their stupid, inevitable misery.

Her finger twitched on the trigger.

Does it ever change? Gwyn had asked of her. *Are people still doing this in the future? Endlessly being cruel and greedy and full of hate?*

Fraction by fraction, Michelle relaxed the finger. *I am better than that.* She took a deep breath. She wouldn't say she liked fighting, but... it was clear cut. You fought and you won.

There was a bigger fight at hand though. She could leave these little people behind.

The gun would come in handy though.

She made the connection with the timepiece and smiled grimly as the blue mist rose around her. Harry's eyes boggled and more screams sounded as she *flicked* from that year.

The screech of the train as it pulled into the station drowned out the rushing wave noise she usually heard when she time travelled. She fell in with the crowd that surged from the carriage, allowing commuters to sweep her along. Back up on the surface, she noted the grim faces and newspaper headlines that read "Poland invaded!"

Michelle scanned her surroundings as she emerged from the tube station. No one watched her. She strolled up the street. It was time to find somewhere private to eat, think, and run her next search.

Seven

96 AD

Gwyn observed Antonia's teenage antipathy fade once the girl realized she wouldn't have to give up her room. It was no villa, but the whole building belonged to the family. They occupied the ground floor while the higher levels were rented by tenants. The only guest room was occupied by Maria so Gwyn insisted a storeroom or pantry would suffice, then offered to help prepare dinner. It was with relief she sat down to eat.

"How long until your baby is due?" Gwyn asked as she passed the dish of broiled asparagus to the pregnant woman.

"A few weeks." Maria nodded her thanks and took several stalks before passing them to her sister.

"We sacrificed a pig to Ceres for the birth," Antonia told Gwyn and looked at her expectantly.

"That's great," Gwyn ventured.

Antonia rolled her eyes. "Not everyone can afford a pig! Last year we only sacrificed bread and fruit and Maria lost the baby."

"Antonia! Bad luck!" Adi tapped her daughter on the hand then flicked her fingers to the side. "We are fortunate your father has come up in the world, thanks to Silva's patronage, but there's no need to tempt evil."

"I feel fine, mother," Maria chimed in, though she looked tired. "I'm well past that time. This baby will be a soldier for sure; he kicks me so! Speaking of soldiers, why were they chasing you?"

This was directed at Gwyn; her breath caught. Her eyes darted around the room. It was just the four of them in the kitchen, eating at the table. The house slave had helped to serve then left.

Antonia was fascinated. "You were chased by soldiers? Why?"

"Hush, my dear," Adi ordered. "They were Praetorians."

The teenage girl looked fearful but could be not subdued. "Why?" she whispered.

"I was in the wrong place at the wrong time." Gwyn rubbed her fingers together then laid her hands flat on the table to still them. "They thought me a thief, and didn't seem like the type to listen to explanations, so I ran."

"Maybe they thought you a spy, or an assassin," Maria commented. She didn't seem too stressed, sitting back and resting her hands on her belly. "Everyone knows the Emperor is terrified of being assassinated. There's a prophecy about it."

"Enough!" Adi snapped. "Don't you know there are informers everywhere? I'll not have our family brought into danger by loose talk! People have been killed for less!"

"Do you have other children?" Gwyn asked Maria, desperate to change the subject.

"Don't be so afraid, mother. We are tiny minnows in this big pond. Nothing we say or do will worry our Master and God." Maria spoke sardonically.

She might not be Adi's biological daughter, but she sure has her attitude! Gwyn thought. *Or at least the attitude Adi had when I first met her.* Twenty years and surviving a war had worn caution into her friend.

"You don't know what the Emperor does and doesn't hear!" Adi hissed. "Our position is dependent on your father receiving patronage from Silva, who is not in favor at this time!"

"Why don't you tell me about what happened to you after you left Masada?" Gwyn blurted, exerting her will that they would talk about something else. Everyone stared at her.

"Masada?" Antonia rolled her eyes. "You're barely older than me. How could *you* remember Masada? I wasn't even born until Mama and Papa had lived in Rome for several years." Gwyn felt like rolling her eyes back at the teenager's self-centeredness.

"Masada?" Maria was puzzled and distressed. "I don't want to think about that." Her lip quivered and Gwyn remembered a wide-eyed child huddling on the edge of the deep water cisterns in the bowels of the Jewish fortress.

"We don't talk about Masada," Adi said quietly. "We are Romans now. We have left all that behind."

Gwyn tried to apologize but the words tripped out of her mouth and landed in an ungainly heap in front of her. The rest of the meal passed in awkward, pointless chatter, after which they cleaned up and doused the lamps.

Later, much later, Gwyn lay on a comfortable pallet in a small storeroom. It was barely more than a pantry, and normally occupied by the house slave. Gwyn had baulked at turning him out of his usual abode but her friend had insisted with quiet authority that she'd be more comfortable there. The slave didn't complain when Adi told him he'd be sleeping in the hall, though Gwyn heard quiet grumbles after his mistress left the room. *I'll not stay here more than a night,* she promised herself. She stared at the dark ceiling. The air smelt of homely spices and dried lentils. It was comforting, but she couldn't let it lull her into thinking she was supposed to be here.

But where could she go instead? She had to find some way of identifying the conspirators and finding out when the plot was meant to take place. What had the guide, Mario, said? Domitian's niece and wife were implicated in the plot, along with palace freedmen.

I can't just sit around hoping I'll bump into them! I don't even know what went wrong and why they got found out. "What am I going to do?" she muttered.

"Gwyn?" Gaius' quiet voice sounded on the other side of the door. She got off her pallet without thinking and opened it. He blinked at her in the flickering light of his lamp. "Gwyn," he said again. "I thought I must have imagined it. I've been thinking about you all evening, how you are here, after all this time." He stumbled over his words and she recoiled, realizing he was tipsy, if not drunk.

"It's strange," she agreed, angry at him for being drunk, angry at him for being older and having a wife, angry at herself for still wanting to be in his arms. It wasn't right, being attracted to a much older man, let alone a married one.

"I thought about you for such a long time." Gaius' voice was low and the shadows added lines to his face. "I never stopped thinking about you. But you were gone. I got married. Adi and I…"

Oh god, he's trying to apologize. Her anger dissipated. "It's alright," she whispered. "I'm glad you two have each other."

He swayed, then gripped the doorframe and leaned forward to give her a gentle kiss on the forehead. "You told me to look after her."

She smiled even as the tears leaked out of her eyes. She gripped the doorframe to hold herself back, glad of the dim light. "That's good. I'm glad."

She stepped back and shut the storeroom door carefully, pretending not to hear as he murmured, "But who looks after you, Gwyn?"

* * *

I look after myself. No one else was going to, she knew that much. She didn't want to bring the Emperor's informers onto Adi and Gaius, and she needed to take some risks to make this assassination happen.

It was morning and she walked the streets, lost in thought. Her connection to the timepiece wavered—like a radio that dropped in and out of signal. *I have to be calm to make it work, but I'm struggling to do that!* The thought of Gaius had once centered and soothed her, but now it intruded and sent her mind tumbling. The temptation to throw herself at him the night before had been strong. She thanked whatever sense she had to know that rather than giving herself closure, she would have started a whole new drama.

Not to mention I'd be cheating with my friend's husband. That thought made her feel dirty. Yes, Gaius wasn't a predator like Vlad, but the situation was too similar to ignore. *Am I destined to fall for people who are already taken?*

"Watch out!" Someone bumped her and she stumbled. Swearing, Gwyn glared at the back of the man who had shoved past. She had been loitering in the Forum all morning, testing out her ability to be inconspicuous, occasionally drifting up the hill towards the palace. Her escape yesterday had been luck; she needed to learn the best way in and out. It was almost noon, and she was hot, hungry and too tired to concentrate. Perhaps that was why the man had pushed past rather than drifting around her like the rest of the crowd.

I need food. Those pastry things I nicked this morning weren't enough. She couldn't keep stealing—it was stupid and dishonest. *I need work. I got lucky in Transylvania, meeting Alina when I did. I need to make my own luck here.*

Some men with business in the Forum were heading home for lunch, while others chose not to venture as far and sought out thermopolia in the streets surrounding. Gwyn followed a group of men who sat at an outdoor table of an eatery. A harried waiter dashed between the kitchen and customers, giving Gwyn—who was trying not to drool at the platters of sausage and cheese—an idea.

She took the shawl from her head and tied it around her waist like an apron. From what she had seen, only the aristocratic or rich equestrian women wore the *palla,* so covering her hair was not necessary for what she wanted to attempt.

As the men at the table complained and demanded service, Gwyn sidled into the thermopolium and straightened her shoulders. She marched up to the inside section of the right angled bar and picked up a tray of drinks. "Which table?" she demanded of the man standing behind the bar. He was hurriedly assembling salads and gawped at her. "Which table?" Gwyn repeated, enunciating. "I was sent to help during the lunchtime rush! You've got customers waiting."

"Uh, in the corner!" he pointed a greasy finger at a quartet of impatient-looking older men. Gwyn carefully lifted the tray and delivered it.

"Finally," one man grumbled.

"Are you legates waiting on food still?" Gwyn asked. "Of course you are. So sorry about this. Lunchtime rush and all. What are you waiting on? I'll chase it up from the kitchen."

They repeated their orders. While the man in the bar and the woman preparing meals in the kitchen gave her strange looks, the waiter was only too glad of the help and despite a few slip ups, Gwyn managed to take orders and serve meals and drinks for the next hour. She was starving, so she managed to scoff a sliver of cheese and a handful of olives when clearing some of the tables.

"We don't allow beggars in here!" The woman from the kitchen caught Gwyn's arm from behind and dragged her away from the half-eaten plate of leeks.

"I'm not begging!" It was hard to be indignant with sauce dripping down her chin, but Gwyn tried.

"Oh leave off, Vibia." The waiter plonked himself down on a bench, running a wrinkled hand through his straggly hair. The caupona was empty of customers now, and the remains of luncheons littered the tables. The waiter helped himself to the dregs of wine from a pitcher.

"That's a disgusting habit," Vibia scolded. "At least add a dash of water. And she's filching food!"

"So am I," the waiter replied, snagging the last two leeks. "The aedile's man said if he found us recycling the vegetables again he'd fine us. She looks like she needs a feed. And she did good work here. I'm getting too old to run about after these pompous pretty boys." He licked his fingers and burped.

"Ohh!" Vibia threw her hands up and glared at Gwyn. "Fine, I won't call the vigiles, but you can beat it. We're an honest establishment—I've no need of bold little hussies working the tables. Get back on the street where you belong."

Gwyn wiped her chin furiously. "Please," she fought to keep her voice calm. "I'm not a beggar, nor a… a lady like you think I am. I just need some work. Not for money—just leftovers. I won't be any trouble, and I'm well-spoken." She glanced at the waiter, who was swilling down the rest of the wine. "If you're that busy every day you seem like you could use the help."

"We've been busy lately, m'dear." The man from behind the bar ventured out to clear tables. "Are ye a runaway, girl? Will ye husband or father come looking for ye?"

"No, sir." Gwyn was emphatic. Imperceptible warmth filled her palm where the timepiece lodged. "I'll be of good use, I promise."

"Hmph." Vibia sniffed. "You can work the evening shift. I'll have no thievery and one whiff of trouble and you're out on your pert little backside."

"Thank you," Gwyn said humbly, bowing her head to hide a smile. *One problem solved!*

"She needs a bath, Vibia," the waiter announced. "She'll sell twice as much wine if you clean her up and put a bit of flash on her. I don't pull the adoring gazes like I once did."

Despite the assertion of being a good establishment, Gwyn caught the look between Vibia and the barman. Money shone in their eyes and Gwyn felt a prickle of uncertainty down her back. *I'll have to watch it with these two. The waiter seems harmless enough but you never know.*

Still, with a bit of food in her stomach, a job and the prospect of a bath, Gwyn perked up.

Eight

96 AD

Gwyn was used to bathing alone, so the communal bathhouse came as a shock. She had known this was how Romans bathed, but knowing wasn't the same as experiencing. She bristled when Vibia mocked her prudishness and tried not to be so visibly self-conscious, but it was hard. They waded through the cold and tepid baths, then sank into the hot water. It went some way towards relaxing her.

"You've run away from a rich house," Vibia decided. "You're certainly not used to slumming it with all us common folk." Gwyn chose not to answer. "Did they want to marry you off?" the older woman continued her needling. "Daddy will have informers after you. What'll it be worth to keep our mouths shut to any as come snooping about?"

"I'm not a run-away," Gwyn said tiredly. *Ohh this water is good.*

"Hmph, if you say so." Vibia was not convinced. Gwyn didn't care.

Hours later, she worked the dinner shift at the thermopolium, smiling insincerely at the clientele who passed through. Bedecked in a cheap gilt necklace and pair of feather earrings, she made a couple of tips. Vibia confiscated those as they packed up for the evening. Gwyn didn't complain. She spooned up the lukewarm soup that consisted of her supper. The waiter tossed her a heel of bread before leaving for the night, and Vibia advised Gwyn she could bunk down on one of the tables if she promised not to steal anything. Gwyn felt like rolling her eyes but murmured her thanks instead.

"There's a bucket in the corner you can use for a chamber pot," Vibia said as her husband dragged the last of the outside tables into the eatery. "I'm locking you in, so don't think about trying to do any extra business overnight. My bedroom is right above and I have the ears of a fox!"

Either I'm a precious little rich girl who's run away or I'm a brazen thieving hussy, make up your mind! Gwyn curled up on a table that she pushed against the wall. She wondered what Gaius was doing.

* * *

"Up! Wake up!" Vibia's grating tone interrupted Gwyn's dreams of Gaius coming to find her. She shook off the dream with a blush and opened her eyes to see her new employer looking down at her smugly. "So you're still here? Help me get the tables out. I've been to the markets already and have fresh asparagus and cabbage for salads."

Where else would I be? Gwyn thought irritably. *You locked me in.* It had taken her hours to get to sleep—the rattling of snores from above seemed to be a marital competition. Then there was the scratching of mice. At least, Gwyn hoped they were mice and not rats. "Can I eat something first?"

Breakfast was a wheaten pancake with the thinnest smearing of honey. Vibia's husband, whose name Gwyn still hadn't heard, wandered in an hour later dragging a handcart with two amphorae of wine. Gwyn used the persuasive powers of the chronokinetor to convince Vibia to send her on some errands. While it was nerve-wracking at first to be out and about by herself, she found if she stayed calm and observed those around her, she could usually bluff or fumble her way through buying ingredients and delivering orders with the help of the timepiece.

Returning from one of those deliveries after waiting on tables at lunch, her elbow was grabbed. Gwyn looked up with a frown into a dark African face. The scar placed him immediately. There were a number of black-skinned men and women in the street, but none quite so distinctive as this man. She had seen pale Celts with blonde and red hair, and plenty of bronzed Middle-Easterners and Egyptians, but the majority of the people in the street were olive-toned to lightly tanned, so with her brown hair Gwyn was nothing out of the ordinary. It seemed that the door-keeper from two days ago recognized her too.

"Is you outta trouble, then?" He grinned. It shifted the scar and

Gwyn realized she was staring. She jerked her elbow away.

"No thanks to you," she hissed. "Don't touch me."

He backed up a step, still smiling, and lifted his hands. "No harm done. Don't be getting your braids in a twist."

"Gwyn!" Gaius' voice startled her into looking across the street. The young African man sauntered off. "Gwyn," Gaius said again, hurriedly crossing to her. Gwyn tensed, wanting to fight and flee at the same time.

"What do you want?" How could she be so cold? She noted more things about him this time; lines on his forehead that furrowed as he frowned, the hair on the back of his arms that was darker and coarser than when she had first met him. His shoulders had broadened but he was not fat. The grey at his temples made him look distinguished, but she was biased.

She didn't know what made her angrier, the fact that he was still attractive to her despite having aged or the thought of him paunchy and bald. Both thoughts ruined her illusion of him.

"Gwyn, are you alright? You disappeared so early yesterday morning—we didn't know what to think." He spoke softly but she heard him clearly despite the clatter of the street. "Where did you go?"

"Make way!" Shouts of lictors sent Gwyn and Gaius dashing to the side. Once the magistrate and his bodyguards had passed, Gwyn started walking and gestured to Gaius to keep up.

"I have errands to run, I have to get back," she said. "I told you, I have business here and I don't want to cause trouble for you and Adi."

He moved in front and faced her without touching. "Please. We just want to understand. This is so strange for us. We were worried about you—I searched for you for some time yesterday."

"Strange for you?" Her tone was unreasonable but she didn't care. "It's pretty strange for me too! Coming back here and finding you two..." She bit off the rest of her sentence and glared to the side. She'd spent a lot of time over the last day brooding instead of focusing on her mission. She wanted to be calm and adult but she was pissed off and here was someone who knew her, around whom she didn't have to pretend to be something she was not.

"Finding us married." Gaius finished her sentence and moved around to stand in front of her again. He was taller than her now. Gwyn scowled at him, not wanting to cry. To her astonishment she saw the glint of tears in Gaius' eyes. "You have no idea how many years I dreamt of you, Gwyn. Wondering what became of you. I imagined you'd come back for me."

This street was not busy, as many people rested after their midday meal. Gwyn breathed out the air she hadn't realized she'd been holding and crossed to a fountain that nestled in a small courtyard just off the street. She drank the clear, cool water and washed her face, drying it on a sleeve.

"I wanted to come back," she bit her lip again. "She told me I could; I just had to do one thing for her. It hasn't been that long!"

Gaius sat on the fountain's edge and trailed a hand in the water. Gwyn sat next to him, nervous and excited to be so close. "It has been for me," he told her in a low voice. He met her eyes and her breath caught. "You told me to look after Adi, and the others. I did the best I could. Silva was angry that I'd lost you—he sent us back to Rome. He didn't want any survivors of Masada to be a focus for further rebellion. I... Adi and I became friends. We talked about you a lot. I taught her Latin. When Silva granted my freedom I asked his permission to marry Adi and adopt the children. Titus was Emperor then and Silva was in favor, so he was generous. Adi always hated being a slave."

"I'm glad you took care of her." The words sounded bitter in Gwyn's ears. She looked at her hands resting in her lap. A sparrow cheeped and fluttered down to the ground in front of her. It pecked at a beetle, then flew away.

"Gwyn." Gaius rested his hand on hers. She glanced up at him, startled. "I never stopped caring about you. But you weren't there."

Did you really expect him to wait? You were off gallivanting with Alina and dodging Vlad! The heat in her cheeks was unbearable but she couldn't move to splash more water on her face. "I understand."

Gaius patted her hand. "You're still so young." The statement was half-wonderment, half-explanation, and Gwyn's misery was tweaked into annoyance by the implication. She straightened and contorted her face into a smile as he said, "Now will you come back home and explain where you've been all this time and why you are back here now? What business is it that brings you here?"

"I have to let my employer know," Gwyn stood. "I found myself a job at a caupona just off the Forum. She'll be wondering where I am. Look," she said to Gaius' puzzled face. "I'll explain to you and Adi, but I don't want to piss off my new boss."

"I'll come with you," he said, clearly not wanting to lose her again. "I'll say you're my wife's cousin and you have to come and stay with us."

Gwyn had to admit that the pallet in the pantry would be much more comfortable than the hard wooden table she'd slept on last night. She sighed and started walking. "It'll be better if you wait outside," she called back over her shoulder. "Come on."

She calmed her mind, preparing to convince Vibia of this new lie.

* * *

Gwyn's tale lasted well into the night. Gaius and Adi frequently stopped her to ask questions, and often the explanations of the answers took longer than the answers themselves. While accepting of her time travel magic, there was much the pair wanted to know about the people of future times—both the fifteenth century and Gwyn's own time.

When it came to the reason she was there in Rome, Gwyn kept her voice low. She knew Maria and Antonia were asleep, as were the house slaves, but she'd heard the fear in Adi's voice when she spoke of the Emperor and his spies. No one wanted to be overhead discussing Domitian's death, let alone plotting it.

When she had finished, Adi whispered in shock, "You cannot mean it."

Gwyn raised her eyebrows ruefully. "I must correct the timeline. That is what I was sent to do in Wallachia—what you call Dacia."

"And Masada?" Gaius asked, his hazel eyes inscrutable in the flicking lamplight.

"Me being at Masada was an accident, like I told you." A burr of irritation nudged her. Did they not believe her?

"Yes, but—how did that woman, Michelle, know to come for you there?" he pressed.

She didn't want to answer, but didn't want to lie either. She hated deceiving her friends, and it was exhausting to remember which lies she had told. "Michelle had a mission there," she said, reluctance clouding her voice. "I completed it by mistake." Gaius and Adi waited. The silence stretched and Gwyn was compelled to fill it. "She had to make sure Masada fell. That the Romans won, and no one was left to fight them." She watched Adi's face grow still, though it was hard to read her expression in the dimness. "I tried to change it." Gwyn was desperate to vindicate herself. "I told Silva to leave it alone, that he'd just be slaughtering women and children and there were barely a handful of men to fight."

"You did," Gaius murmured. "I remember." He reached out a hand and touched Adi gently on the arm. She twitched and stood up, wrapping her shawl tight around her.

"That is all in the past," she said abruptly. "I am a Roman now. Best to forget the rest." She went to the door of the living area and said over her shoulder. "I am going to sleep now. Husband?"

Gaius got up wearily. "It is very late. Gwyn, do you know where you are to sleep?"

"She does," Adi replied for her. "Gwyn." She turned to face Gwyn now. "I think it would be best if you did not stay past tonight."

Gaius looked shocked. "But Adi, she is our friend and guest! We can't just throw her out into the street. She needs to be kept safe. You wouldn't let Antonia out to wander the streets alone!"

His words niggled Gwyn. She didn't like the comparison to their daughter. "I'm more than capable of looking after myself," she said. "I'll be working at that caupona, and like I said, I don't want to cause trouble." She looked straight at Adi. "You've both done more than enough already. Thank you," she added, softly. She was hurt by Adi's change of heart, but understood. It had been painful to confess her role in the fall of Masada, but it was a relief too.

Adi nodded and left the room.

"Good night," Gwyn told Gaius awkwardly. The tension between them was still strong, though she guessed that his feelings were paternal. *Which is just messed up.* This guess was confirmed when he moved to stand close. Gently putting his hands on her shoulders, he kissed her forehead. Her breath caught.

"Be careful, Gwyn." He looked down at her seriously. She wanted to wrench away from his grip but it was hardly a grip at all—she could have shrugged him off, so what was the point? *He's the opposite of Vlad.* "I do not see how you are going to achieve this thing, it is much too dangerous. But if I cannot stop you, I have to protect my family. I won't seek you out, but if you need me, I will come."

The boy she had known—the kind, carefree young lad with the sunny smile—had grown into this responsible, dependable man. But he was still kind, and it was his kindness that was breaking her heart.

"I'll be fine. Thanks." She had to be tough. She didn't want him to compromise his duty to his family. "I'll be gone in the morning and hopefully you won't see me again until this is all over. I... I'll say a proper goodbye this time." She broke away and hastened from the room, hurrying through the kitchen and into her pantry. Tomorrow was time to get serious.

Nine

1922 AD

Michelle stared at the hologram in exasperation. The tracker was visible but nothing else. How could that be? "They've bloody moved him in time!"

Shit. She sighed and leant against the rough bark of a tree. It sheltered her from the snow flurries that decorated Hyde Park with chilly blankets. She couldn't stay in this time—there was nothing for her here. Tired as she was, she took several meditative breaths and tuned her mind to jump again.

Stopping to check every few years, she worked her way back to the end of the nineteenth century. She began to make out the shape over not just one, but five bodies out of time in her mind. She had no way of knowing where they were—until she matched times with Owen, the geographic search function wouldn't work.

As she hit 1890 she slowed to jump just a few months, then weeks, each time stopping to search. The hologram lit up like a starship and Michelle punched the air. "Finally!" She activated the geographic search and her smile dropped faster than a meteor.

Owen was nowhere near her. Not in London, not in England, not even in Europe. The holographic map of the world rotated and zoomed in on a continent shaped like an overgrown comma. The zoom continued and the name of a city appeared in text.

Buenos Aires.

What to do? She could travel forward again and endure multiple, painful jumps to reach a time where she could fly straight there. But why had Owen's captors picked this time? Was there something she could learn by absorbing her surroundings over several days or weeks?

Either way, she didn't have the energy to jump again. She risked burnout, and that would make her vulnerable should she have to disappear in a hurry.

You need to eat and sleep. You're not a machine. She growled at the logic of her brain and set out from the park. She needed to find a pawnbroker. She'd been issued with small precious stones and strips of gold—currency in almost any time, as long as one knew where to change it.

* * *

"Inheritance, did you say?" The bespectacled man peered through his magnifying glass at the tiny sapphires Michelle had placed on his counter.

"I didn't." She smiled but no trace of humor entered her face. "But yes, an aunt left them to me. She had no daughters of her own." Michelle waited.

Either the pawnbroker believed her, or didn't care, for he gently put down the gem he'd just scrutinized and peered up at her. "Four pounds, these are worth. You won't get a better price than that, my dear."

Michelle placed her hand over the jewels and said, "Good day to you, then. I'll try the broker up the road."

"Wait!" He took off his glasses and rubbed them urgently with a cloth. "Let me take one more look. Perhaps they are worth six pounds—I thought I saw a flaw but it might have just been dust."

"Twenty." Michelle did not remove her hand. "You know full well you could get four pounds for each stone, even without mounting them in a necklace or a ring. There are eight here."

"Twenty! Outrageous!"

Michelle covered a yawn. "Good day."

"Fifteen." The massive jump told Michelle she had won.

"Twenty. Or I go up the road."

"Eighteen."

Another yawn. She didn't bother speaking this time, just eyed him with boredom, hand unmoving.

The broker heaved a sigh. "You drive a hard bargain. Twenty it is."

Michelle took back her hand. "You'll make three times that much if you set them in a brooch, let alone a necklace. My money, please. And don't even think about sending your heavy after me." She eyed the thick-set man loitering at the back of the shop. "I do have some protection." She slid out the pistol she'd taken from 1941 and rested it briefly on the counter before tucking it away. The heavy shifted at that, but a signal from the broker stilled him. Michelle smiled and held out her hand.

* * *

Two nights in London allowed Michelle time to secure a first class cabin from Southampton to Buenos Aires. It also meant she could arrange an appropriate wardrobe. Clothes were always an issue in any pre-space age. On specific missions she came prepared, but now she was forced to improvise. Walking into a London tailor's she strode to the service counter and remarked in a Russian accent, "Travel dresses, ready-made. I am in a hurry." She placed a circumspect amount of money on the bench and gazed about as if expecting a garment to leap out at her.

"Very good, madam," the clerk was professional and didn't blink at her outlandish trousers and jacket. "We have several items that might suit. Would madam care to step this way and measurements can be taken?"

It was the fourth tailor she had tried. Her initial attempt resulted in scandalous looks and a polite but emphatic ejection from the shop. Not knowing the exact value of clothes in this time, nor having the right outfit to be seen as a respectable lady, it required trial and error before she had the confidence and knowledge to bluff her way through a purchase.

Pretending to be foreign helped. If there was anything Michelle had learned in all her time travels was that in-groups and out-groups defined most humans' mindsets. People would believe anything of a person from a different culture. The measuring, fitting and purchasing of three long, cumbersome dresses went smoothly as a result. Upon arriving by train in Southampton she went straight from the station to port side, her small wardrobe packed into a discreet carry case.

Now she stood on the deck of SS Margaret. Passengers all around Michelle waved and shrieked farewells as the ship's foghorn made her teeth vibrate. Michelle stood still as she watched the shore of England slip away.

"Is there someone down there for you? Or have they already left?"

Michelle turned with surprise. A young lady stood by her at the rail. She was dressed in the same navy blue as Michelle, but there the similarities ended. Michelle's dress was severe and cut for ease of movement; the young lady's dress had ruffles and lace and even a bustle. Her pale round face seemed ethereal against such a dark color, framed as it was by regimented blonde curls.

Michelle disliked her immediately.

"They've left," she replied brusquely and turned back to watch the receding dock.

"You looked so forlorn, standing there. I thought you must have left a sweetheart behind. I wish I had a sweetheart—I'm going home to get married but it would be so much more romantic if I left a bereaved beau behind." She flung out a dramatic hand then clasped it to her chest. Michelle almost choked with laughter. Forlorn? Her?

"This is my normal face," she said, eyebrows raised in challenge. If this silly duck was going to spout romance at her, Michelle had no problem being rude.

The blonde girl looked knowingly at her. "I know what it is like. I shall have to hide how I feel when Father marries me to some local ranch owner's son. I imagine I shall cry for weeks."

Michelle gripped the rail. Her knuckles whitened for a moment, then she relaxed. *No punching allowed.* "Please go away," she requested. "I don't want your company, and if you had any sense you wouldn't want mine."

"I am Miss Penelope Morton. You will forgive me for introducing myself, but it is going to be an awful long voyage and I thought I'd best make acquaintance with other respectable ladies."

Michelle's eyebrows almost shot off the top of her forehead. Had this empty-headed sheep not heard?

"Penelope, darling, there you are." A harried looking man with thick sideburns shuffled through the other first class passengers. "My dear, I do hope you are not bothering this lady."

Why yes, sir, actually she is. Michelle wanted to say.

"I am trying to make acquaintances, Papa," Penelope Morton protested. "I don't know anyone on board and I must practice meeting strangers if I am to succeed in Argentine society."

Michelle changed her mind. This girl was silly, but Michelle had done far more challenging things than befriending a brainless teenager, and the connection might prove useful. "She is not bothering me, sir, and I owe her an apology for my initial rudeness. I was preoccupied with a personal matter. I am Lady Michelle Stucely. May I have the pleasure of your acquaintance, sir?"

Penelope Morton's father introduced himself as Mr Morton, of Mendoza. "Not the usual way of meeting someone, I am sure, but I suppose shipboard etiquette is somewhat different to normal polite company."

Michelle permitted herself a thin smile. She had no idea why introducing oneself was not the done thing. She did receive an invitation to dine with the Mortons, if, begging her ladyship's pardon, she did not have prior arrangements.

"I do not." Michelle tried to sound aloof. "I thank you for the invitation."

"We will see you at six o'clock then!" Mr Morton ushered his daughter away. Michelle left the ship's rail, deciding it was time to brush up on her South American history.

Ten

1890 AD

Dinner with the Morton's proved tedious, but Michelle persevered. She affected an interest in Mr Morton's business affairs.

"It was cattle, you see, Lady Stucely. I have several thousand acres near Mendoza, in the west of the country, but a year ago we discovered silver."

"Mama decided I ought to go to finishing school back on the continent," Penelope interrupted. "So Papa came to fetch me."

"And to secure a contract in London," Mr Morton coughed, his cheeks ruddy from the wine. "Not that you'd be interested in the financial details. Ledgers and figures and so forth. But it should set Penelope here up nicely for her entrance back into Argentine society."

"I've kept to myself since my dear husband died," Michelle told her table hosts. "And we lived in the country before that. I'm not much of a social creature, but I'd appreciate any detail you can give me about the people on board or in Buenos Aires."

That, Penelope was happy to do. Her father disappeared to the smoking room after dessert and the ladies were escorted from the dining room into the first class salon by white-gloved waiters. Michelle and Penelope hovered at the edge of the room, watching ladies who chatted over small glasses of Madeira.

"My sister married into Buenos Aires' society, but Papa hoped I might snare an English lord. That is why he sent me to Paris and London for schooling," Penelope confided.

"And you didn't?" Michelle scanned the room. Should she shed her companion? She was bored but she doubted anyone else in the room would hold a more interesting conversation. Gossip over who had been seen with whom at whose parties reached Michelle's ears and her eyes rolled. At least Penelope didn't seem to find Michelle's ignorance on society matters strange.

"Oh there was Lord Buck's son—he seemed interested. We danced at several balls in London. But his father arranged a marriage for him. Then there was..."

She chatted on and on until Michelle's eyes began to droop. "I'd best take you back to your room," she said to the girl. "I'm surprised your father hasn't fetched you yet." Other men had entered the salon and were circulating. Michelle projected an aura of disinterest. Perhaps another night she'd engage other passengers in conversation—tonight she wanted to get the lay of the land. She did notice several young men eye her young companion with interest.

"Oh, Papa is probably gambling." Penelope was so blithe that Michelle's eyes shot wide in surprise. "He'll be up until midnight at least. I can see my own way back."

"Not on my watch," Michelle muttered. She admired the girl's independence but refused to be responsible for any trouble that might be encountered. *Especially in first class. I don't actually have the clout to see justice for anyone who might harass her.* "Come on, let's go."

Eyes followed them, but nothing else, so it was without drama that Michelle deposited Penelope back at the Morton's suite. A maid opened the door and Michelle waited until it was firmly closed before she went in search of her own bed.

Quiet male voices made her pause in a doorway. Two gentlemen entered the corridor from the stairs and passed Michelle's hiding spot without noticing her. "Seems flush with money," one well-dressed man said.

"Just secured a silver contract," the other replied. "His credit's good, but can he deliver?"

"I reckon it'd be worth it for the daughter—she is quite the dish."

The voices faded and Michelle breathed out quietly through her nose. Penelope would have no lack of suitors while her father's prospects were good, it seemed. She wondered if the girl's outspokenness would scare some away though. Michelle grinned at the thought.

The rest of the voyage passed with little event. Michelle was treated with bemused respect as the rest of first class seemed unsure of her legitimacy as a lady but unwilling to call her out on it. She was invited to the captain's table several times and made the acquaintance of various ladies and gentlemen. The ship made port in Portugal, Rio de Janeiro and its ultimate destination, Buenos Aires.

Michelle made sure she was out on deck as the ship steamed into the wide mouth of the Rio de la Plata. *Silver.* She mused. She hoped Mr Morton could fulfil his contract and not gamble the cash away, if only for Penelope's sake. Michelle had grown fond of the girl, in the same way one would a pet. She enjoyed planting new ideas in Penelope's brain—many of which the girl rejected at first, but Michelle could see the cogs ticking over and sometimes the girl surprised her with a poignant comment or question.

"Will you take ship straight to Valparaiso?"

Michelle didn't take her eyes of the myriad of ships and boats crowding the waterway as they approached the port. "I might stay a few weeks." She had to discover if Owen had been moved again. She hoped not. Running a search whilst the ship was moving had given her erratic results.

"I would offer you hospitality, of course." Penelope looked forlorn. "But we stay with my sister in her Recoleta house. I do not know if there would be room."

"It would be an imposition," Michelle overrode her smoothly. "Perhaps your father can recommend a hotel."

"Of course! I shall ask!" Penelope scooped up her skirts and was off. Michelle felt an indulgent smile creep across her face. Penelope was a nice child, if silly, and had been a distraction from the history texts stored on Michelle's computer.

Buenos Aires spread out to the north and west as the ship docked. Michelle accepted the offer of a carriage ride from the Mortons. They rattled north through La Boca, seeing immigrants everywhere. The construction work on La Casa Rosada spilled out onto Avenida Paseo Colón, delaying them, but the carriage finally rolled up outside a boutique hotel a block south of the cemetery.

"Thank you," Michelle attempted a curtsey as Mr Morton handed her out. "Your kindness and generosity will not be forgotten." She meant it too.

"Shall we see you again?" Penelope's voice tremored. Michelle realized that the girl was nervous about re-entering a society she had left several years ago.

"Perhaps." Michelle projected calm and waved as they drove off. The porter took her bags to a room and she welcomed the quiet as she entered the small suite. She needed to be frugal—perhaps she should have angled for a room at Penelope's sister's? But no, she needed independence.

In the quiet of her room, she ran another search.

"Dammit!" She would have thrown the computer across the room if it hadn't been clasped to her wrist. The search hologram showed her an unwelcome display. Owen wasn't there in Buenos Aires. His captors, whoever they were, were moving him westward.

Why? Where are they taking him?

Another, far more unsettling thought crept into her mind.

What if... what if he wasn't kidnapped? What if he defected?

Either way she had to find him.

* * *

Was their destination Valparaiso, or even California? Surely they would have taken a ship south through the Strait of Magellan if that was the case. Michelle knew the Panama Canal wouldn't be complete and operational for another twenty-four years, so Cape Horn was the only option.

A helpful clerk at the hotel answered her questions about overland travel. "They build the railway from Mendoza to Valpo, but many years before completion," he said in heavily accented English. "By horse, or donkey, yes, you can cross the mountains, but is dangerous for a woman."

"Thank you. But to take train to Mendoza?"

The clerk looked alarmed at the thought of her catching the train without an escort. Michelle sighed. "My brother is to meet me in Mendoza."

But the clerk refused to divulge any more, politely but efficiently shutting down any further enquiries regarding solo travel. Michelle frowned—she would try elsewhere.

The ticket office at the central train station was more helpful. She dressed conservatively and could pass for middle class—as a result people were generally polite. The price of a ticket would leave her without sufficient funds to cover her hotel bill, however, so she ventured into a less salubrious neighborhood in search of a pawn shop or jeweler's.

Spanish and Italian flooded Michelle's ears. Her chronokinetor translated the talk straight into her brain. As an English lady on her own she might have been shunned or harassed, but the second she opened her mouth anyone near her relaxed, and directions were given freely.

Gold nuggets were the currency of exchange this time. Michelle spun a story about her deceased husband prospecting in the west before he had died. She used the influence of the timepiece to increase the shop owner's sense of pity for a poor widow so he didn't cheat her.

"Gracias, Señor." She wiped away a non-existent tear and turned, secreting the money in a leather pouch and her boots. It was too late to return to the train station.

Michelle paid her hotel bill the next morning. She could have easily skipped out—she'd done it before when needed—but she was flush with cash so decided to do the right thing. A different clerk attended the desk that morning, and was happy to direct the doorman to summon a two-wheeled cab to take her to the station. She tipped him generously and he grinned a gap-toothed smile at her and touched the brim of his hat.

The train journey took several days. Every time it stopped to take on coal or passengers or water Michelle ran the computer search. Owen's tracker moved slowly now—horses or travel by foot seemed likely. *But why? What do they hope to achieve in this time and place? Geographically, it's isolated, and historically—how can they hope to influence the future from here?*

These questions gave her a headache, making her surly. Other passengers left her alone and the train staff were polite but wary. So when the train slowed to a halt in the middle of the night Michelle didn't expect to have someone hammering on her door. "¡Abre la puerta!"

Open the door? "¿Por qué?" she yelled back, scrambling into her boots and shoving arms into her travelling coat.

She heard men's voices murmuring in Spanish and she wished she'd thought to answer in English. She liked to take every advantage in a fight, and from the tone of these men, Michelle felt like she was about to have a fight on her hands.

Opening the door never occurred to her.

A massive thump shook the door and splinters showed near the hinges. Someone was kicking it hard. Michelle held the pistol she'd liberated from 1941, but it had only three bullets. She might use all of them on these men and have nothing left for later. Of course she could fight them hand to hand—the narrow cabin doorway was an excellent pinch point—but the screams and yells and gunshots she could hear further down the train told her these men were not alone.

Michelle threw the cabin's small stool and bedclothes to the foot of the door—they might hinder the men for a second—and opened the window, sliding it up as far as it would go. She peeked out quickly then slung out her always-packed bag, holding onto it by a strap. As another tremendous kick smashed the door from its hinges, Michelle shimmied out of the window and, bag dangling from her shoulder, clambered up onto the roof of the train.

She heard shouts from her cabin. Securing her bag over both shoulders, Michelle ran low and fast towards the front of the train. Flaming torches on either side of the tracks showed dozens of horses. Cries rose from below as the bandits snatched money and valuables from passengers at gunpoint.

Michelle leapt from carriage to carriage, glad the train was still. Athletic as she was, it would have been suicide to try it in a dress on a moving train. She slowed as she neared the locomotive, creeping over the tender that was half full of coal. The fuel shifted. Michelle held her breath, hoping the noise of the raid and the chuffing of the stationary engine would mask her approach.

"Please don't shoot me, I have a wife and family!" a man sobbed as he knelt on the floor of the cab. A rifle was pressed to his neck. Michelle couldn't see their faces; the man with the rifle had a bandana tied around his.

The bandit's gravelly voice held notes of disgust as he kicked the kneeling train driver. "Don't cry, you whimpering milksop. I won't shoot unless you try to start the train moving." The locomotive rumbled—it was at rest but still fired. Michelle guessed that the bandits wanted enough time to rob the train and then they'd let it move on. Perhaps.

Wait and see, or intervene? It was so hard operating in a timeline without knowing where the turning points were! Was this train meant to be robbed and would she be upsetting history if she intervened? She sank back into the tender and opened her mind to the timepiece.

Nothing jumped out at her from the timeline, so she'd have to take the chance. She didn't have the computers or programs used by the Agency to map the interweaving threads of cause and effect. All she knew was that these bandits were slowing her down from catching up to Owen, and that pissed her off.

The masked man with the rifle tensed at finding a cold metal barrel pressed under his ear, but had enough sense not to fire his own gun. "Don't move," breathed Michelle in the deepest voice she could manage.

"Who the devil are you?" the man snarled.

She ignored him. "Get up," she ordered the train driver in the same deep voice. "Get this thing ready to move."

The train driver rose and looked at her, astonished. "But you are—"

"Holding a gun," she finished for him with a warning glare then spoke to the bandit. "Put down your rifle slowly."

As the driver grabbed a shovel and began to stoke the firebox, the bandit crouched, then launched himself backwards in an attempt to disarm her. Michelle expected that, so wasn't where his elbow swung. She faded back, he overbalanced. She kicked him in the groin and snatched the rifle as he fell.

He was a fighter, so he took the kick with an anguished grunt and came up swinging. Infuriated when he realized his assailant was a woman, he simply tried to push past her pistol.

She shot him in the shoulder.

He screamed and clutched the wound. Michelle was backed against the tender now. She used it to stabilize herself and kicked again as hard as she could. The bandit ricocheted off the half wall of the cab and fell over the side. Michelle leant over the edge of the footplate and shot him in the head.

The driver was staring in open-mouthed terror when she turned back. *Only one bullet left.* She pocketed the pistol and examined the rifle quickly. She nodded, confident she could use it. "What?" she asked the driver. "Get the train moving, hurry up!"

He gabbled as he shoveled more coal in from the tray at the bottom of the tender. The gap there permitted the fuel to slide slowly through. "They killed the stoker! I can't shovel and drive at the same time!"

"Here." Michelle leant the rifle against the tender. She grabbed the shovel from the driver's hands and started stoking. The heat of the growing furnace beat against her. Sweat trickled down her face and neck.

The driver climbed onto his platform, moving levers and checking gauges. He continued to glance fearfully at Michelle. She kept one eye on him as the sensation of pressure built in the locomotive. Slowly, slowly, the train began to move.

"More coal!" the driver called, and Michelle shoveled faster. The bag on her back was a hindrance but she didn't for a second consider abandoning it.

It saved her in the next second when a blow to her back almost sent her face-first into the furnace. The shovel got in the way and her chest thumped onto the handle end. She was bruised both front and back. Dropping to a knee she thrust the shovel handle up and behind while she swiveled to see who had hit her. Another bandit, drawn by the gunshots and the movement of the train, had abandoned whatever robbery he had been committing to come and see what was going on.

The shovel handle thwanged into him, then he wrested it from her. She let him have it and used the momentum of his drag to dive in his midsection to knock him down.

The cramped cab worked against her—in a similar move to the one Michelle had pulled earlier, the bandit braced himself against the wall of the tender and pushed back. She fell onto her butt and lashed out with a kick that tripped him.

The train was gaining speed now, the whistle screaming and the wind blowing through the cab. Michelle jumped up and the man launched himself at her. She hit the edge of the cab's half wall—the bag on her back saving her once again from serious injury—and grabbed the man's arms, twisting him to the side so he'd fall backwards off the locomotive.

This move was successful, except the man held onto Michelle as he fell.

She fell with him.

Eleven

96 AD

Vibia made a number of scathing remarks but took Gwyn back in. Scaurus the waiter was happy. He spent less time waiting tables and more time flirting with some of the young men now that she had returned. Gwyn didn't mind—she wanted to keep him sweet. Vibia's husband was tight-lipped in comparison, but quick to slide a greasy paw towards Gwyn's breasts or buttocks if his wife wasn't around. Gwyn stayed out of his way.

"It's not worth messing you around, Gwynia," Scaurus declared, scratching his neck. "Your papa or fiancé will show up eventually to claim you. I'm too old to fight over your honour."

Annoyed that he was fixed on the idea that she belonged to someone, she went to retort, then stopped. *Silly old fool is teasing you.* "If only I had whiskers, Scaurus, then I might win your heart."

That startled a laugh out of him. He winked. "You know, Gwynia, if you give your tips to me I'll only keep half. Then Vibia won't get her hands on them." Gwyn shook hands on the deal.

In addition to waitressing and running errands around Rome, Gwyn eavesdropped. As she spied she tried to formulate a plan. The caupona's location near the Forum was perfect for loitering in the wake of important men, as well as gossiping with their hangers-on. After watching other women in the street Gwyn altered the way she wore her outfit—Maria's dress, scarves and Vibia's cheap jewelry—to change her appearance. Housewife, unsupervised maiden, freedwoman and slave— she gathered information about the Emperor. It was hard, because conversations were guarded. Still, Gwyn persisted. She heard some of the best gems while waiting tables—men discussing business during their lunches and dinner, with snide remarks about who was in whose pocket, and who had recently fallen out of favor.

"It's a bad business, with Clemens and old Epaphroditus," one voice uttered as the evening drew on.

"Ain't it just." A curly head nodded. Gwyn poured him more wine. The man waved vague thanks.

"Shush!" A stage whisper from the third man. "I've no wish to trip on a sword on my way home."

"You're right, you're right," the first man soothed. His was a more cultured voice than the other two. "Let's talk no more on it. We should call it a night—you've a long journey tomorrow."

The other two men groaned. "Don't remind us."

"Well, one more drink then, tug my toga." The cultured speaker chuckled and signaled Gwyn to top up their jug. She scooted to the bar and complied, ears straining.

"Oh, if you could carry a message for me I'd be much obliged. Only since you're heading that way."

"Mhmm." Curly-haired man drank noisily. "Where to?"

"The captain of the *Scipio's Fury*—at port in Ostia." He sounded too casual. "I've business in the Campagna that I have to leave for first thing in the morning. The letter is personal, so I want someone who won't just pass it into the nearest slave's hands."

"Of course! You've been good enough to see us dinner." Toasts were made and Gwyn was called to another table. When she circled back the men were leaving; tipsy back slaps and cries of affection. They wandered into the night, leaving Gwyn to clear their table and think.

It's a murmur of discontent with a healthy dose of fear. Or unhealthy. Whatever. People don't like the Emperor but they don't hate him—he just is.

"Who are Clemens and Epaphroditus?" she asked Scaurus.

"Who?"

"Clemens and Epaphroditus—who are they?"

The old waiter's expression became closed. "They're no one now, Gwynia. Our master and god saw to that."

"What happened to them?" Gwyn rubbed persistently at a wine stain on the table. It was no good asking for salt to try to clean it. She'd tried that and been told she wasn't a soldier to be paid in such an expensive commodity.

"Why do you want to know, Gwynia? Just smile your pretty face at the legates who grace us with their presence and maybe one of them will pick you for a wife."

Gwyn made a rude noise. She switched tactics. "Look, if you don't know, that's fine. I just thought you knew all the gossip, but if you don't, that's okay—I don't judge."

Scaurus glared at her. "Look, everyone knows our dear Emperor isn't the friendliest of fellows. He's not his dear old papa, tight-fisted piss-taxer that he was. He's not his dashing big brother, the much mourned war hero. But Rome muddles along well enough under him. He builds us arenas and puts on games. So if he happens to take against someone—in this case his niece's husband and a crusty old Greek—that's his business. We'll just keep muddling along."

"What did they do?" Gwyn asked quietly. There was no one else in the caupona at this late hour. Vibia had taken her husband upstairs to their apartment when he'd complained of bunions, promising a swift return to lock up. That was an hour ago.

Scaurus shrugged. "All I hear is rumor. Some say Clemens copped it because the Emperor fancied his wife. He's got a thing for his nieces, you see." Gwyn pulled a face. "She's in this hocus pocus new religion though, and wouldn't have a bar of it, not like poor old Julia, so she got exiled and he got the chop."

"And the other guy?" Gwyn wanted to know.

Another shrug. "Just an old Greek bastard freedman who probably dates back to Augustus. Arrested on the pretext of not having saved Nero from topping himself." He spat. "I lived through that bastard's reign. Domitian's a kind old soul compared to that monster. Mind you, Clemens and Epaphroditus were pretty close to him. I suppose a few people are scared now. If it can happen to them, it could happen to anyone."

"Who'd be scared?" Gwyn needed names. Her knowledge of who might be involved in the plot was sketchy. The problem with eavesdropping was she didn't know what she was listening for.

"What are you two standing around gossiping for? That doesn't get tables cleaned!" Vibia's caw set Gwyn to jumping. She quickly made herself a plate of leftovers and cleared the rest, washing dishes and straightening the bar. Only when everything was tidied to Vibia's satisfaction was she allowed to sit and eat her cold meal. Then she was locked in for the night after Scaurus tottered off to whatever hole in the wall he called home.

* * *

The next day she was to deliver a luncheon order of Lucretian sausage, goat's cheese, salad and a jar of pickled herrings to one of the regulars. It was a slow day at the caupona when the slave arrived on behalf of her master. Scaurus preferred to commandeer the tables when business was quiet—that way he kept the tips for himself—and he declared himself too old to go running up the hill where the customer lived.

"Cook's away wit' mistress," the slave explained. She was an adolescent girl, with the lighter skin of a Gaul. "T' master don't like me cookin', so I is sent runnin' for lunches and dinners all this week."

"No wonder you're so skinny," Gwyn panted. Fit as she was these days, she was hard pressed to keep up with the little imp as she skipped up the hill.

"Skinny is best, missus. T' master likes 'is girls plump."

Gwyn shuddered with disgust and was tempted to stop and spit in the man's salad. She delivered the food to the house and was tossed a couple of coins as a tip. Gwyn tried to palm them to the girl when the man wasn't looking.

"You need this more than me," she muttered.

Wide-eyed, the slave girl shook her head. "He'll say I stole it. Best you is havin' it, missus."

Dejected, Gwyn saw herself out the door. She wandered back down the street, not keen to return to work. If she was late back she would simply talk her way out of trouble with Vibia. Despite her gruff tongue and accusatory ways she wasn't the worst employer Gwyn could have.

A brawl in the street sent her cutting down an alleyway and across a marketplace. She was fairly sure it was the alley she escaped down that first day, but the crisscross of Roman streets disorientated her. Turning back to examine the alley from the other side, she saw the man from the caupona, the one who had wanted a letter sent. Gwyn recalled him saying he had to leave for the Campagna first thing. *You're running late, buddy. It's mid-arvo already!*

He didn't look dressed for travel. Gwyn wondered idly if he'd had to change his plans. On a whim, she decided to tail him for a bit. Maybe she could inveigle herself into conversation with him and find out some more about the two men Domitian had killed. Or find out who was afraid they might be next. She mentally patted herself on the back for her cleverness and slipped after him.

He was a man on a mission, not stopping to talk to anyone. Gwyn remembered movies she'd seen where spies hid in doorways and pretended to shop while stalking someone. She had to run to keep up, dodging through crowds and rounding street corners in a hurry so she wouldn't lose him.

This is pointless. I'd best give up now and get back before Vibia gets really *cranky.* She halted. The small street before her had chickens and people and a snorting mule, but no mysterious man. *Ah well, that settles that then.*

A vice-like grip took hold of her arm. "What are you following me for, girl?" The man hissed and shook her. "Are you spying on me, or do you think to rob me? You're a poor excuse for an informer or a thief." He shook her again.

Gwyn struggled. "You've made a mistake, Legate! I'm just on my way to visit a friend."

"In this neighborhood? A young girl like you shouldn't wander alone here." His skin was pale and his brown eyes hard. "You were waiting tables at Vibia's thermopolium last night, but I've never seen you there before last week. You think I didn't notice you eavesdropping? And now this?"

"Domine, please, this is a misunderstanding." Gwyn half chuckled. She injected conviction into her voice. "Yes, I work at the caupona, but I also get sent out to run errands, which is why I'm here. I'm sorry you thought I was following you." Her lie came all too easily—she was getting good at it. *Give me a minute and the pocket watch will have him convinced.* She ventured an innocent look.

"Save your lies, slut." The man snarled and hauled her down the street with him. Gwyn was too shocked to resist. A dull-eyed pair of vigiles propping up the wall of an eatery perked up as the man dragged Gwyn up to them. "Here's a silver apiece to shove this little bit in the prison for a night or two. She's an informer, or works for one, and she was harassing me as I went about my day."

Gwyn was appalled. "Wait. What?" she cried.

"As you say, Domine." The vigiles didn't seem to care they were being ordered about by an arrogant stranger. The silver disappeared into their red tunics faster than Gwyn's confidence. The situation had changed so rapidly she was left speechless. The man stalked away and the vigiles grasped her arms. A short march to their station house and a heavy clank of a cell door took place before Gwyn could fully process what had happened. *Shit! Ok, calm down—just connect to the timepiece and jump out of here.*

There was one problem with that. She was not alone in the cell.

Twelve

96 AD

The cell wasn't large, and the only light squeezed in from a shuttered window high in the far wall. Gwyn peered into the shadows.

"What's this—try to empty the purse of a customer while he was emptying hisself into you, did you, love?" A shape unfurled from the gloom and took on the appearance of a short, weedy man with pockmarked skin and a black eye.

"Don't even think about touching me," Gwyn declared, pressing her back against the cell door.

"I don't have to think about it," another voice chuckled, "I'll just do it." A bigger man, with a fat lip and fat hands to match rose from the floor and approached Gwyn.

Fuck! She projected dullness, greyness. It had worked in the past.

It wasn't working now. Gwyn sought to divide her mind, one part searching for the timepiece's connection, the other watching the two men and deciding which one to hit first. She'd grown slack in the last few days, not bothering to practice the moves that Meric taught her back in Transylvania. She thought her ability to persuade others was enough to protect her. She understood now that the power of suggestion couldn't deter those who had their minds fixed. When Vlad Dracula had attacked her it had been the same—only the intervention of others had saved her from being raped.

"Back off, I saw 'er first!" Weedy Man snarled. Fat Man growled and came at Gwyn from her side. They both looked as though they'd been in a fight. Had they been fighting each other? They certainly didn't appear to be friends.

Gwyn was not a natural fighter. She lacked the instinct that told her where an enemy's weakness was, but even she could work out that hitting a bruise or a split lip would intensify the hurt. When Fat Man grabbed her waist she elbowed his mouth. He howled and clutched his hands to his freshly bleeding lip.

Weedy man was more cautious, snatching Gwyn's wrists and trying to push her down. She braced her back against the door and kneed him hard in the groin. As he curled over she thrust her head forward into his black eye. Gwyn jerked free and shoved him backwards as hard as she could, her forehead smarting. He went sprawling.

Sausage fingers groped Gwyn's arm and pulled her sideways. She stumbled and landed on the dirt floor. Then fat man let go and froze.

Gwyn looked up to see a dark skinned face grinning over at her, white teeth gleaming. Dark hands held a small knife to Fat Man's throat. "How about you is leaving the nice lady alone, and I is not making a mess of you all over the floor. Same goes for you," he shot back over his shoulder. Weedy Man was crouched in the corner, one hand on his face, the other between his legs. "Huh. You wasn't even needing me," the African man said to Gwyn in his deep voice.

"Well, maybe you sped things up." Gwyn got to her feet breathlessly and brushed her hands on her dress. She was assessed her rescuer carefully. He kicked the fat man, who scuttled into one of the dark corners.

"I know you," Gwyn said. "You're the doorkeeper. I saw you in the street the other day too." Was he going to threaten her with the knife? He didn't seem about to, though he towered over her. The scar on his face was hardly visible in this dim light, but she felt sure it was him.

"Izem is my name." He smiled and twirled the knife between his fingers.

"Gwyn," she replied, watching the knife.

He noticed and his smile became even broader, before he slipped the knife away into his belt. "I is not needing it for those two." He jerked his head at the sullen men sitting in opposite corners glaring at each other. "Just gets their attention, like."

"Yes, well, thanks." Gwyn relaxed a little, and worked on putting out calm, peaceful vibes. *I'll chat all day if it keeps me out of a fight.*

"You is in trouble, Gwyn, to be ending up in here. Or is trouble finally catching up with you?"

"Just a misunderstanding," Gwyn replied shortly. "And you?"

"Fighting these idiots." Izem nodded at their cell-mates. "They is brawling in the street and I is breaking it up. Stupid vigiles is grabbing me with them. My master is being along to bail me out, present-like."

Gwyn raised her eyebrows. She knew Ancient Rome as a sophisticated society but had never thought about the finer legalities of its justice system.

"Someone is coming for you?" Izem picked at his teeth with a fingernail.

"I... I don't have a way of getting a message to them," she realized out loud. "Has this happened to you before?" *He sounds very nonchalant.* "Do masters often bail out their slaves?"

"I is not a slave!" Izem glared at Gwyn.

"His mother was a slave, and a whore to boot," Weedy Man was dumb enough to pipe up. Izem whirled and snarled into the darkness. Gwyn put a hand on his arm. She didn't know what possessed her—it wasn't the safest move—but she didn't want to witness a murder. *I've seen enough death lately.*

Izem stilled and looked curiously at Gwyn. She wondered if she'd made a mistake. "He's not worth it," she said.

"He would have raped you," Izem pointed out. "Same as that idiot." He nodded towards Fat Man in the other corner.

"Rapists deserve to die, but–" she cut herself off, feeling tired. A quote rose to her mind. *Many that live deserve death. And some that die deserve life. Can you give it to them?* "I just don't want their deaths on my conscience. Not if I have a choice." Perhaps that was a coward's way out. She was here to murder a man, to set history to rights. Could it be she didn't have the guts to see it through? Her stomach dropped. *This is real.*

"Fabius Izemus?" The shout from the other side of the cell door made Gwyn jerk. Izem steadied her.

"Yeah?" Izem called lazily.

"Your bail has been paid." The door opened a crack and a shaven-head vigil peered in. Gwyn welcomed the light, then saw the sullen faces of her would-be rapists examining her afresh. She took a sharp breath.

"I isn't leaving just yet." Gwyn stared at Izem in astonishment. He shot her a small smile. "There is someone you can get a message to, someone who can help? They is needing money."

"I'm not a bloody message boy," the vigil complained. "What's it to you if the wench stays here?"

Why was Izem helping her? *Maybe it's the pocket watch influencing him. Who cares?* "Um." Would Vibia come if she sent for her? Gwyn doubted it. She wasn't worth that much to her.

There was only one other person in the city of Rome Gwyn could think of who would come to her aid. With a sigh she fished out a few coins—her tip from earlier—and dropped it in the guard's hand.

* * *

It was several hours before Gaius arrived. Izem waited in a corner beside Gwyn. They didn't speak—the presence of their cell mates was a deterrent. Fat Man's brother showed up after two hours, bribing the guards to release him. No one came for Weedy Man.

A thump on the door got their attention. "You going to piss off now?" the vigil asked Izem as he beckoned to Gwyn.

The young man's scarred face broke into another grin and he bowed as he and Gwyn left the cell. The sergeant's desk played host to an anxious Gaius who slammed a purse down on the table and grabbed Gwyn by the shoulders. "Are you alright? What happened?"

"Outside," she shook him off, comforted and embarrassed.

Izem brought up the rear, saluting the sergeant as he went. "I is seeing you next time," he said.

"I'm starving," Gwyn sighed and looked at Gaius. "Can we get something to eat before I explain?" She jerked a thumb at Izem. "And I owe him a meal at least. I have money, just not on me. I'll pay you back."

"No need." Gaius eyed Izem warily. The African man was a head taller than Gaius, and lean with muscle. He wore a simple brown tunic with plain sleeves. It looked to be good quality, as did his sandals, though scuffed and dirty in places. *Probably from the fight he was in earlier.*

He was not attractive. His nose was too big and his ears stuck out. His grin held a challenge and he held Gaius' stare.

The older man huffed out a breath and gestured for them to follow him.

They found a tolerably clean bar that served food. Gwyn expected Izem to flirt with the waitress—she was clearly flirting with him, but aside from a wink to her as he ordered, he watched Gwyn. This clearly irritated Gaius, and she found herself under intense scrutiny as she ate. "Will you two stop staring at me?" she demanded at last.

"You is interesting to look at," Izem announced, adding more water to his wine.

"I wasn't staring." Gaius retorted.

"Look, he saved me from getting raped in there," Gwyn told Gaius. "I don't know why he did it, but I'm grateful. I was...following someone in the street and they took it amiss. That's how I ended up in there."

"Why did you help her?" Gaius fired off at Izem. "And why were you in there? What's your name, anyway?"

Oh bloody hell, he's acting all protective. How embarrassing. She glared at Gaius.

Izem took it all in his stride. He leant back on his stool, spreading his hands on the table. "She is not fighting too badly. I is figuring she didn't want to be meat for those dogs, so I is lending a hand. And my name is Izem. Fabius Izemus if you want to be looking me up. Got picked up by the vigiles when I is breaking up a fight."

"Like to fight, do you?" Gaius interrogated. Gwyn rolled her eyes.

"Might be I is a public-minded citizen trying to stop his neighbors from hurting each other." Izem grinned again. Gaius snorted. "Who is you following, Miss Gwynia, that took so against you? Boyfriend? Husband? Customer who didn't tip?"

Gwyn observed that if Gaius' eyebrows furrowed any further he'd go cross-eyed. "Just a person of interest," she replied. She didn't think he was too bright if he kept getting into fights, or sought them out.

"Yes, well, eat up and I'll see you home," Gaius ordered. "You can go," he told Izem.

"You her father?"

Gwyn and Gaius both blushed and she spluttered on her wine. "No," she coughed.

"No." Gaius was emphatic. "She's my… wife's cousin."

Gwyn caught the look Izem slid between the two of them. *Maybe he's not as stupid as he seems. He was pretty decent, actually, to save me in the cell and not trying anything himself. Bit arrogant though.*

Gwyn scowled at both men; Izem with his knowing smile and Gaius studiously frowning at his half-empty plate. "Is you eating that?" Izem asked.

"Be my guest." Gaius stood and placed coins on the table. "Gwynia?"

She ate a few more mouthfuls deliberately. "Let's go," she mumbled, taking one last sip of wine as she rose.

"See you round, Gwynia." Izem winked and helped himself to the others' plates.

* * *

Gwyn and Gaius trudged in silence through the dark streets, dodging carts and wagons. Now that the daytime ban on wheeled vehicles was lifted the roads were busy. Gaius apologized, "I don't have the money for a carrying chair."

"You know I can handle walking." Gwyn thought of their time together at Masada, when they had walked through the night and she'd rather ineptly lost her virginity to him. She went on hurriedly. "Besides, you used your money for my bail. I'll pay you back, I swear." She felt his silence and rankled. "I'm working as a waitress, not a prostitute! I've saved my tips!"

He put a hand on her arm. "In most taverns it's one and the same. And I know a woman with no family or supporters has to make hard decisions. I don't judge. But… I didn't think that was you."

Gwyn rolled her eyes, then realized he couldn't see it. They climbed a hill. "It's not like I have the skills to be a seamstress or hairdresser."

When Gaius spoke again she could tell he was puzzled. "And what does your work have to do with… the other business you have here?"

"Nothing." Gwyn couldn't keep the dejection from her voice. "I've made no progress so far. Hey, are we going the right way? I'm kinda lost."

"This is a short cut to the Forum. It should bring us out near your tavern. I would rather not take you back home again." Gaius sounded cautious.

Gwyn blinked sudden tears from her eyes. She knew Gaius was protecting his family. "Does Adi know you came out to rescue me from jail?"

"No. I didn't tell her."

She had no reply to that. She was angry at herself for getting into trouble in the first place, let alone having to call for help and risking danger to Gaius' family.

They neared the Forum and Gwyn turned down the side street where the caupona was located. It was busy. Light spilled out as laughter and conversation flowed behind it. "Wait here," Gwyn said to Gaius. "I'll get the money I've saved."

She ran inside and caught Scarus' arm when she saw him. "My tip money, Scaurus, I need it."

"Gwynia, where have you been? Vibia is livid!" The old waiter didn't look too happy either. He was as flustered and busy as when she'd first seen him.

"Please," she begged. She lifted his tray and he pointed to an inside table with a frown. She delivered the drinks and returned to badger him. He gave a frustrated growl and fumbled inside his belt pouch, passing her several coins. She looked at them and glared at him. He huffed and a couple of bronze sesterces were added to her palm. She sighed, knowing she'd been royally short changed but unable to do anything about it.

"Girl!" A customer at an outside table yelled and Gwyn saw Vibia's head shoot up from the kitchen. Gwyn skipped out past the table and dumped the money into Gaius' hands.

"I know it's probably not enough, but I'll try to make the rest up soon," she told him.

"Girl!" Vibia lunged out of the doorway and caught Gwyn a solid slap over the back of the head. "Where have you been, you skulking, thieving slattern?" Gwyn dodged the second slap. Several customers on the outside tables cheered the unexpected entertainment.

"It wasn't my fault!" Gwyn's head throbbed. *Cow!* "I got… mugged."

"I don't care, you unreliable little bitch! If this is your father he ought to take you home and beat you, and if he's your lover then good luck to him with a runaway trollop!"

"Gwyn, come away from here," Gaius steered her away from Vibia's livid form. Gwyn shook him off.

"I don't need your help!" Her anger bubbled out. She was being bogged down by this stupidity and not making progress in her mission.

"Just come on!" His normally gentle voice snapped with impatience.

She scowled and allowed herself to be dragged away. "What?" she demanded when the hoots and whistles receded behind them. "You can't take me home—that was the only other place where I could sleep and get food!"

"I'm not taking you home. I'm taking you to stay with my sister, Junilla. But first, there is someone I think you ought to see."

Thirteen

96 AD

It had once been a wealthy villa, Gwyn decided as she waited nervously. The vases and frescos looked expensive but were layered with dust. Gaius had brought her in through a side door, and they had passed through enough rooms and halls for her to see that the place was extensive. The few slaves they passed nodded to Gaius while giving her sidelong looks. Gwyn would have liked the opportunity to have a quick wash but it was getting late.

Whoever's house this was had company. She heard voices across the courtyard and saw figures in a well-lit dining room. Every other room in the house that she could see, including the dusty little study in which she waited, was dark or only half-lit by oil lamps that hung at skewed angles—as if a drunk had put them up.

Maybe it looks nicer by day. She cracked her knuckles and yawned. The day's events, not to mention tramping back and forth around Rome, had worn her out. She sat on a stool in front of the desk and put her head down on her arms.

She jerked awake when two men came in, leaping to her feet and tripping over the stool. Gaius grabbed her arm and set her upright. "Gwynia, it's alright." He lapsed into the Latinized version of her name as she stared at the other man who sat behind the desk.

Silva was now in his mid-fifties, and looked it, but Gwyn saw traces of the steadfast Roman general who'd sponsored her care as his forces laid siege to Masada. She was glad of Gaius' introduction to confirm her recognition, though Silva frowned as he searched his memory for Gwyn's face. "You tell me, Gaius, that this is the girl who gave us critical information about the Jews and then disappeared right after the fortress fell? Do you take me for a fool? If that were so then she hasn't aged a day! This is a poor time for a joke, lad."

Hardly a lad, anymore. It was clear to Gwyn that the relationship was a long-standing one, as Gaius didn't alter his demeanor. "Sir, you know I wouldn't lie. Antonia Gwynia has been sent by the gods to us for a reason. She was at Masada to help make sure you, and Rome, would triumph. She has come to help Rome again."

Gwyn frowned. This was a garbled version of her tale, but she kept silent, trusting Gaius had a purpose here. She understood now why he didn't want to talk about magic—the risk of being overheard and reported to one of Domitian's informers was not worth it. From the wary gossip she'd heard at the caupona people were being arrested in their homes to be tortured and then executed for crimes against the Emperor.

"There are people who think the same," Gaius continued cryptically. "I wondered if you might know them."

Silva stared at his freedman, then ran his hands through his short-cropped greying hair. He tapped one ringed finger on the desk. "This is ludicrous, Gaius. You know I'm going back to my country estates tomorrow. Why would you come to me with this foolish tale?"

"Please," Gwyn interrupted. "Sir, you were kind to me, at Masada. Your centurion Drusus brought me in to see you late at night. I slept on the couch. You questioned me the next day and I told you I thought the siege was hopeless. You had Gaius look after me, but insisted I stay in the tent. We discussed Herodotus. I reminded you of your daughter, a little." She swallowed and continued. "I asked to be sent to Joppa, but you couldn't spare the men. You were going to write to my cousins." She kept her eyes fixed on him, not glancing at Gaius at all, not wanting Silva to think she had been prepped with this spiel. "I wore a blue dress—taken from the spoils you wanted to gift to your wife. I had been wearing a brown dress when the scout found me. I climbed over the wall at the Eastern Gate and came down the Snake Path in the dark. You gave me wine."

Silva was too refined to gape at her, but she could tell her words impacted him. He shot a look at Gaius. "Even if I were to believe this…

fancy, I'm not in a position to do anything about it. As I said, I'm leaving Rome tomorrow."

He seemed far more flustered than the capable military man she remembered. She remembered Adi's comments about Silva not being in favor with Domitian. Gwyn went on. "I have been sent to make sure certain things happen, sir, so if you know of anyone I should be talking to, or whose household I should be familiar with, you need to point me in the right direction. Before it is too late… for you."

She guessed his fear of the Emperor had become more real in recent times. Silva would have been buddies with Titus and had no doubt risen during his brief reign. The memory of his older brother might have stayed Domitian's hand thus far, but if the rumors she'd heard in the last few days were anything to go by, closeness to the Emperor was no longer any protection. Everyone was at risk.

Silva fidgeted. Gwyn tried not to copy him but clenched her toes in her sandals. She maintained eye contact. *I'm not bound by your rules of social subservience. You will help me.*

Silva stared at her then Gaius. "Is there something I should know, my lad? I thought you enjoyed the quiet life, with your family."

"I'm thinking of you, sir." Gaius was serious. "I owe everything to your patronage, including my quiet, family life. If something should happen to you…" The implication was clear. Domitian's disfavor would have a chain reaction. Anyone who looked to Silva for social, political or monetary support would suffer. In looking out for Silva, Gaius was protecting himself. Gwyn admired his survival instincts.

Silva huffed, then sucked air through his teeth. He seemed to be wavering still so Gwyn jumped in. "Sir, when I met you, you were the calmest, most practical general I'd ever met." *The only general I'd ever met.* "You need not fear for our discretion." She waited.

"Flavia Domitilla," Silva said. "If there's anyone who'd know anything, it'd be her. I tell you this only because you've been part of my household and family for more than twenty years Gaius. I trust you. I hope that trust is not misplaced."

"It is not," Gaius said quietly.

The silence between them was heavy, before Silva went on, "But I don't see how this will help. You're just as likely to be taken for a spy if you try to approach her. She's been banished to the Isle of Pandateria."

"Let me worry about that," Gwyn told him. "I just need to know where to start. I don't intend to take a direct approach." She hoped this was the breakthrough she needed. If she could position herself close to the conspirators, she would have better luck ensuring their attempt was successful.

"Thank you, sir. Good luck with your trip."

Silva shook Gaius' hand and, after a moment's hesitation, patted Gwyn on the arm. "I must be mad to believe you, or my memory is failing, but you do look just like the girl from Masada."

Gwyn smiled. "It's good to see you again, General."

Gaius let them out a different door and they trudged down the street, watching shadows warily. Silva had offered to send slaves with them as bodyguards but Gwyn preferred no one else to know where she was going. She told Gaius to be quiet and just lead the way. He held her arm and she concentrated on projecting an aura of poverty, seeking to deter muggers.

Gaius' sister Junilla was not impressed at being woken. It took her some time to answer the door, peering around the frame with a large knife in hand. Gaius explained by candlelight that Gwyn was from Silva's household and needed a place to stay for a night or two. He pressed a purse into Junilla's hand and asked if he could doss down for the night too. "I'd rather not push my luck by tramping back home—I'd be robbed for sure."

"Your wife won't be impressed," Junilla sniffed.

"I'll explain to her tomorrow."

Gwyn thought he'd have a lot of explaining to do, and felt bad for him, but that still didn't stop her from falling asleep as soon as her head hit the mat.

* * *

It had been well after midnight when she finally went to bed, so Gwyn was not pleased with being woken by a caustic voice.

"Rise and shine," The heavy wooden shutters clattered back and sunlight fell hard upon Gwyn's face.

"Ugh, seriously?" She covered her eyes with a hand to fend off the unwelcome brightness, but nothing could block out the noise of her hostess smacking clay pots and plates down on the table.

"I suppose he expects me to feed you, too? Gods all know he eats like a horse. Well you'll just have to put up with yesterday's bread until I go to the markets. You can get up in the meantime and make yourself useful. I'll not wait on anyone, *friend* of my brother's or no."

Junilla. Gwyn remembered where she was. "I'm sorry to be a bother to you," she apologized. It came out sarcastically since she was grumpy from being woken. She also recalled Gaius handing his sister money. She crawled off her little pallet and shook the creases from her skirts. She was dying for a bath but the last few days had taught her that Roman baths tended not to open until much later in the day.

"Hmph," was Junilla's only reply. She was a thin woman who looked much older than the mid-forties Gwyn knew her to be. Frown lines etched their way across her pinched face, and brown eyes glanced back sharply at Gwyn. "What are you peering at, girl?"

"Where's Gaius?" Gwyn wanted to know, not answering.

"Gone home, left at dawn while sluggards like you were still snoozing. Pass me that bread board there."

Gwyn complied. "When is he coming back?"

"Didn't say," Junilla snapped. "So I suppose you're my burden until then. As if I don't have enough to be going on with."

Gwyn took the bread she was given. Junilla kept up a litany of complaints throughout the morning as they visited the markets, bought food, came back to the little apartment and cleaned. Gaius' sister did piecework weaving in the afternoon, so at least Gwyn could help with the spinning. She made more mistakes than not, though, and by the afternoon her ears were blistered with criticism.

This is not helping! She was annoyed at Gaius for not reappearing sooner, forgetting that he'd been put out enough the evening before when he rescued her from prison and escorted her around half the city.

"I suppose he'll come just as I serve dinner. Typical. Probably because that wife of his can't cook proper Roman food. That's what he gets for marrying an Easterner. Foreigners always bring more trouble than they're worth."

Gwyn felt compelled to defend her friend. "Adi cooks exceptionally well," she remarked. "And a nice variety of dishes."

"Oh, I suppose you'd rather eat there then? Rather than stomach my poor fare? Oh, I understand." Junilla sneered and went back to slicing vegetables to stew in the pot.

"I didn't say that." Gwyn rolled her eyes. Junilla noticed.

"Well, why didn't he house you there in his own house then? Or did she throw you out? I'm surprised at him, taking up with someone so young, but it's typical of men. Never mind what I taught him. Never mind everything I went through to feed him and clothe him and put him through school." She shut up suddenly, as if realizing she'd said too much. "Not that that's anyone's business but mine!" she snapped.

She thinks... I'm Gaius' mistress or something! Never mind that it was close to the truth in Gwyn's own unhappy imagination. The reality of being viewed as such stung her. She set down the bowl of pearl barley she had been rinsing. "Look, Adi is a dear friend of mine, and Gaius has never been anything but a perfect gentleman to me. He said he learnt how to treat women from you. He got me out of a tricky spot last night and not once asked for repayment of any kind. I'll be out of your hair as soon as I can manage but he did give you money so I don't know why you are carrying on so much." She kept her tone level, picking up the barley again and pouring it into the pot.

Junilla pursed her lips, then used the knife to point at Gwyn. "You are far too young to talk to me like that. Mind your tongue." All the same, Gwyn thought she didn't sound upset at being stood up to.

It was indeed dinnertime when someone showed up for Gwyn. But it wasn't Gaius. It was Adi. When Junilla saw her sister-in-law the almost companionable atmosphere that had grown shattered. "What do you want?" Gaius' sister demanded.

"I've come with a message for Gwynia," Adi replied in clipped tones. "I won't be long, I've a chair waiting."

Gwyn looked between the two and sighed. "I'll come down." It was two flights down to the street. If she hurried she might get back to her stew before it went cold.

"No," Adi responded. "It's best if no one else hears." She moved across the small kitchen to Gwyn, careful not to touch any of the furniture. "There's a barge going to Ostia at sunrise from the Probi Bridge—Gaius will meet you there and travel with you. It's his business now." She glanced at Junilla. "He inherited it from his uncle."

The uncle who had abused Junilla, Gwyn remembered with anger. *If he inherited a river transport business, why is his sister living in this poky little apartment? Surely he would have provided for her?*

"He's arranging things now, which is why I'm here," Adi said in Hebrew. "When you get to Ostia you must find a ship that will take you to Pandateria. When you get there find a way to speak to Flavia Domitilla. She and her late husband are of the faith." Gwyn was startled by the change of language, even though she understood the words. She was distracted by Junilla angrily leaving the room.

"Will you remember that, Gwynia?" Adi asked harshly. "I take a big risk coming to you like this."

"Okay, yes." Gwyn's face must have shown her confusion.

"Jews are not popular in Rome, and especially not popular with the Emperor," Adi hissed in Latin. "And that band of Jews calling themselves 'Christians' even less so. I've tried to leave all that behind, to not put Gaius and my family at risk." An unimpressed 'hmph!' from the doorway showed that Junilla hadn't gone far. "But I still hear some things, whether I like it or not. From what I hear Flavia Domitilla has good reason to help you, and she will have the connections you need. And now I have to go."

"Thank you." Gwyn lunged forward to give a sudden hug. Adi stiffened, then patted Gwyn on the shoulder, before disentangling herself and exiting the apartment.

Junilla was silent when she re-entered from the other room.

"You see?" Gwyn said, sitting back at her bowl of barley and vegetable stew. "I'll be gone by dawn."

Her host sniffed. "You'd do best to stay away from people like her," she remarked acidly as she picked up her wooden spoon. "Like I said, foreigners are trouble."

I'm more foreign than you'd believe, lady. Gwyn sighed, and ate her dinner.

Fourteen

96 AD

Gwyn followed the streets downhill to the River Tiber in the pre-dawn light. Carts and other wheeled vehicles that had to be out of the city limits by sunrise rattled by, raising welcome zephyrs. The day promised to be hot again. At the bridge she was anxious about spotting Gaius, but he found her immediately. He must have been watching for her.

"Here, Gwyn—this way." He ushered her down stone steps and steadied her as they stepped on the rickety little wooden jetty. Once on the barge he seated her in the middle and called to push off. There was a pair of donkeys penned near the bow, and a handful of men crewing the oars. Gaius talked to them while Gwyn hugged herself and watched the river traffic come to life as they drifted past.

After a while Gaius returned to Gwyn with a small parcel. It contained a warm pie and mulsum in a flask. "I figured you wouldn't have had time to have breakfast," he said, squatting beside her.

"No." Gwyn didn't tell him that his sister had said 'good riddance' and watched Gwyn carefully to make sure she didn't steal anything. "Why don't Junilla and Adi get along? Is it because you and she were once so close, and you went away then came home with someone different?"

Gaius frowned and ran a hand through his hair. "What did Junilla say?"

"Oh, she just seemed a bit... critical." Gwyn didn't want to gossip, especially if both women pretended to be nice in front of Gaius.

"She's bitter, it's true," he replied. "And yes, she hates foreigners. Sees them as a threat. The... work she used to do—she was undercut by a lot of cheaper girls. Poor things were just as desperate as her. I got my manumission just in time or she would have starved. Then our uncle died, and left everything to me, and nothing to her. I tried to give her half but she was so angry she refused. Said she could still make her own way in the world. That's the other reason I took you to her. She won't take charity but every chance I get I slip her something."

Gwyn was sad for Junilla. Surviving years of prostitution would make anyone hard, though it didn't excuse her rancor for Adi. "But surely she wants you to be happy?" she asked. "I know not everyone likes their in-laws but I always had the impression your sister cared about you very much."

The city was falling away to either side of the river now—the apartment blocks getting smaller and greenery filling the space between. The sun had risen but the river breeze was refreshing.

"I think she still does," Gaius sighed. "I worry about her. But perhaps it's best if she has nothing to do with us at this time."

"When we get to Ostia," Gwyn began, but Gaius shushed her.

"Not now," he said.

Gwyn saw a member of the crew smirk and nudge his mate. Annoyed, she sat straight and refrained from chatting. The ease with which she'd once spoken to Gaius was gone. The feeling of comradeship dissipated into awkwardness, and Gwyn felt exposed in the bright sunlight with the sound of waves swashing against the barge.

* * *

Ostia was crowded like Rome, but with a distinctly nautical air. The barge bumped against the stone wharf and one of the men leapt out to secure it to a bollard. The movement jolted everyone, including the donkeys, who brayed, adding to the cacophony of the port. As soon as they disembarked Gaius showed Gwyn into a small office on the side of a warehouse. "Wait here and stay out of trouble. You'll be safe—I lease this place for the barge business. I'm going to see if there are any ships sailing to Pandateria. There have to be some to take supplies to Flavia Domitilla. I hope," he added quietly.

"What do you mean, you hope?"

Gaius caught her gaze. "Pandateria is where Emperors Tiberius and Claudius sent their own relatives—imperial ladies—to starve to death. Nero's first wife was sent there and killed. I daresay the only reason our Master and God has stayed his hand thus far is because he has a fondness for his nieces."

Ew, that's right—he got one of them pregnant. "Can't I come with you?"

"No. It'll be quicker if I go alone. You need to stay here."

"Can I at least go get something to eat?" Gwyn wanted to know, miffed at the implication that she chose to find trouble.

"Fine. Just—don't go far! Here's some money." Gaius handed her a few coppers and went out.

Gwyn watched him from the door, noting the direction in which he'd gone. She pulled her shawl up over her head, breathed slowly until calmness washed over her, and ventured out amongst the wharves and warehouses of the seaport town.

Concentrating on being inconspicuous, she wasn't harassed as she located a public latrine. She could never decide if it was better to breathe through her nose and risk fainting from the stench, or use her mouth and then wish she could scrape the taste from her tongue afterwards. Spilled effluent pooled in gutters on the floors, so Gwyn tiptoed to the nearest of the multi-hole benches to hitch her skirts. The public slave attending the latrine offered her the communal sponge on a stick. "No, thank you," Gwyn whispered. Her skin crawled. She had taken to carrying scraps of cloth for the essential times she couldn't go without some form of toilet paper—anything was better than sharing someone else's fecal matter. *Education, roads and the aqueduct they may have given us, but sanitation? Monty Python got that wrong.*

Afterwards she washed her hands, arms and feet thoroughly in an outside fountain, disdaining the basin inside. As usual she wished for soap, bleach or possibly even napalm. She promised herself to get checked out by a doctor when she returned to her time.

Gwyn wandered past shops and stalls in the wharf-front market. Slops from a pungent barrel of fish heads tempted bile into her throat, but she skipped over it and sought fresher air. It was hard to find. Her eyes were assaulted as much as her nose and ears, with colorful tunics and vendors' yells filling the space all around her. Fish, squid, oysters and octopi were just some of the ocean fare on display. Trade goods such as olive oil, timber and iron trundled down gangplanks and luxuries like Baltic amber, spices and silk were guarded closely as shipments were offloaded and inspected for customs tax.

Gwyn navigated the sights and smells to find cooked food at a street vendor. She settled on a bollard and was about to eat her lunch—fish skewers balanced on flat bread—when a voice said, "And what is you doing here? Seems like everywhere I go, you is there."

Gwyn fumbled. Izem's large hands scooped under hers and steadied her food. She smiled and realized with stupid excitement that she was glad to see someone she knew. Especially someone whose behaviour was a cut above the other men she'd met in this time. "Are you following me?" she asked.

"Seems like you is following me, Gwynia" he winked. "Not that I mind."

Gwyn blushed hard. *Woah, he's flirting big time.* "What are you doing here, really?"

He shrugged. "Every time I end up in the watch house my master is sending me away for a bit as punishment. This be the second time in two months so I is being given a long holiday." He grinned. He'd lost a tooth to one side of his mouth, but the rest were white and strong. Despite her cynicism she smiled back.

"Maybe you should stop getting into fights?" she joked. Her hands were sticky from the fish juice and her lunch was going cold. She wanted to eat but not in front of him. Making a mess would be embarrassing.

Almost as if he'd read her mind, he said, "Is you eating your *prandium?* It's going cold."

She blushed again and nibbled delicately. *I don't like eating in front of people. Especially not flirty guys who, despite not being handsome, are kind of attractive.* It made the meal less satisfying.

"Wait here," Izem said, and strolled away. Gwyn gratefully wolfed her food and wiped her face with the edges of her scarf. Another trip to the fountain would be needed. But she didn't want to lose the opportunity to keep talking to Izem. She found herself wanting to learn more about him, and he seemed to like her. *He probably just flirts with every girl,* she scolded herself. *You should get back to the warehouse and concentrate on approaching Flavia Domitilla, not hanging about here like you're on a date!*

"Just the thing." Her non-date was back, proffering a ripe pear. He bit into his own. "So if you is not following me, and I is not following you, what is you doing here?"

What if he's an informer? The cold thought trickled into the back of her mind. *Rubbish.* She shook it off. There was no way he could possibly know what she was up to, unless he'd followed her to Adi and Gaius' house and eavesdropped somehow. Still, it paid to be cautious. "Going on a holiday too," she said flippantly before biting into her pear. Juice ran down her chin, to her dismay. *Oh for fuck's sake, Gwyn, stop worrying about impressing this bloke and get back to the warehouse before Gaius comes back and has conniptions!* "Look, I'd better go." She got up off the bollard, but lingered. The odds of running into him again were slim. They'd probably used up all the coincidences they were owed.

"Can I be walking with you?" Izem gestured for Gwyn to lead. "I is kicking my heels till my master is done at the whorehouses. He don't pay for me."

Gwyn stiffened as he fell into step beside her. "Would you rather he did?"

"Naw." Izem slung the word out lazily, without pause. "No fun in being with someone you pay for. You is never knowing if them really wants it. Chances are they don't." He glanced over at her slyly, "I might not be pretty to look at, but I is knowing how to have fun." He winked again and Gwyn almost tripped. Red-faced, she veered gratefully to the fountain as they passed and took a long drink. She washed her face and hands carefully and dried them on her scarf. Izem drank too, then splashed her.

"Hey!" Gwyn dropped her scarf as she flipped a hand into the fountain and splashed him back. He laughed and sent another spray of water her way. She skipped back, bumping into a passing fishwife.

"Watch it, girl!" the rotund woman bellowed and Gwyn apologized as Izem grabbed her hand and dragged her clear. She giggled despite the fishwife's glare and leaned against a cool stone wall. The sun had passed its zenith and cast shadows back towards Rome.

Izem held up her scarf. "You dropped it." He shook it out and draped it carefully over her head, looking down at her. Excitement frissioned in Gwyn as he arranged the scarf under her chin and over her shoulders. She straightened off the wall for him to do so. They were only inches apart. She could see the muscles under his tunic; smell his faint, cinnamony sweat. She met his eyes.

He leaned down and brushed her lips with his own. She melted with a sigh and his hands caught under her elbows. The kiss lasted forever and only seconds at the same time, and when they broke Gwyn was hungry for more. She knew she should be heading back to the warehouse. She knew this was a foolish distraction and she was behaving like a trollop in a public street. But the feeling of being so wanted was intoxicating, and her brain went '*meh*' and settled in for the ride.

Then common sense prevailed and Gwyn pulled away to clear her throat and blush heavily again. "I really should go."

"But how is I finding you again, Gwynia?" He looked forlorn. "I can't just be waiting around hoping you is turning up."

Probably best if you keep the ball in your court. You've got things to do. "Can I find you at your master's house? That street down from the palace?"

He raised his eyebrows and she saw the way the scar on his face moved. Funny, she'd hardly noticed it these past few minutes. "You is finding me there or leaving a message. The slaves and other freedmen will all think I is so popular, to have girls coming knocking at the door for me," he teased.

Gwyn gave it right back to him. "Oh, are there so many? Will I have to wait in line? Maybe I won't bother then."

"No." Izem caught her hands and kissed them. "There is being no others. If you is coming to find me there, I is waiting for you." He shot her a sultry look and she shivered, almost losing her resolve to walk on.

"I'll be seeing you then, Izem." She extricated herself gently and tried not to grin like a loon as she walked away. As she reached the wharf to turn back into Gaius' warehouse, she turned to see if he still watched.

He did. He raised an arm slowly in a salute and she smiled into her shoulder and turned away.

Sheesh, what a bit of foolishness!

Her heart still raced as she let herself back into the warehouse.

* * *

Gaius was unimpressed. "What took you so long? I thought you were just going to get something to eat?"

Gwyn's good mood popped like a bubble. "I did. I didn't think you were going to be back for ages so I didn't rush. I didn't exactly want to be cooped up in here all afternoon."

He huffed with frustration. "I found a ship much quicker than expected. Called *Scipio's Fury*. A coastal trader. But it's no good. The captain has ordered everyone aboard tonight so he can put to sea before dawn, and I don't know how to convince him to take us."

"Us? Oh no, you've done enough. Just point him out to me and I'll take it from there."

Gaius frowned. "You cannot possibly think I'll let you travel alone on a ship full of rough men to an island where women are sent to die!"

"Gaius!" she snapped. "You're not my father; you don't need to babysit me. I'll dress as a boy and convince him to take me on as a ship's lad or something. I just need to disguise myself." Part of her laughed hysterically. *So it's come to this has it? The old 'girl disguises herself as a boy' trick!*

The man who was not her father turned red. "That's hardly respectable!"

When did he turn so stuffy? "Didn't I pretend to be a camp follower to escape Masada? Or don't you remember whose idea that was?"

"That's just... that was... that was then!" They were practically shouting. Gwyn realized as a spy or assassin she was shit at discretion.

"Look." She stopped and took a breath. "Gaius, why are you helping me? You and Adi are putting yourselves in a lot of danger by doing this. Do you think it might have something to do with the fact that I can influence people? This!" she thrust the chronokinetor absorbed in her left palm under his face. "This lets me speak other languages, persuade people to help me, as well as travel through time." Her gaze was fierce, but her voice quiet. "You've done enough. I can take it from here. Go home. Go back to Adi."

His lips twitched in a frown. "And let you just disappear again?"

They stared at each other, a picture of disagreement. Gaius huffed,

Gwyn's shoulders sagged. "It's getting late. I need to find men's clothes and get some supplies before the sun goes down. Can you… can you help with that? Please."

Another sigh. He nodded. "There's some old clothes in the chest over there. Might be a bit moth-eaten."

She changed behind a screen and they tucked her hair up into a cap. "You should cut it, if you really want to disguise yourself," Gaius said.

"I'll take my chances," she replied. "I might need to be a girl again in a hurry."

Gaius bought a cheap, woven bag for her and filled it with what he deemed to be essentials: a wheel of cheese, the last bread rolls from a bakery, a cup, a strigil and a knife. Gwyn stuffed her dress and scarf in as well. "I will find a way to repay you," she told Gaius as he treated them to an early dinner at a dockside caupona.

He looked at her oddly. "Gwynia, you have no money. Better that I pay for these things than you have to steal or…" Their meal arrived, plonked on the table by a sour waitress. A man at a neighboring table groped the woman's backside as she walked past. She slapped his hand away.

"You want it, you pay!" she snapped and disappeared back into the kitchen. Gwyn shuddered.

"I intend to avoid *that*," she muttered.

"Besides," Gaius poured their wine, "if you succeed it'll be for the best. For Silva, for Adi, for me."

"I suppose. I'd rather pay my own way, though." She wondered how Michelle dealt with it. She supposed the Agent wouldn't stress over someone else paying if it got the job done.

Perhaps it was easier to accept his help because she didn't feel as though she owed him anything physical. Back when they'd been at Masada, he was the first person to have liked her that she liked back. So it had been all muddled up—needing his help, wanting him, him wanting her. Now it was clear cut. And what she'd just had with Izem— *what was that even? A flirtation? Halfway to a fling?* It had sparked out of the blue and was totally unrelated to the work she had to do. She liked that. No ties. No broken hearts and pointless longing like with Alina. Maybe she was getting bolder, but if she succeeded in the plot against Domitian she'd reward herself with a little freedom. It wasn't as if she had anyone to answer to here. Especially not Gaius.

"Gwynia?"

"Huh? What?" She snapped out of her daydream and looked at him.

"I said, come on, eat up—we have to get you to the ship soon."

"Oh. Sure. Sorry." She tucked into the lentils and fish, pulled a face and sipped her well-watered down wine. Eating, she looked at Gaius. It was easier to see him as a friend now, not a weird kind of ex-boyfriend. The worry on his face aged him.

Her attraction to him was gone. It made her sad, but it was for the best.

* * *

The captain of *Scipio's Fury* was unimpressed when Gaius approached. "A ship's boy? I don't need a ship's boy—my men can shift for themselves." They stood on the stone wharf in the shadow of the ship's mast. The sun was low in the sky and working men and women everywhere were packing up for the day. Plenty more were getting started: prostitutes, pickpockets, hustlers and pimps.

"The lad's determined to run away to sea," Gaius lifted a purse. "We thought to let him get it out of his system then come home and work in the family business. He'll not complain about a hard life once he's had a real taste of salt."

"Hmph! Thrash him!" The captain was a stocky, broad-shouldered type who looked as if he'd dealt a few thrashings in his time.

"His mama's soft on him. I can't have her babying him—he needs to learn how to be a man. A short voyage should do that. You just run down the coast and back, do you not?"

The captain stroked the rough stubble on his chin. "Aye, and a few islands." He hefted the purse Gaius held out, and peeked inside. "You're a fool but I'll not rob ye. He can come learn the ropes; I'll make sure he gets fed. Skinny weed, looks like he needs toughening up."

"My warehouse is two wharves over. If you can send him back to Gaius Flavius Junillus in a few weeks I'd be grateful." Gwyn blinked in surprised. She'd hadn't known his full name.

"Come on then, lad." The captain gripped Gwyn's shoulder and towed her away from Gaius. She looked back after she'd scrambled on deck. Gaius nodded, turned, and walked away.

Fifteen

96 AD

Standing at the rail of the small merchant ship, Gwyn watched as the sun crept over the horizon. She marveled at the array of vessels crowding Ostia's harbor. Most ships were steered by two rear oars—rudders not having been invented in this time and place. She tried to keep out of the way of the gruff sailors as they rowed out of the port, but a shout of "Move, boy!" greeted her wherever she went. The captain finally set her to scrubbing the deck at the bow under the supervision of the lookout.

"So ye run away to sea, have ye, lad?" the lookout asked without taking his eyes off the horizon.

"No, sir." Gwyn kept her voice low and her head down. Scrub, scrub. She was starting to feel queasy. They'd left the gentle waters of the harbor and were now out at sea.

"Get a girl in trouble, did ye?" Why was he still asking questions? All the other men on board were too busy to chat.

"No sir." *Ugh, I do not feel great. It stinks like fish guts here!*

"Father sent 'im to get a taste of real work," the captain lumbered up in a rocking gait that matched the ocean swell. "Too bad this isn't a war galley or I'd put him to oar. 'Cept a weedy, skinny lad like him probably be useless at rowing."

"Use 'im for bait," the lookout joked.

Oh god, I'm going to be sick. Making it to the rail just in time she heaved to the echoes of laughter that burst from the men. The captain grabbed the back of her tunic and held on, preventing her from fulfilling the lookout's suggestion of turning her into bait. She gasped in fresh air, grateful for the spray that dashed against her eyelids.

"His father paid me decent coin—I'd best not feed 'im to the fish." The captain hauled her back in. Gwyn sagged and groaned. "Finish that deck now—I want it clean before we make landfall later." He stomped off, roaring at the other sailors to get back to work.

"Sit tight, lad, ye'll have ye sea legs in no time," the lookout said as he kicked the brush over to Gwyn. "Best get back to work, though. Cap'n might not let ye drown but he's not above giving stripes."

"Yes, sir." Gwyn took several deep breaths, feeling better. She'd better toughen up, fast. She didn't want to seem like a shy boy who would be a target for bullying, or worse, give the captain excuse to strip off her tunic and whip her. The thought made her shudder. She wouldn't be able to talk her way out of that one.

The heavy linen sail caught the breeze and the coastline fell away behind them. It was not a rushed journey. The ship put in several times to offload goods and take on others over a number of days. Gwyn suffered several more bouts of seasickness before she grew accustomed to the rocking of the ship and the smells that clung to it. She lent a hand where she could, earning gruff thanks from the sailors amidst the teasing and finally a copper denarii from the captain. "Not so useless after all, boy!" he exclaimed.

When she had nothing else to do she practiced knots, remembering her desperate escape over the wall at Masada. She was atrocious at first and sailors laughed at her efforts. "Soft hands!" they called her. She smiled and played the gullible lad, awed by their tales of sea monsters and sirens.

I'll have to try male disguise again! It was good to only have to duck out of the way of a few graspy hands, rather than fear them all. She hid with a bucket under the spare sail when she needed to pee, projecting a 'go away' vibe as strongly as she could. She wondered how other women in similar circumstances had managed. *Books are full of stories of women disguised as men but they don't often talk about going to the toilet!*

Finally the captain gave the order to steer west. The ship sailed away from the coast and across the expanse of blue-grey sea to the small island that rose steeply from the waves. Long and narrow, the shore of Pandateria was not welcoming. They had to drop sail and row to angle into the small harbor that nestled amid grey cliffs. Gwyn stayed out of the way as the men shouted and heaved. She was relieved when they docked safely. "We'll stop a day," the captain told his crew. "Lad, ye can come with me up to the villa. I've got letters to deliver."

They trudged up the track from the tiny fishing hamlet that hosted the dock. "My legs feel strange," Gwyn muttered.

The captain barked a laugh. "That's being on a ship for ye. Ye either love it or ye hate it. Some can't wait to be on solid land again. Me, I never rest so easy as when I've a deck rolling under me."

You can keep it. She sighed, knowing she'd have to leave the island the same way.

* * *

Gwyn leaned against the cool marble wall off the atrium, still feeling as though she was rocking to and fro. The captain had ordered her to stay put while he delivered his missives, but the household slaves drifted in, seeking news and gossip from Rome.

Gwyn told them she was a Christian convert. She whispered that she greatly admired the lady Domitilla's adherence to the new religion despite the trouble it had caused her and her family. The irony of Domitilla's husband Flavius Clemens being executed for atheism did not escape her. Refusal to acknowledge Domitian as God was dangerous

No wonder Christianity turned out to be such a violent religion. It's like the bullied child growing up to be a bully themselves. Not an excuse, but the thought depressed her.

Raised voices caught her attention and she straightened. Peeking along the length of the rectangular atrium into the audience chamber, she tried to glimpse the speakers. A lady's voice—it had to be Domitilla—and a man's could be heard. Gwyn sidled along from column to column, pretending to look at the frescoed half-ceiling until she was close enough to hear.

"I trusted you, Stephanus, and this is how you repay me?"

"Domina, this evidence is false, spun up by jealous types who wish me removed from your service." The man, Stephanus, had the voice of a weasel; whining, sycophantic.

"Forgive me, Domina, but 'e speaks rot." That was the captain. "I was told to tell ye that the evidence in those letters is backed up by verbal testimony. He was embezzling money from yer estates, even before yer late husband died."

"And what jealous type would envy your service to me here?" Flavia Domitilla sounded angry as well as hurt. "To be banished to this rock, with none of the comforts and entertainments to which you are accustomed." Stephanus protested but Domitilla rode over the top of him. "What would my husband say if he could see us now? A widow in exile, bereft of friends, stuck with her cowardly, thieving steward!"

"Domina, please, you have to understand…"

"Get out of my sight! I'd throw you off this island if I didn't think it would be a reward for your treachery. Go!"

A thin, dark-haired man burst out of the room and shoved past Gwyn, almost tripping into the central pool of the atrium. He wore a look of disgust and fury on his clean-shaven face. With a gentler expression he might have been handsome, or certainly refined, but a sneer twisted his features. "What are you looking at, idiot?" he snarled at Gwyn, before stalking around the pool and out through another doorway.

The captain stuck his head out and spotted Gwyn loitering near the doorway. "What are ye doing, lad, eavesdropping there? Scat!" His frown was deep.

"Please, Captain," Gwyn began.

"Scat! Or I'll tan yer hide when we get back aship!"

She fled, cursing silently. *Now what? I need to talk to Flavia Domitilla. Should I reveal that I'm a girl and ask for sanctuary? Then I'll be stuck here. It's not as though there are many ships passing by I can hop on. Bloody hell!*

She needed to think. She hated not knowing what to do.

Wait. How had she known this was the time she had to come to in the first place? She had seen history change, felt back along the timeline and located the aberration with her mind. She could try that again.

Looking about, she decided to find somewhere out of the way to sit and concentrate. She found herself back in the entrance hall. That was no good. The captain would find her and haul her back to the ship. She ducked back into the atrium and cut across, darting through a doorway she had seen a number of slaves use. It took her along a hall, past work rooms, storerooms and the kitchen, and deposited her out into a rather sad looking garden.

It must have been nice once. Lank, scraggly bushes drooped over small rock walls. The fish pond was mossy and choked with weeds, and tufts of grass spurted through the unraked pebbles of the path. Only the herbs—sheltered in the corner nearest the kitchen—looked maintained. Gwyn pinched off a sprig of parsley and chewed it. She'd forgotten to find a decent tooth-brushing stick while in Rome.

OK. Deep breaths. She sat cross-legged in the shade, leaning back against the garden wall. The smell and taste of the parsley helped push other thoughts aside, and she sought the timepiece in her mind and examined the now.

What she saw was a series of overlapping, looping and merging threads of light. Examining each thread, flickering images, sounds and movements entered her awareness. The time and place she was in bubbled out around her and she felt along into the future.

The zigzag she'd identified was looming, but this close to it she realized the timeline had already started to veer off course. The images she'd glimpsed centered on the man Stephanus.

Of course! Mario the guide had said the failed assassin was a man named Stephanus. Surely this was the same man? But if he was out of Flavia Domitilla's good graces then how could he be a part of the plot?

Think, Gwyn. He was accused of embezzlement. Perhaps he had been going to do a runner when he saw the family fortunes going downhill under the Emperor's paranoid eye. Perhaps he had even informed on Flavius Clemens. Gwyn shivered. It was a selfish person who would throw another to the wolves like that—even in Rome, and Rome was renowned for wolves.

She opened her eyes and inhaled deeply, smelling the parsley along with other herbs. She would have to hide out and find a way to speak to Flavia Domitilla privately. That meant becoming a girl again.

Sixteen

1890 AD

Ropes. Someone had tied Michelle's hands with ropes. Rough twine bit into her wrists. She would need to free them soon or her hands would be too stiff to fight. She already felt like one big bruise from the fight on the train. The fall must have knocked her out.

Keeping her eyes closed and her body relaxed, she listened. She was lying on uneven ground with rocks jabbing into her back. The smells that assaulted her were unwashed skin, soot and horse sweat. She heard men speaking Spanish, and from the conversation she knew she was in the hands of the bandits.

Well, shit. She could time jump away, but she didn't have her stuff, and untying her hands without help or a knife would prove problematic. Then there was the issue of jumping back to match times with Owen again. She could do it, but she ran the chance of running into the bandits again unless she made a significant move geographically.

Better to see if she could get out of her predicament first.

She could hear tension in the talk around her. One man complained about a botched job, while another replied that if he couldn't handle danger he should have stayed home with the women while the real men did the work. Another man told them to shut up.

Michelle had her eyes half-open by now, and watched the exchange with interest while taking in the rest of her surroundings. It was a camp, filled with swarthy men who moved with purpose. They were grubby and tended towards long black moustaches. All had big knives sheathed at the hip. Some were cheerful, clapping each other on shoulders or breaking into song, but a few were subdued, tending horses or cleaning their guns with quiet preoccupation.

Michelle returned her attention to the men closest to her. The two who had been arguing picked up tack and saddled their horses. The third man glanced over at Michelle. She looked at him squarely. "Señorita, you are awake," he declared in a deep voice, and strode over. He wore well-made leather boots with small spurs, a bandana around his neck and a big knife like all the others.

"That's Señora." She'd say her wedding band had been stolen. "And you are?"

He squatted down beside her and picked up her bound hands, examining the ring fingers. "Please forgive me, but you don't look like a Señora." His eyes lingered over every part of her, especially her breasts.

Michelle had been looked at many times before in her missions, and depending on her guise she usually ignored it. No modern man would be so crass, but humans in the past were far less civilized. The persona she wanted to adopt now, however, wouldn't let such an insult pass. "Unless you are about to cut these ropes, you will take your hands off me. I have had my wedding ring stolen and was thrown from the train in the middle of the night. If you are to have any hope of redemption you will let me go!" She threw all the force of her willpower, amplified by the chronokinetor, at the mustachioed bandit. She wasn't certain that he was the leader, but the swiftness with which he'd stepped in to handle the two bickering spoke of authority to her.

Michelle kept her indignant defiance in place as the bandit considered her with dark brown eyes. He drew his knife in a sudden movement. She tensed, ready to jump if need be, but he sliced through her bonds and pulled her to her feet. "My apologies, Señora." Despite her directive he continued to clasp her hands in his large palm. She looked at his hand— dirt under the fingernails, fine hairs. He grinned, and lifted her hands to his lips. She tensed but refrained from punching him.

"Now will you tell me where I am, and how I came to be here?" She continued with the haughty tone. "Have you kidnapped me in hope for ransom?"

Several other bandits had gathered around. "She keep on like that and we be paying to give her back," one muttered. Michelle glared at him.

"Bulls' balls," her bandit said, looking around at his men, still grinning. "She has a fire. I would take great pleasure in dousing it, but first I want to know how she came to be lying next to a dead Guillermo. She will answer my questions."

Michelle tried not to sneer at the implied rape threat. She settled for the appearance of seething instead. "Don't you dare touch me. The Lord have mercy on any man who thinks to harm or dishonor me."

"Dishonor?" The chief bandit let go of Michelle's hands and threw up his own in shock. "Our sacred Mother preserve me, we are not monsters, Señora. We are but poor farmers struggling to take back a little of what is rightfully ours! We have wives, and children." His men laughed and nodded.

"Chief," a somber man interrupted. "Guillermo and Manuel are wrapped up, ready to go."

The chief nodded. "Then we shall move out. They deserve a Christian burial. Cover all signs of our camp and tracks." He ordered a man to bundle Michelle onto a horse.

"Where are you taking me?" she demanded. She didn't want to lose ground, and she didn't have her bearings.

"You are coming with us until I decide what to do with you," the chief said. "Don't try to escape, Señora—you would die out here in the wilderness by yourself."

You want to bet? But she kept silent. She'd have to jump too far forward to reach any kind of time that had decent transport or communication. She sighed. She hoped this delay meant she wouldn't lose Owen.

* * *

Much to the amusement of the men, Michelle refused to ride side-saddle, despite not having the appropriate split skirts. "It's bad for your back," she announced. "I had a bag with some clothes when I was pushed from the train—where is it?"

The bandit leader raised his hand and signaled. One of his men, a short, hairy character with a lopsided frown, produced Michelle's backpack. "It's here, Diego." He held it up.

"Gracias, Miguelito." Diego took it and offered it to Michelle.

"Is there somewhere I can change, *in private?*" She glared around, trying not to laugh at the interested expressions of the men.

"This way, Señora," he gestured. "Miguelito will stand guard. No one will bother you. But, ah—don't think of running off. You won't get far, and we will track you. That's if we don't decide to let you be eaten by mountain lions."

Michelle gave him a disdainful look and deigned not to answer, but she took the warning to heart. She was used to the most dangerous animal around her being humans.

Her money, she discovered as she rifled through her bag behind a clump of bushes, was gone. She was annoyed but not surprised. She would have to exchange more of the precious gold nuggets or synthesized jewels she had shoved into her underwear. Her clothes were there at least. She took the opportunity to relieve herself and then pulled her trousers on under her skirts. That would have to suffice for modesty. Her pistol, which had been in her pocket, was gone. She wondered if it had fallen out or if it had been taken, and what they would think of a poor widow carrying such arms.

Michelle looked about, toying with the idea of escape despite Diego's warnings. The bandits had camped in a rocky gully. Her surroundings had changed drastically from the rolling grasslands dotted with fat brown cattle that the train had chugged past the day before. The landscape was drier, the hills more sparsely vegetated. No wonder the bandits had been able to climb aboard and stop the train—it would have been creeping up the gradient while the passengers slept. A cool breeze encouraged her to dig out a scarf as well. It certainly wasn't the thought of being eaten by mountain lions that made her shiver.

They didn't tie her to her horse but she was flanked by Miguelito and a tall, hard-faced man. The evidence that she wasn't a skilled rider was plain to see, so they relaxed their guard after a few minutes.

They rode all day. Michelle counted thirty men—they wore boots, wide-legged trousers and white shirts with grey leather vests. She didn't count the cloth-wrapped dead ones slung on the back of a horse. The sun was warm but the cool breeze trickled down the mountains to the west.

The Andes were on her left. The train would have deposited her in Mendoza, and she would have made plans from there. Now she was being diverted north, against her will. "Where are we going?" she asked Miguelito. He ignored her. She persisted to the extent she thought was in character then fell silent, observing everything instead. The bandits rode easily, as confident in the saddle as she was time-jumping. All were armed—the knives each man carried were complemented by guns, lassoes and whips.

At noon, after a brief stop to water horses and humans alike, it began to rain. Michelle growled and twisted around to retrieve her all-weather hooded jacket from her backpack. She shrugged it over her coat, not caring how ridiculous it looked. She was uncomfortable from riding, hungry, bruised from the fight and fall of the night before, and now she was wet.

Diego fell back from his position at the front of the line. He, like the other bandits, wore a broad-brimmed hat, which shed the droplets in tiny rivulets. "We need the rain, Señora," he said. Michelle threw him a sour expression. "The grass does not grow so easily here in the hills, and the cattle need to eat."

She considered his words, then looked again at the men who held her captive. A number of them dug out brown woven ponchos to shield them from the wet. The weapons, she realized, were standard tools for anyone who ventured into this wilderness. "You're a farmer," she stated flatly.

Diego swept her a wide-armed bow. His horse snorted at the movement. "But of course, Señora. You thought we were bandidos?" The corner of his lip curled up.

"You robbed a train." Same flat tone.

Diego shrugged. "We have been pushed to the edge of our old farmlands, driven out of our homes by the government, which is controlled by the English. They said it was to build a railway, but now other men, city men, own our pastures and raise fat cattle there. They have the best access to the railway, while we are forced to scratch a living in this dirt as our families grow poorer and thinner."

Michelle didn't respond straight away. She had read about the immigration of English into Argentina. They had established themselves as a prosperous middle class, often to the detriment of other Argentinian social groups. "Not everyone on that train was English," she said.

Another shrug. The rain was coming down harder. "Those who can afford to travel by train have more than we. They will not miss it. And they will not find us. We have covered our tracks."

"And what do you propose to do with me?" They couldn't let her go and report them to the authorities—distant though any government might be.

She caught the look Diego gave her and guessed that legality aside, he'd like to do a few things with her. She filed that information away in her mind and gave Diego a level look. "Well?"

He winked at her. "I haven't decided yet."

* * *

The rain abated as the sun went down, just in time for the raiding party to ride into a small village. Cries of welcome met them, and Michelle peered through the lengthening shadows to see women, children and older men spill out of small timber houses to encircle the horses and men.

No woman came to greet Diego, she noted. The leader clapped his men on their shoulders as they dismounted and drifted into their fire-lit cabins. He bowed his head solemnly to two women as the poncho-wrapped corpses of Manuel and Guillermo were presented by their comrades. The village priest came forth to make the sign of the cross over each dead man, and Michelle clenched down on the guilt she felt at the sight of the widows weeping.

"This way," Miguelito tugged Michelle's elbow, his dour expression made droopier by his rain-slicked moustache.

"Where are you taking me?" Her demand was half-hearted. She dismounted, stiff and bow-legged, and sneezed. She didn't care where she was going as long as it involved a fire, dry clothes and food. Then a bed. She'd even sleep with Miguelito if that's what it would take, but the sour look he gave her as they entered a small cabin made her think that such a demand was unlikely to be made of her.

Miguelito struck tinder and flint and brought candles to life. As Michelle shucked her wet outer layers the little man knelt and laid the fire. Her torso and feet were dry thanks to her all-weather jacket and boots, but her legs were damp and her hands ached from holding the reins. Her whole body ached. She gritted her teeth but a small moan escaped her lips as she eased herself onto a wooden stool.

"Wait here," Miguelito told her. "Diego will come. Do not run."

Michelle was scarcely in any shape to run. She doubted she would ever stand normally again. But she dragged off her boots and said, "I won't be going anywhere, Miguelito, unless it's to find something to eat."

"I will bring something." He left, and Michelle sighed in relief. Except for a few toilet breaks, this was the first time she had been alone all day. She enjoyed the fire and the silence, warming her toes as she leaned onto the small table at her back.

"You are not used to riding, Señora." Diego came in and sat in the single chair by the fire. He toed off his boots with a satisfied grunt. "Here, we are born in the saddle. A man is not a man if he cannot ride."

"That's nice." She heaved herself upright as Miguelito brought in a tray with bowls of hot stew. Michelle managed to swivel on the stool and face the table, mouthwatering.

Diego chuckled and got up to commandeer a bowl. Miguelito disappeared and returned again with a warped glass bottle. He stuck a knife in the cork and levered it out, pouring a sour-smelling red wine into a tin cup for Diego and himself.

"Is there water?" Michelle knew she was dehydrated, and wine certainly wasn't the answer to that. She took a mouthful of stew and sighed with contentment.

"There's a well in the yard," Diego put down his bowl. "Allow me."

Michelle shrugged as the big man disappeared through a rear door. Miguelito glared at her and disappeared also, taking his meal and wine with him.

Diego reappeared, but his offsider didn't, which suited Michelle just fine. The village leader, or raiding party leader, or whatever he was, was preferable company and much easier on the eyes.

They ate quietly, him in the chair by the fire and her at the table sipping water from the pitcher he'd brought in. The warmth and the food were making Michelle sleepy, and she reminded herself to keep her wits about her.

"You are an Englishwoman," Diego said out of the blue.

"Hmm? Oh no, I'm not." Michelle tried not to yawn. A shower would have been nice, but she suspected plumbing, if any, was outside.

Diego got up and put down his finished bowl on the table. He leant over Michelle. She kept eating. "You speak Castellano well, but you are an Englishwoman all the same."

She chewed her final mouthful and took a sip of water. "And I said, I'm not. If you're trying to intimidate or trick me into saying I am, you'll have to wait until I'm less sore and tired." He could overpower her, she knew, and at this close range she wouldn't be quick enough to dart away. She stood with effort, forcing him to straighten but bringing herself even closer to him. "Are you planning on torturing me, murdering me or ravishing me, or can it wait until the morning?"

He gave a shout of laughter before his eyes became intent. His arm snaked around her waist and his large mouth bent to hers.

As he kissed her Michelle sighed mentally. *I really would have preferred some sleep first.* She remembered that indignant kidnapped widows should protest this sort of thing, and pounded her fists—not too hard—on his chest. "How dare you!" seemed the appropriate exclamation, and she added a shocked expression to her face to go with it.

Diego searched her face even as his hands groped her backside. If Michelle hadn't been in the mood she would have punched him, but it had been awhile, and while the circumstances were less than ideal, at least it might warm her up.

Diego bent to kiss her again and Michelle decided she couldn't be bothered with protesting anymore. She hated that sort of thing anyway—if someone wanted sex with another consenting adult, good for them. She just pitied the human females in this time and so many others whose protests were ignored or even considered part of the ritual.

Kissing back, she felt Diego's surprise and enthusiastic response. At least he wasn't someone whose arousal was based on resistance or fear. One hand slid lower and reefed up her skirts, only to be thwarted by the trousers she'd worn all day for riding. "Damn it all," he muttered.

"Tell me you're not going to take me right here on the table," Michelle countered. "Where do you sleep?" Her voice was somewhat breathless as Diego's other hand found its way into the front of her dress. With no corset—Michelle refused to wear them—he cupped one small breast easily and bent to kiss her nipple.

"Of course," he murmured, kissing again. She moaned. It had been too long. He picked her up and she wrapped her legs around his waist, feeling his urgency. Perhaps it had been a while for him too.

Diego pushed through a doorway and deposited Michelle on the bed that filled the tiny room. He hauled up her skirts and yanked on her trousers. She scooted back, forcing him to kneel on the bed, and tugged his shirt from his pants.

The rest of their clothes followed quickly and kisses became more ferocious as Michelle matched him. This seemed to excite him more and more, and he cupped his hand under her butt and tried to flip her over. She resisted. "It's good manners to ask," she admonished.

The surprise at being told to consider his partner made Diego pause. "Please," he said hoarsely, quivering with tension but held by her gaze. She allowed the tension to build a second more, then smiled seductively and rolled over.

He was on her and in her in a second and they both groaned with pleasure. An amused voice in Michelle's mind said he must have been inspired by the stallions, then they both cried out and collapsed on the bed.

* * *

When she stirred, it was morning. She stretched and felt Diego hard up against her, in more ways than one. Feeling her move, he lost no time in making his desire known and despite her aches, Michelle was happy to comply. Afterwards she let the relaxation wash through her body as she lay on her stomach, sighing sensually.

A click and the cold barrel of a gun pressed against the back of her neck in the next moment brought her fully awake.

Seventeen

96 AD

Flavia Domitilla stared out of the wide window at the darkening ocean. Grey waves smashed against the cliffs, sending foam to clutch desperately at the sky. Each burst of spray hung for a second, then fell back into the maw of the relentless swell. Always falling; never clinging to the outcrop of dejected isolation that was now the noble lady's home.

She watched the visiting ship sail out of the narrow bay. She watched as shadows consumed the cliffs and water alike, leaving only gloom. The lamp that had been lit earlier by a slave hung at her back. Echoing the darkness of her thought, Flavia Domitilla could not bring herself to turn her face to the light.

My dear Clemens. You trusted Stephanus. And he betrayed us. He betrayed you. Had their steward been the cause of her husband's fall from grace? She would never know, short of a confession from Stephanus or her uncle the Emperor. She clenched her fists, wishing that her husband had never manumitted their steward. She wished he was still a slave she could torture for evidence. Now she didn't know what to do with him. She was powerless here, reliant on her uncle's whim for her existence. He could forbid any ships from visiting the island, starving her like Agrippina and Julia Livilla starved before her. He could send an assassin to strangle her in her sleep. Why not just kill herself now? Wouldn't that be simpler, less painful than waiting for her end?

Except she couldn't. It was a sin. She believed in that just as firmly as she believed in every other aspect of her new God. Her devoutness had convinced her husband, and together they had protected and supported Christians in Rome, denying her uncle's self-proclaimed divinity. He was not a god. He was a man. A paranoid, selfish, tyrant of a man who pushed people away even as he complained that nobody loved him. She hated him. Hated what he'd done to her husband, what he'd done to her cousin, dear Julia. She wished God would strike him down and punish him for all his sins.

A noise behind her disturbed her angry thoughts. She frowned but didn't turn. It would be one of her slaves, clearing away the uneaten tray of food. Flavia Domitilla had little appetite—the evidence of her steward's betrayal churned her stomach.

"Domina, are you going to eat that?" It was a girl's voice—not one of her slaves. Domitilla whirled. "Because I've been hiding out all day waiting to speak to you and I'm really hungry."

It was a slim, short girl, with tanned skin and plain brown hair bunched messily under a cap. She wore a long tunic and a pinched expression. She gestured at the uneaten meal.

"Who are you?" Domitilla demanded. "Where did you come from?"

"My name is Gwynia," the girl plopped herself down on a chair, eyeing the food. "I'm here to sort out your problem with Stephanus."

At the mention of the steward's name, Domitilla deflated, her indignation gone. The knowledge of his betrayal hit again and she sagged onto a couch. A corner of it flaked off. She glared at it. Everything in this villa was decrepit; a reminder that the women banished here deserved nothing but what was used and discarded.

The girl was still looking at the meal on the tray. It rested on the low stone table—also chipped—and while the soup showed no steam and the bread was hard, the girl was practically salivating. "Oh, go on," Domitilla flapped her hand at it. It wasn't as though she was going to eat it, and wastefulness was a sin.

"Thank you, Domina." The girl dipped the bread in the soup and chewed with a sigh. "I didn't want to steal from the kitchen, and I was staying out of sight so I wouldn't get sent back to the ship."

"You came on the ship?" Domitilla asked dumbly.

"*Scipio's Fury*," the girl—Gwynia—said. "I disguised myself as a boy on board, and came up here with the captain. I needed to meet you."

"You disguised yourself?" Confusion must have written itself across her face because Domitilla saw a flicker of annoyance cross the girl's eyes. "Please explain yourself," the noble lady said haughtily. "You come into my chambers, eat my food, claim you need to see me—what is all this about? Who sent you?"

Gwynia chewed her bread, striving to clear her mouth, then slowed down. She finished her mouthful, drank the rest of the soup straight from the bowl and sighed with relief. "The enemies of your uncle sent me. The time has come for your husband's murderer to pay, and you have a choice. You can wait out your days here, hoping for a pardon that might never come, or you can join with those who would see a tyrant brought down. Do you truly believe he is a god?"

Domitilla gasped. "No," she whispered. "There is only one God."

Gwynia frowned. "Then you know that he is only a man, and a man can be brought down."

"Vengeance." Domitilla leant forward, urgency in her voice. "Vengeance is mine, sayeth the Lord, but I cannot wait. That is wrong, I know, but I am weak. I am a sinner, and I want revenge for the death of my husband."

"Then, Domina," Gwynia leant forward as well. "Tell me who has sent me to you, so I know you are true in this." A sheen of sweat covered the girl's forehead, though the night was mild.

"Parthenius," Domitilla breathed. "He, and the other freedman fear my uncle's fickleness. They know they are in danger now—no one is safe. He spoke to me—Parthenius was the one who warned me of Stephanus' embezzlement of my estate's funds. He said he would find evidence." The return to the thought of her steward jolted her. "But what has *he* to do with all this? Stephanus cannot be trusted."

Gwynia sat back and smiled. "You have evidence against him now, do you not?"

Domitilla nodded, elegant eyebrows furrowing.

"And you can arrange for charges to be pressed against him? Even from here—you must have family or friends back in Rome who'd litigate on your behalf? It would destroy him—the Emperor doesn't like those who flout his moral code. Even with you out of favor, it's still an insult to the imperial family."

"This is true." Eyebrows furrowed further still. "But I don't see—"

"Offer to pardon him," Gwynia advised. "Hold the evidence as a guarantee of his cooperation, but offer to forgive all charges if he joins in what needs to be done."

Light dawned on Domitilla, and her smile became fierce. "Yes," she whispered. "He shall strike the blow. But…" Sudden uncertainty. "How will that even be possible? My uncle is so fearful of attack that the very marble of his palace is polished to give reflection. Everyone is searched. No weapon could even come close to his person."

Gwynia looked solemn. "I have an idea for that. Let me tell you, and when the time comes, you can tell Stephanus."

* * *

Gwyn spent the next few days working on Domitilla. The lady's feverish devotion to her dead husband and the Christian god made Gwyn uncomfortable, but she ingratiated herself with the noblewoman and her servants by helping out wherever possible. Assisted by the timepiece, Gwyn convinced the household that she was working to improve the lot of their beleaguered mistress. The only one who continued to distrust her was the one she really needed to control.

Stephanus the steward hadn't improved from Gwyn's first impression of him. Handsome yes, but disdainful. The two kitchen maids doted on him, Gwyn noticed with disgust, and he obviously slept with whichever one took his fancy on any given day. He was rude to the other slaves and to any villagers who delivered fresh produce to the villa. Gwyn he actively disparaged, so she did her best to stay out of his way.

Flavia Domitilla, on the other hand, became enamored when she learned that Gwyn had been to Judea. The lady quizzed her about the Jews she had met, and propounded her theories on religion late into the evening. Gwyn was flattered by the attention but felt unqualified to deal with the subject matter.

"Don't you believe in the Roman gods anymore, then?" Gwyn ventured as the cold sea breeze gusted through the open shutters. She shivered.

"Are you cold, Gwynia? Come sit here," Domitilla ordered. Gwyn obeyed and submitted to a blanket being wrapped around her shoulders. "God's light and love keep me warm," the lady said. "The idols of Rome hold no sway over me now. When I learned of their falsity I was confused, but my teacher opened my eyes to the depravity of Rome and the need to save it. That is why I led my husband to the truth, so his soul would be saved and we could commit our efforts to spreading God's word before the End of Days."

"Oh." *No point telling her that Judgment Day isn't going to happen any time soon.* The righteousness reminded Gwyn of the desperate situation at Masada, and she sighed. "You said the ship will be returning in another week, Domina. Have you thought what to put in the letter to Parthenius?" Once again, the adventure was wearing thin and Gwyn heard the voice of doubt in her mind. She was afraid the ship would never return, and that she'd be stuck on this rock forever.

"If the good weather continues we might see it sooner, but a week certainly. I will compose my missives soon. Can you write, Gwynia? You can take them down for me if your hand is good."

Gwyn vowed to practice her handwriting on wax tablets over the next few days. Domitilla had bemoaned the scarce supplies of her writing desk, so Gwyn didn't want to waste the few sheets of papyrus that were there.

The days went by. Stephanus continued to be abominable to her, so Gwyn tried out an authoritative air and ordered him to leave her alone or it would go the worse for him. He glared but complied, contenting himself with shooting filthy looks her way.

"It's been a week, Domina," Gwyn mentioned one evening. "The ship must have run into bad weather." She paced by the window, watching the darkening sky.

"Nonsense, Gwynia," Domitilla said as she toyed languidly with a braid. She had become more confident and relaxed during the time Gwyn had been there. Accepting her steward's betrayal had been hard, but the plan for revenge had re-established her faith that all would be well. "It's only been five days."

Gwyn paused, then reddened. "Forgive me, Domina," she coughed. "I lost track of the days." *Two more days. How infuriating.*

Flavia Domitilla laughed, a tinkling sound that grated on Gwyn's nerves. As much as she pitied the woman, Gwyn was irritated by Domitilla's quirks and mannerisms. "Never mind." Amusement was in the lady's voice. "I shall summon Stephanus into my presence tomorrow, and force him to join our conspiracy. My displeasure with him must be well felt by now, for I haven't given him a favorable word in all this time."

I'm not sure he cares, Gwyn shifted uncomfortably. The steward was still polite to his mistress' face but Gwyn noticed he didn't try to establish his innocence either.

"And then we shall write my letters." Domitilla sounded almost jolly. Gwyn quashed her impatience. Why should she deny the lady the enjoyment of her revenge? *I just want to get back to Rome.* She needed action to make her feel as though she was making progress, and she wanted the chance to run into Izem again.

The thought of the charming street-Romeo entertained her as she went to sleep that night. She promised herself that if she succeeded in this mission she'd reward herself by looking him up. *Why not?* she asked. *I'm an adult, making history-altering decisions. I deserve a little fun.*

The next day was anything but fun. Stephanus correctly blamed Gwyn for his drastic change in fortune and while he didn't attack her directly, the food she received from the kitchen was even poorer in quality than the usual household fare. The two kitchen maids whispered venomously that Gwyn had better watch out, or she might find herself falling from one of the many high cliffs that girt the island.

Writing the letters was painful too. Gwyn exerted all her influence to get Domitilla to leave out religious overtones. "Does Parthenius share your—our—beliefs, Domina?" Gwyn asked. She was reluctant to pen a dogmatic missive to a political pragmatist.

Domitilla paused from her dictation and frowned. "No, not yet. I am sure he will come to see the truth, especially in the light of my uncle's blasphemy." She was warming to the theme, transforming from vengeful widow to the righteous agent of her god.

Gwyn sighed. "I'm sure you're right, Domina, but would I be right in saying that Parthenius would not have risen to his current post if he wasn't… practical?"

Domitilla turned from the window. The sea breeze whipped some of her smaller curls loose, contrasting the pale stillness of her face. "Perhaps you are right, Gwynia," she conceded. "Though with his mortal body so at risk he would do well to consider his soul. But I acknowledge that such men can become… preoccupied with survival, rather than salvation. Very well, write this: I send Gwynia back to you, in the company of Stephanus, to do what must be done."

Gwyn omitted 'back' and added in 'my trusted servant'. This would serve as her letter of introduction to Parthenius, but Domitilla still believed it was he who had sent Gwyn.

"Stephanus has agreed, for I have promised in return not to charge him for his heinous acts against my husband and my estate. This has bought his cooperation. I feel it best that Gwynia, who knows the details of the plan and has proven herself at discretion and disguise, prepares him for the act."

Gwyn changed her name to 'Gwynius' and wrote 'himself'. A male servant or slave would be safer. She would convince Domitilla of that before she left the island.

"I trust you to arrange things with the Praetorians," Domitilla continued. "And to be discreet. Our opportunity arises soon, and with *divine* guidance we shall restore things to how they should be." Gwyn hid her smile at the emphasis on 'divine'—it was a nice compromise.

"Very good, Domina." She finished the letter on the wax tablet and looked it over. "Would you like me to read it back to you?"

Domitilla waved a languid hand. "Just transcribe it to parchment. Here is my ring for the seal."

Gwyn took the proffered ring, examining it carefully. It was heavy and silver, topped with a flat circle. The words DIVA DOMITILLA AVGVSTA were engraved on the piece.

"It was a coin issued in honor of my mother," Domitilla said quietly. "I had it made into a ring for my seal so I would always remember her." She fell silent. Gwyn said nothing, afraid of disturbing the lady's thoughts. "I will pray now," Domitilla declared and turned away.

Gwyn worked slowly with ink and sand. When she was satisfied she dripped the red wax from the small heated bowl and pressed the ring firmly into it. She was concentrating so hard she didn't hear the shouts from outside at first.

"It's the ship!" Domitilla leant out the window, looking down into the island's small harbor.

Gwyn leapt up to join her and smiled. It was difficult at this distance, but she could just make out oarsmen pulling hard to angle the *Scipio's Fury* in to shore.

* * *

When the captain stomped into the villa the next morning, Gwyn disguised herself as a boy again. She cringed under his verbal attack and bit back tears when he clipped her over the ear. She bit her lip and tried not to glare at him too much. *Bastard.*

"Where have ye been ye lay-about, cock-brained whoreson? I ought to thrash ye and trail ye behind for the sharks all the way to Ostia!"

"Captain, please." Domitilla entered the atrium from her solar, gliding down the steps in an elegant white gown. Her hair had been curled, she wore large earrings and a heavy necklace of lapis lazuli. Gwyn whistled quietly in appreciation. The fretful, dejected woman Gwyn had met the first night was gone—this lady was imperial without being imperious. Flavia Domitilla was ready to assert her rights as the noble mistress of her household, and that included ordering all those lower in rank to behave as she wished.

"Domina," the captain apologized, not taking his rough hand from Gwyn's shoulder. "The lad is lucky to get nothing worse. I had to sail without 'im. I hope 'e was not bothering your maids, though truth to tell I didn't think 'e had it in 'im."

"No. Do not punish the lad. He brought me a message from fellow believers back in Rome. He is sorry for the deception but you know our religion is not… popular with many. He feared persecution on your ship."

Gwyn thought if the captain's tight lips were anything to go by she'd be in for a hell of a lot of persecution when they got back on board. Her stomach tied itself in a knot.

Stay calm. You can handle this. She relaxed her tense shoulders. The captain's grip loosened slightly. "Well, Domina, if 'e delivered 'is message, and you have the evidence from me, I'll take our leave unless you have further instruction. Tide waits for none."

"Actually, that's what I wanted to talk to you about—the evidence that is." Domitilla seated herself elegantly and called in an authoritative tone, "Stephanus!"

The sour-faced steward sloped into the room. "I am at your command, Domina." Gwyn thought he sounded sarcastic.

"You are," Domitilla said. "As we discussed yesterday, you are to take ship with the captain back to Ostia, and then travel to Rome accompanied by Gwynius, who will take you to trusted associates of mine. If you do the thing we agreed on, I will destroy this evidence and no charges of embezzlement will be laid against you."

"Domina!" the captain protested. Domitilla turned a steely eye on him.

"I have made an arrangement with my steward, captain. I thank you for bringing this evidence. Your continued service to my husband's family and to me is most appreciated. Please take this note to my bankers in Rome and you shall be paid well for your efforts." It was a dismissal.

"Well... is 'e ready to leave?" The captain sounded skeptical. "My ship is waiting—I'd rather not delay for the packing of fine shaving kits and fripperies." Gwyn muffled a snort.

"I'm packed," Stephanus replied, voice dripping cold disdain. "If your lad could but help carry my things, I'd rather be on our way." It was clear he'd rather do something else entirely, possibly strangle his mistress and stab the captain and kick Gwyn while he was at it, but his self-control showed he was not stupid, even if he hid his emotions poorly.

You'll need to do a better charade when we get you in front of the Emperor! Gwyn held her tongue but turned to look up at the captain, seeking permission. "Oh, go on, and hurry up!" the stocky seafarer barked. She bolted from the room, giving one last bow to Domitilla who acknowledged her with a disinterested nod.

Stephanus had more things than Gwyn thought were necessary, and she cursed him silently as he ordered her to carry a small but heavy pine trunk. It was locked, and she added lock-picking to the list of skills she needed to learn. *I wonder if it's got his embezzled money inside, or if he squirrelled that away somewhere else.*

At least Domitilla had issued her some cash for when they got back to the mainland. She didn't want to go running to Gaius again.

Once on board ship, the steward perched himself atop his things and sneered around at all the goings on—sailors securing gear and making ready to sail. Gwyn was given a swift kick to the rear which sparked tears in her eyes, and set to scrubbing the deck again. She bent over her work, trying not to cry, lifting her face to the wind only when she thought she risked sea-sickness again.

Now just to get him back to Parthenius. How the hell am I going to manage that?

Eighteen

96 AD

Stab! The fly's body twitched helplessly, speared by the sharp pen nib. The man who had stabbed it considered it dispassionately, then reached a careful finger and thumb to pluck free the tiny, gossamer wings.

"So perfect," he breathed. "So tiny, yet so perfect." He brushed the wings from his skin and watched them flutter and slide through the air to land on his scroll. "But still part of the rotten corpse."

Wings were like words, he decided. They could be pretty, and they fluttered about his head filling his ears with buzzing, buzzing, buzzing. But they were fragile and tainted by the ill-intent and malice of what lay underneath. Words were without substance—people used them to hurt or hide truths. Well, he would prize out the truth under all the pretty words. He would find the substance, good or ill, and punish any who thought to deceive him.

Rome had a disease, and he had been sent to cleanse it. There was a reason the gods had taken his smiling, popular brother, with all his war trophies and good looks. Hadn't they shown their displeasure, with the eruption of Vesuvius and another great fire in Rome? Of course, Domitian had ordered him deified, like their father had been before them, because how else could an emperor be treated? Good precedents must be set, bad ones eradicated. That was why he had ordered that old fool Epaphroditus executed. Assisting in Nero's death—completely warranted though it was—was not an example Domitian wanted any of his freedmen or slaves to even consider as a possibility. They had to know—treachery would be punished with the ultimate price.

I'll clean this city, this empire, of the rot that plagues it. They'll love me again—

they must. Look at everything I've given them. Games and spectacles and stability! I've continued my father's legacy, with none of the back-stabbing and treacheries of Nero's and Caligula's reigns. If they're afraid it's because they plot against me. If they plot they should fear me!

Another fly buzzed through the window. Domitian sat very still, alone in his private chambers, just as he liked it. His person was sacrosanct—he was a god, after all—and he preferred the calm silence of his own company over the murmured advice and information imparted to him by his household staff, let alone the obsequiousness of togate senators, most of whom hated him.

Buzz, buzz. Yet a fly would dare disturb him! Domitian watched as it swung against the warm September breeze that shifted the drapes beside the windows. *Buzzzz, buzzzz.*

It landed. It walked a few tiny, insectile steps across his desk, pausing to inspect the ink pot. *Buzzzz, buzzzz.* Up and down. Walking again. The Emperor barely breathed.

Stab!

Another dead fly.

Nineteen

1890 AD

"What is this, Señora?" Diego's voice was dangerously quiet.

Michelle's eyes had flashed open but otherwise, she did not move. "A gun, by the sound and feel of it," she answered levelly. *Devious bastard.* She couldn't help but admire the wiliness of someone who would ensure she had her guard down and was vulnerable. Yes, a time-jump was always a possibility, but with a two-year range and no clothes she'd scarcely be in a better predicament. Plus she'd lose the few things that made her travels easier.

Diego grabbed her shoulder and flipped her roughly, pointing the gun at her forehead. "A gun that came from your pocket, right after you fell from the train, with two of my men dead beside you."

"What's your point?"

He stared, then snarled, "I have never seen a gun like this before! This is an English gun! You are an Englishwoman."

Voice still calm. "I'm not, and while I did take it from an Englishman, he wasn't that happy about it. And yes, I shot your two men. They tried to kill me."

Her bland admittance stumped him. The barrel wavered. Michelle was very aware of it. At point blank range she'd never jump away in time, but she let none of her fear show.

The gun barrel snapped back onto her forehead as Diego refocused. "Why are you here?" he hissed.

Michelle sat up slowly. He kept the gun trained on her head but did not stop her. "I was on my way to Mendoza when you hijacked the train. Your men tried to break into my cabin so I climbed out the window. I found a man holding the driver at gunpoint so I ordered him to stop. He attacked me instead. Your other man also attacked me. Hate the English as much as you like, but preying on women and unarmed civilians is a weak and cowardly thing to do." She was standing now, facing him down despite the difference in their heights.

One bullet. There's only one bullet in there. Michelle flicked her eyes to the door behind Diego and widened them. He turned slightly and her hand flew up to strike his as she ducked to the side. The pistol fired, putting a hole in the wall behind her. Michelle let go of the gun immediately.

If she let the fight last he would overpower her. He was too large, too strong, and it was too small a space for her to maneuver. He brought the gun to bear on her again, expecting her to be frightened, so she kicked him hard in the testicles and then the kneecap. The gun clicked as Diego pulled the trigger. Michelle kicked his knee hard again, then chopped down on his forearm. She wrenched the pistol from his grip as his fingers spammed and brought the butt of the gun down hard on his skull.

Diego collapsed.

Michelle checked his pulse. Alive. She used his belt to tie him to the bed and stole his knife. She dressed swiftly and peeked out into the other room of the cabin. No one was there. Fresh bread was, however, along with cheese, dried meat strips and a jug of milk. Miguelito, or someone else, had been and gone. Were they close? It didn't matter—someone would have heard the gunshot. Michelle gulped the milk and stuffed the food into her bag, then went back into the bedroom. She stepped over the prone Diego and climbed out the little window. She landed lightly on the soft ground and pushed the shutters closed. Her boots made prints in the mud but that couldn't be helped.

In the lean-to that stood on one side of the cabin, Diego's horse stood, munching on hay. Michelle took several deep breaths and concentrated on being calm and assured, so the animal wouldn't start. It eyed her suspiciously but permitted her to slip the bit and bridle on, snuffling through large nostrils. The saddle was another matter, and when the stallion shuffled and almost stood on Michelle's foot she decided she'd have to attempt the ride bareback. Her legs screamed in as she hoisted herself on—the horse was far too broad for her—but she bit her lip and swore silently.

Where to? A reading from her wrist computer was essential now. Even if she fled the village unseen, someone would find Diego soon. She hoped they thought she and he were still having sex, and not want to interrupt.

The map search she ran displayed her location as north of Mendoza. She was surprised. She had surmised they'd moved north, but once the rain had started she'd lost sight of the sun and hadn't realized they'd come a fair way west as well. Mendoza looked to be a day's ride to the south. Could she outrun her captors to the town? Unlikely, but she wanted to try.

Her next search changed that plan. Owen's tracker was not in Mendoza. Neither was it over the Andes as she'd feared. It was due west of her. And much closer than she could have hoped. If she could outrun the Argentinian villagers she might reach it by noon.

They would expect her to ride south, back towards the train line.

She would do her best to hide her tracks and ride west instead. Find Owen, time-jump out of there, and get him back to 2623.

She smiled grimly and cracked her neck. With a squeeze of her legs, she coaxed the horse forward.

* * *

None of Diego's people caught up with her that day, though the going was rockier and harder than she'd expected. It had been pure luck that let her escape the village unseen, but even in her state of constant ache, Michelle figured she was due some luck. The stallion coped well despite the terrain and it was the third day in a row it had embarked on a long ride. Michelle weighed less than Diego, and no saddle probably helped too, but she spent the day anxious that she would be caught if she rode too slowly, or that the horse would wear out if she rode too fast.

When she stopped by a stream to rest them both, it was mid-afternoon. Michelle ran the search for Owen again. The hologram displayed her friend in a cave, surrounded by workbenches and strange computers. Again, Michelle battered her mind to think of why he had been brought to such an isolated spot and time. There had to be more of a reason than hiding him, surely?

The stallion she left grazing, untethered so it could flee if necessary. Her need for a mount was done—as soon as she could touch Owen they were jumping out of there.

She crept through low scrub to the top of a small ridge. Below lay another rocky gully with a large cave entrance. There was no one in sight, but the distance given by the hologram and her own instincts told Michelle that Owen was in there.

She didn't like the idea of trying to sneak in during daylight. Perhaps walking the horse through streams and over rock had worked, and Diego's people hadn't tracked her this way. If that was the case she'd be smart to wait until dark, rather than plunge in blind.

Her muscles ached as she crept up and down the ridge, observing the cave from all angles and searching for signs of life through the late afternoon. She found a rubbish pit containing biodegradable wrappers of protein bars and a worn path to a latrine. They were smart enough to keep their waste far from the cave entrance, though no forcefields or security lines were in play, as far as she could tell.

They don't expect anyone to find them out here. It was a fair assumption. No towns or villages lay near and the railway was miles to the south. She wondered how they'd got the technology to time travel back here—had an Agent turned traitor? Maybe even two—the amount of gear they must have, told her that serious planning and logistics were involved.

She holed up in some bushes and rested. As evening fell she stretched and ran a search for Owen again. His location hadn't changed. She was glad to move—while it hadn't rained, the day had been overcast and the wind rolling down off the Andes was cold. Her all-weather jacket done up tight, Michelle adjusted her backpack and crept towards the cave.

Proof of human habitation assailed her nose. Hot food was in there somewhere. It was enough to make her mouth water—all she'd had to eat that day had been the cold bread, cheese and meat she'd stolen from Diego. *Don't get distracted!* She'd been hungry before—she'd survive. Rescuing Owen was paramount.

Silent as a shadow, Michelle ghosted through the entrance. There was no sentry. Voices and more smells of cooking drifted out from a passage to her right. She considered investigating, but Owen should be down and left.

The cave narrowed and angled down. A hard right turn had her worried but natural steps in the rock twisted back to the left and took her to a lower level. Now she was in a narrow passage lit by crystal lights along the floor. How far would she have to go? The further in she went the more nervous she became, though she quelled it. To be trapped down here... She calmed herself. She could always jump a week or a month from now—surely the tunnels would still be intact? The chronokinetor would prevent her from jumping into solid rock, but the possibility of a cave-in frightened her. She didn't mind small spaces usually—sleep pods and upright baths—but that was with the protection of technology that had a thousand safeguards. To be enclosed by dark, raw rock with no way to call for help...

Get it together. The crystals ended at a doorway. She wondered why they hadn't generated a forcefield. The setup was extensive—supplies and lights and computers, judging by what she'd seen in Owen's hologram. Was that the limit of the technology they had been able to bring?

She was sick of questions. Time to get some answers.

Twenty

96 AD

"Keep moving," Gwyn snapped at Stephanus when he stopped to look around again. The afternoon was getting on—it had taken most of the day to ride back from Ostia—and she didn't trust the man she had corralled into coming back to Rome.

"Keep your tunic on," came the contemptuous reply. "I'm scarcely about to 'do a bolt', as it were."

"How can I be sure?" Gwyn ground out, keeping a firm grip on the reins that led the mule. Stephanus' belongings were cinched onto the beast, along with her small bag. She hoped that by controlling his things he'd be less inclined to run off.

"Be sure," Stephanus retorted, lengthening his stride. This forced Gwyn to speed up to match him.

The Via was not crowded at this time of day—most people sought the coolness of the baths or the shade gardens up on the hill where there was a breeze. Gwyn desperately missed the fresh sea air—the stench of Rome in late summer made her gag—although she was glad to be back on solid ground.

Stephanus ignored Gwyn's muttered cursing and continued. "I know where my vines are planted. If I do this I'll be a free man. I'll be persecuted forever if I don't—by my mistress or by *him*. The likes of me are always ill-used by the upper classes. Even when we try to make a little something for ourselves we are held down and punished."

I don't think embezzling counts as 'making a little something' for yourself! Gwyn was sick of his whinging. Every time he opened his mouth it was to bemoan his situation. "If you were so hard done by as a steward, why

125

didn't you get work elsewhere?" she demanded, brushing a fly from her face.

"And end up somewhere worse? No, thank you! Besides, even when you've been freed as a slave the family still expects you to serve them," he said bitterly. "You're beholden forever. Don't you know anything?"

Gwyn didn't answer him. "Scat!" she told a young boy who sidled up next to the mule. "There's nothing for you to steal here!" *Uh, when did you get so callous?* She felt ashamed until the boy gestured rudely and ran off. "Are we almost there?"

Stephanus stopped again. "Don't you know where we are going?" he demanded.

"Of course I do!" Gwyn bluffed. "I just haven't been this way—I normally get there from the opposite direction."

"Hmph. It depends. It isn't far to Parthenius' home, but I want to bathe first and dress in clean clothes. There's a bath house just up ahead."

Uhoh. Gwyn realized the massive flaw in her plan. On ship she'd kept her tunic on and used the pocket-watch to dissuade curiosity about her. How would she keep an eye on Stephanus without revealing herself to others in the bathhouse? "I'll stay and watch our possessions," she said when they reached the bathhouse.

"That's what slaves are for!" He shot her an incredulous look. "I know Domitilla gave you money; pay for one of these lazy sods to guard the damn mule. I'm not showing up with a companion reeking of sweat and fish brine. You'd better have a clean tunic, or you'll need to buy one. Might as well spend our cash. You can pay for me too."

She hesitated. He grabbed her elbow and towed her behind a column at the top of the steps. Thrusting his hand between her legs, he gave a quick squeeze. Gwyn almost shrieked at the assault but didn't wish to attract more attention. Stephanus snarled, "Now if you don't want me to cause a fuss and reveal that you're a woman to every man in this place, you'll pay for me to have a bath and go sort yourself out too!"

Gwyn jammed her thumbnail into the webbing between the forefinger and thumb of his free hand. He yelped. "Don't touch me," she hissed. He withdrew the offending hand, but she dug her nail in harder. "If you don't want to end up in more trouble with Flavia

Domitilla you'll do as I say! I am important to her." The lie sounded good to her ears.

Stephanus obviously thought otherwise. "You're not part of her household—I've never seen you before and I've known her for years. You're not one of her skulking Christian friends who came to parasite themselves on Flavius Clemens.

Gwyn was losing control of the situation, but rallied. "Just because you didn't see me doesn't mean I wasn't there. I'm here to make sure you follow through with this, whether you like it or not. You've no choice."

Something in her voice must have had him believing because he slumped. She stopped pinching. "The only reason I'm here is because I have no choice. I don't fancy exile; Rome is the only place worth living, but my life won't be worth living if I don't do this thing. So you don't need to harry me. Go bathe yourself. I won't be going anywhere." He stalked off, flipping a coin to the attendant and disappearing into the bathhouse.

* * *

An hour later they arrived at a private villa on the Caelian Hill. Gwyn tied the mule to the metal ring fixed in the thick wall outside and tipped the door porter to bring a bucket of water for the animal. Lugging the small trunk and her bag inside, she sat in the atrium with Stephanus. Being clean and perfumed did not improve his demeanor; he was still sour to her. She for one had to find a bathhouse around the corner that was running a women's session. She quickly and self-consciously progressed through the pools, using the strigil Gaius had bought for her to scrape herself clean. At least there had been snacks there. She had bought several crumbly almond cakes and a pastry to fortify herself for the evening ahead.

A quiet Greek slave admitted them into an inner study. Unlike the shabby room in Silva's house, this study was spotless, airy and elegant. Coy maidens danced around an urn, the nudes in the frescos showed no bestiality and not a phallic decoration was in sight. *Maybe the more exciting decor is in other rooms of the house.* She'd been astonished at the number of penis statues, lamp shades, fountains and other household fittings in the homes she'd been in thus far. *Seriously, these people are obsessed!*

Parthenius' taste appeared conservative by comparison. The man himself was dressed in a white tunic with a few plain rings on his fingers. He was overweight, had a shaved head and dark eyes over a big nose. "Stephanus," he greeted. "You have some gall coming to see me here. You have one minute to explain why I should not throw you from my house."

Gwyn wondered if it was the man's attitude or actions that made everyone dislike him. Probably both.

"Flavia Domitilla sent me." The steward's voice was a croak. His shoulders slumped. "She sent money with her servant here, to buy the right people." He indicated Gwyn. "She ordered me to carry out the deed that must be done, and sent me to you to make it happen."

Parthenius folded his fleshy hands over his paunchy stomach, looking now at Gwyn. "Is this true? Did your mistress really send him for this purpose?"

It was her time to shine. She was dressed as a male slave, short, undyed tunic and her hair shoved under a cap. Handing over the letter, she bent all her will to make Parthenius go along with the plan. "My lady Domitilla sent me, yes, and Stephanus here. Is this room a safe place to talk?"

The door had been shut behind Parthenius, but he went to it and opened it, dismissing the slave who stood outside. Closing it once again, he walked around the desk in the center of the room and sat in the high-backed wooden chair set behind it, resting thick fingers on the polished wood. He moved quietly for a big man, and had better posture than the skinny and handsome Stephanus. "Speak softly, but tell me what you intend. Then I shall decide whether I trust you or not. It will have to be something extreme for me to believe you, Stephanus. What you did to your master was disgusting, and then to try to steal from your widowed mistress…" He pursed his lips, then ordered, "Speak."

Gwyn spoke. She outlined the contents of the letter, which remained gripped in Parthenius' pudgy hand. "She did not put much detail in, for fear it would fall into the wrong hands, but she meant for Stephanus to feign an injury in order to wear bandages around his arm. In those bandages he will hide a dagger, and approach the Emperor with word of a plot." She watched Parthenius stiffen in alarm, but plunged on. "Stephanus will give the Emperor a letter describing this plot, and while Domitian reads it Stephanus will use the dagger to kill him." She spoke quietly, but the room was so silent that every rustle of cloth, every breath, could be heard.

"Treason." Parthenius blanched.

"No." Stephanus leant in and hissed. "Not to Rome. We will be the saviors of Rome. And not for some Judean god, either." He shot a black look at Gwyn. "For the true gods, and for the people of Rome."

Parthenius looked down at the scrolled parchment in his hand and broke the seal. Scanning it, he nodded, seeming to approve of Domitilla's sparsity of language. He paused for a very long time. Gwyn and Stephanus held their breaths. Would Parthenius join in with the plot? If what Gwyn had learned about the Emperor's chamberlain was true, he would have considered this course of action already. His position and his life were under threat. There was no telling who Domitian might turn on next. And the fact that Domitilla had named him as a supporter suggested he would be the ringleader of any assassination plan. Gwyn stared at him intently, willing him to realize this was just the opportunity he had been waiting for.

"I will make the arrangements," Parthenius said at last. "It will take more than a disguise for a knife. The Emperor keeps a dagger himself— under his pillow—and the guards will need to be... distracted. Or distant." He tapped a thick finger against his lips. "I must talk to one or two other people. With the utmost discretion, of course. And she means for it to take place three days hence?"

Gwyn glanced at Stephanus. His face could have been carved from stone. "As the prophecy dictates, Domine."

Parthenius shook his head. "He is already in a state of vicious anxiety. He will be alert to anything that smells odd. The prophecy says that his death will come in the fifth hour."

"So tell him it is later than that," Gwyn suggested. "Let him think the danger has passed, so his guard is down."

Both men stared at her. Stephanus' smile was grim. Parthenius nodded soberly. "Very well. I will arrange for the dagger under his pillow to be false, a handle only, perhaps. And I will need to think how to deal with the Praetorian Prefects. Even if we succeed, they are our biggest danger."

"Bribe them," Stephanus said. "I can kill Domitian, but I can't fight off guards. They'll murder me. Domitilla sent funds." He nodded at Gwyn. "He has a writ to release money from her banker."

"Give it to me," Parthenius ordered, holding out his hand.

Gwyn quailed inside but shook her head. "We need a watertight plan before we start splashing money around. Flavia Domitilla entrusted this writ to me and I serve her interests." She didn't want Parthenius to sell out Domitilla to the Emperor. He already had the letter from her—a note to her banker would damn her doubly and the conspiracy would never succeed.

The imperial freedman looked offended. Sniffing, he said, "I have funds of my own we can use, I merely wished to keep the writ safe."

"No one goes through my paperwork," she pointed out. "You have too many clerks who might read it. You should burn her letter."

"I will," Parthenius retorted. To emphasize his words he thrust the parchment into a small brazier kept on the end of his desk. They all watched the flames lick up the sides and flare as they took hold, charring the evidence into ash.

"If that is all for this evening, we will go to my mistress' house here in Rome. I'm tired," Stephanus stood and cracked his neck. "I must behave as though I have been sent back to take care of her business, which means I must actually do some of that. Which means I need sleep."

Gwyn stood. Parthenius looked at them both. "I will speak to whom I must in the morning. Return tomorrow at the eighth hour," he instructed Gwyn. "You speak truly when you say I cannot be certain of my clerks. You can disguise yourself as a scribe?"

"Yes," she replied. *Well, I'll get a sleep in at least.* She realized just how tired she was, and sighed at the thought of one more trek through the streets of Rome before she could rest.

"I'll order my chair," Parthenius said. "Wait here."

She exchanged a glance at Stephanus, who sneered and looked away. It wasn't long before Parthenius beckoned them out of the room and instructed a slave to take them to the entrance, nodding solemnly as they left. Gwyn admired his aplomb. For someone who had just had conspiracy thrust upon him, he showed no sign of unease.

The sullen door slave tried to turn them away at Domitilla's town house, much to Stephanus' fury. He berated the slave and glared at Gwyn as if it were her fault. "Come inside," he ordered, then to the slave, "Inform me immediately if any other visitors come."

"Are you expecting anyone?" Gwyn asked the steward.

"No," he replied shortly, stalking up the tiled hall, leaving her to trail in his wake. She dragged their travelling bags which she had unloaded from the donkey.

"Is there anyone else here?" she puffed.

"Just the doorkeeper and a kitchen slave. When my mistress was exiled, those that chose not to follow her were either dismissed or sent to her country estates. This way."

They reached a private room. Stephanus gestured for Gwyn to enter. "Put my bags there," he ordered. She dumped everything where he indicated and extracted her own bag.

"I suppose you want to sleep since you're so tired. Where can I sleep?" She kept a wary eye on him, standing as he was between her and the door.

"I'm hungry too," Stephanus snapped. "That hypocrite Parthenius could have fed us. Go and get us something from the kitchen, and don't harass the kitchen slave."

Gwyn's temper boiled. "I'm not the one who harasses kitchen maids," she shot back.

He sneered. "Firstly, I'm the steward, they should be grateful for my attention. Secondly, I know what you unnatural types are like. Don't think yourself a man just because you dress like one."

She gaped. "You're disgusting," she spluttered. "Grateful? Ugh! And I know what I am, thank you very much. Get your own damn food."

She stormed out, blinking tears from her eyes. The slur that she was unnatural—that dressing as she liked or liking women was unnatural—mortified her. *There's nothing wrong with me.*

She blundered into an empty bedroom and pushed the door shut. She wouldn't inflict her affections on anyone who didn't want them, of that she was adamant. Not after what had happened to her, not after what she had done.

Hurt and depressed, she rolled herself onto the bed and slept.

Twenty-One

96 AD

Gwyn's delightful dream about Izem was interrupted by Stephanus shaking her awake. "Will you sleep all day? I must be about my business as if all were normal and I need you to fix the bandages. Get up."

Groggily, she complied. "What time will you be back?" she wanted to know. She sat up and stretched, blinking at the room where she had spent the night. She was on a double bed with a high side that backed onto a wall. Several shelves adorned the other walls, their only occupant, a lonely statuette. Gwyn's bag rested by the chest on the floor; an empty table near it. *It feels like a cheap motel room.*

"I shall return in the evening. I have been gone for several months— there is much for me to do. You must go to Parthenius at the eighth hour so I suppose you can loll about here all morning if you've nothing better to do." His tone indicated he doubted it.

"Have you got bandages?" she snapped. He proffered them. "Sit down, I can't reach all the way up there!" He sat on the edge of the bed and she huffed impatiently, yanking his right arm over.

"Not that arm!" He snatched it back. "I need to use that hand to pull the knife."

Gwyn stared at him, exasperated. "Well, give me your other damn arm so I can bloody well bandage it! I can stick a knife in it to make it more realistic, if you like!"

Stephanus glared then held his left arm across his body. Gwyn levered herself off the bed and sat on his other side to make it easier. Bandage after bandage she wound, trialing different wrapping techniques and getting Stephanus to practice pulling his dagger from

133

them. He got tangled several times before she changed the way she fastened the bandage at his wrist. It was essential that this disguise would hold up under the guards' inspection, and under Domitian's paranoid gaze.

"We can refine it tonight," she yawned once she was happy with the knife and bandage arrangement. She was still tired despite her night's sleep. "Now, what do you tell anyone who asks you how you hurt your arm?"

"I sliced it on a smashed jug," Stephanus retorted. Gwyn ignored him.

"Favor it if you can, even wince now and then but don't overdo it. It'll be better if you don't draw attention to it."

"I'm not stupid," he snapped and stood up. Gwyn glared at him. "If you are not here when I return, try to be in the house before nightfall. Janus will bar the gate after that."

She nodded stiffly then slumped when he left. Yawning, she lay back and closed her eyes.

"Excuse me?" A hoarse, female voice startled Gwyn awake.

"Crap, what time is it?" Gwyn cast about. She had fallen back asleep.

"Almost noon." The slave shuffled in, a slouching, middle-aged, dark-haired woman. Her voice made her sound like a chain-smoker. She peered at Gwyn. "Miss?"

"Um, yes." Gwyn cursed the lack of a cap on her hair. She scrambled upright and straightened her tunic. "And you are?"

"Marcia." The slave ducked her head. "I work in the kitchen. You came with Stephanus last night? He said you'd be wanting some food and that you were due over on the Caelian by the eighth hour. I thought you'd be wanting some time to bathe also."

"Thank you, Marcia." Gwyn tried to recover her dignity. She helped the slave drag in a small iron hip bath and washed in cold water. With Marcia's help she disguised herself once again. "You're very... kind. You don't even know me."

The slave chuckled, revealing only half a mouthful of teeth. "Oh, but I know Stephanus, and he don't like you. So I figure, you can't be all that bad." Marcia leant in and whispered conspiratorially, "I'm sure he's up to no good."

Gwyn's heart sank. She appreciated the good will but didn't want to encourage gossip. "That's why I'm here, to keep an eye on him. I've got to get going, sorry, Marcia."

"Of course, of course." The slave let her out the front door and pointed out the quickest road to the Caelian Hill. Gwyn sighed and trotted off.

* * *

Gwyn waited over an hour for Parthenius, so she was not in a good mood when the Chamberlain finally waddled out to the atrium where she kicked her heels.

"Palace matters kept me," he explained shortly, "so I was late home for lunch."

Oh I'm fine, thanks for the offer! The hard bread, boiled eggs and cheese that Marcia had brought her were long forgotten and Gwyn was hungry again.

She was given a sturdy mule to ride, but was forced to trot it behind Parthenius' litter. They travelled through city avenues and down the wide Via Tiburtina that ran out past the Campus Cohortium Praetoriarum. It was better than walking, she knew, but the mule was a finicky creature—balking at passing traffic and yanking the reins from her hands. *I'd take a horse any day.*

Acting as a scribe, she kept her eyes down as she walked into the Prefect's office. Parthenius indicated a stool where she could sit. A short, heavily muscled man came in the opposite door.

"Parthenius!" he barked. "What brings you to my humble camp? This ain't the gladiator circuit—I've got no toy-boys for you!"

"Petronius Secundus." Parthenius bowed and seated himself again. "Just a small matter regarding the rostering of palace guards. I wanted to confer with you as to the exact numbers and timing of the shifts—a clerk has alerted me to the fact that the Treasury might not be allocating sufficient funds to your cohort and I wanted to apologize and rectify the matter so no confusion as to fault arises."

Secundus' beetle-black eyes fixed on the portly chamberlain. "I ain't aware of any dis-crep-pan-cies…" He sounded out the word through his teeth, finishing with his bottom lip jutting. Gwyn thought he liked to make out that he was less intelligent than he actually was, playing on the stereotype that Praetorians were brutish bullies.

By contrast, Parthenius was the polished, smooth Greek—a palace bureaucrat who'd risen through the ranks by deception and sycophancy. Gwyn could see the tiniest beads of sweat behind his ears, but no nervousness leaked into his voice. "A mere clerical error, if it is that at all. I can easily order the release of funds, but in the interest of mitigating any bad feeling, perhaps a direct payment to yourself and Norbanus, and you can trickle down the funds to the correct soldiers. I just need to know who is rostered on for the next two days, and that will allow me to make the necessary calculations."

Silence reigned. It was a bizarre request, and Secundus would have been a fool to think otherwise. He was no fool, however, and he tapped his stubby fingers on the table as he considered. "Mayhap I've rostered on too many guards. I ain't wanting to be draining the imperial treasury." Gwyn stifled a snort.

"I'd still be most grateful if you allowed me to fund the compensation of those soldiers who were rostered on. The scribe who noticed the discrepancy seemed to think that four more guards than necessary were on duty. That would make..." He named a sum of secestres that caused Secundus' fingers to twitch, then resume tapping.

"I'd have to check with Norbanus—make sure he ain't made the same mistake as me in the last few weeks." The atmosphere was tense, despite the apparently relaxed scene in front of Gwyn. Secundus leant back, his fingers drumming.

Parthenius sat quietly, manicured hands resting on his stomach. Gwyn barely breathed. "Perhaps twice that would cover it, to ensure that neither you nor Norbanus are put out. After all, I understand the extra paperwork takes time away from your more important duties."

Several eternal seconds passed. Secundus nodded and sat up straight. "Mayhap that'll do. I ain't wanting any trouble over this."

"Oh, no trouble," Parthenius said smoothly, the relief palpable in the air. "I'll send my secretary here over with the correct funds, not a copper denari less, and we'll consider it all sorted."

"Aye," Secundus grunted, standing up. "Send him to my house; I ain't wanting a pretty-boy like him to get molested by my men. I'll be there for dinner tonight, with Norbanus too, so I'll make sure any rostering of guards at the palace is sorted for... the next two days."

"I'm most grateful for your understanding." Parthenius, too, rose and held out his soft-skinned hand to shake Secundus' rough one. The handshake lasted a second longer than necessary, and Gwyn could almost see the thoughts transmitting between the two men.

You are in this now, Parthenius seemed to say.

I ain't committed to nothing, Secundus' eyes replied. *If this don't succeed I ain't going down with you, and you ain't got nothing on me to prove otherwise.*

It will succeed. The tiniest smile gripped Parthenius face, though no mirth was in it as he turned and gestured to Gwyn to follow him out. There was no chance to discuss the meeting as she bumped along on the mule back into the city, though she was burning to ask him if he thought the Praetorian Prefects would co-operate.

Back in Parthenius' marble-walled office, he penned a note to his banker, then sent Gwyn with two bodyguards to visit the kohl-eyed Assyrian who kept the palace chamberlain's personal funds. The day was getting on now—Gwyn was astonished to realize how much time had passed—but she still had an hour or so to kill before dark. She and the bodyguards trudged back towards the Viminal Gate where Secundus' house was located. From the funds Domitilla had given her she shouted dinner for herself and her companions.

They sat quietly on the high stools on the caupona, nibbling at illegal pork skewers and sipping watered-down wine. Gwyn had no wish to fall into the trap of getting tipsy and robbed, though the prices were enough to make her want to call the barman a thief. *Incredible how I've only been in this time a couple of weeks and already I feel like a local.* She laughed at herself. Food put her in a better mood and she was confident that the plot was coming together.

Don't get too cocky, she warned herself, but smiled all the same. The day after tomorrow and it would all be done.

At last the sun set and she nodded to the bodyguards. "Time to go," she told Antonius and Tertius. They grunted and finished their drinks, flanking her as she walked the final block to Secundus' villa on the Viminal Hill.

"Watch out!" a man shouted as they drew close to their destination. Gwyn gasped as a pair of men barreled into her group. A third figure, shadowy in the fading light, collided with her and tugged urgent hands at the heavy purse tied under her tunic.

"Oi!" she yelled, grappling with the man. *Shit! They must've followed us from the bar or something!* Her bodyguards were busy. Panic spewed through her chest as a knife cut first one string, then the other and her fingers were all that were left to hold onto the large bribe. The mugger growled as the blade tangled in her clothes. He tried to elbow Gwyn's face, but she dodged sideways and the blow glanced off. Cheek stinging, she head-butted the man, sparking a yell of pain from her attacker. "Fuck off!" she roared, fury and desperation making her far more aggressive than she would have believed possible.

Then the mugger's knife was at her throat and Gwyn was mortified to feel urine trickling down her leg. *Fuck!* her mind shrieked, and everything froze.

Wham! Tertius had finished with his attacker and was earning his fee. A single, solid blow from a ham-like fist sent the mugger flying and only a razor sharp scratch nicked Gwyn's neck. Antonius had disposed of his opponent too. The hulking bodyguards breathed heavily as they scanned their surroundings for more trouble, but passers-by sensibly steered clear of the scuffle and no more muggers made their presence known.

"Shit." Gwyn wiped furious tears from her eyes and stuffed the purse back into her tunic. She hoped neither bodyguard noticed her incontinence. It was one thing to read about people pissing themselves in fear; another thing entirely to experience the humiliation.

"Let's go," Antonius' voice was gruff.

"Come on, lad," Tertius gripped her elbow and towed her along. "Not been in many biffs? Don't be afeard—ye only piss yeself once or twice afore ye gets used to it."

Oh Christ. Gwyn felt her skin flush beet-red. "Thanks," she muttered with a choked voice. How would she ever handle Domitian's assassination? Shamefaced, she was snappy with the doorkeeper when they reached the villa, and asked to use the latrine while she waited to be shown in to see the Prefects.

Rinsing her face and legs with a pitcher of fresh water helped her composure, and she took a minute before venturing back out. She could feel her cheek swelling into a bruise but her neck was no longer bleeding.

"Petronius Secundus will see you now," a shaven-headed slave informed her brusquely as she re-joined her bodyguards. Gwyn coughed, then nodded, unable to relax her hold on the bribe purse.

They were shown into an over-decorated salon. Secundus and another man whom she took to be the other Praetorian Prefect Norbanus, reclined on dining couches. Gwyn ignored the risqué frescos and phallic lamps and focused instead on being a discreet, urbane and unassuming palace slave. "Sir," she crossed the blue and red patterned tiles and bowed to Secundus, then Norbanus, and proffered the purse.

"Right then!" Secundus swung his feet to the ground and accepted the purse with a crocodile's grin. "Let's see if our greasy Greek friend puts his money where his mouth is." He upended the purse onto his wide lap and used pudgy fingers to count the secestres. Norbanus looked on, his tanned face flush with wine. He was much fitter than his counterpart and took less to get drunk.

"Come sit here, lad," he ordered Gwyn. "Secundus counts slow; you might as well be comfortable while we wait." He grinned, and Gwyn's skin crawled.

"It's all there," she murmured in a low voice to Secundus.

The Prefect paused and flicked beady eyes up at her. "It ain't all here till I say it's here, lad. Now go keep Norbanus company while I count. I may be slow but I ain't stupid."

Norbanus grinned. Gwyn drifted reluctantly to Norbanus' couch and perched awkwardly on the end. "That's no good!" the Prefect slurred. "C'mere and tell me what it's like being the bum-boy of those greasy-Greeks."

"I'm just a scribe," Gwyn whispered. *Leave me alone,* she thought hard. *You're not interested; I'm grey, boring, flat, dull. I'm nothing, nothing, nothing to you.*

Secundus grunted, distracting Norbanus for a second. Gwyn edged away but the Praetorian pushed himself up and dragged her closer. He groped her bottom, making her feel sick. "Ooh, bit of tension there, lad." He squeezed. She watched Secundus pick up the last handful of coins, stomach in her mouth. Secundus' lips moved as he counted. Norbanus' hand crept around her hip, headed for her groin.

"It's all here!" Secundus declared and Gwyn leapt to her feet.

"Thank you, sirs, I'll tell my master that all is to your satisfaction!" She willed Secundus to override his partner, whose hand still rested on her butt.

The Prefect's eyes flicked from the money to her. He leant back and waved a lazy hand. "Leave the lad be, Norbanus. I'll order in one of mine for you. Got to keep our friends at the palace happy."

Amidst Norbanus' grumbling, Gwyn fled.

Twenty-Two

96 AD

The plot was set. The pieces were in place. It would be one more day before the assassination, so all Gwyn had to do now was wait.

She was proud of herself. Her daring, quick thinking and nerve had taken her from a helpless teenager to a bold woman who dodged guards, organized herself, work and allies to further her cause, and set history to rights. *Yes, Gaius helped a bit,* she admitted, *but I did the hard work, convincing all those people. I put myself at risk to fulfil this… this mission.*

She allowed herself to feel a touch of smugness, imagining casually telling Michelle how she had not only identified a problem in the timeline, but fixed it too. She smiled, and turned off the main Via. Confidence was a nice feeling, she decided. Novel and nice.

Knock, knock! She rapped on the door of the elegant villa. It was the tradesman's entrance, made for those who worked, not guests. A sleepy slave opened it. "Yes?" she yawned.

Gwyn frowned. It was early, but surely the household would have risen by now? "I'm looking for Izem. He told me to find him here." Now that she was faced with it, all her confidence shattered. What if he had forgotten about her, or worse, hadn't been serious? She could have read the situation all wrong, and he could be just an opportunistic flirt who stole kisses from passing ladies. What if—and now a thousand thoughts ran through her mind—this rather good-looking female slave had just risen from bed with him? Was this going to be one of those scenarios like in the movies where the heroine found out the man she liked was a two-faced, lying, cheating cad?

"Izem?" Another slave, a bulky, muscled specimen with a face like an angry buffalo moved into view, patting the first slave's bottom with his hand. This didn't reassure Gwyn. The female slave might not have a choice about who she slept with, and the impression Gwyn had received earlier was that Izem was given fair license to carry on as he wished. "That feckless, good-for-naught–"

"I is being here." Izem stepped out from a side corridor and smiled brilliantly at Gwyn. Her stomach sprang into butterflies and everything from the slaves to the street noise from the Via faded away. "Gwynia. You is coming to see me. I was wondering if you had forgotten me. What is happening to you? Is the man who is not your father beating you?" His deep voice had started off pleased, and she knew she hadn't misread the signs. He examined the bruise on her face, frowning, then waved a hand in dismissal of the two slaves. They shook their heads and disappeared.

"I'm fine—it was an accident. Were…you sleeping?" Gwyn asked for something to say. She wanted to look at him yet she didn't want to at the same time. Was she here to ask him on a date? For conversation and kissing? For sex? She knew she wanted to see him; that the thought of spending time with this confident and charming young man was far more appealing than bringing danger and plotters back onto Adi or Gaius' trail. She had a day to kill, why not reward herself with a little fun?

"I is not being asleep. My master—he had party last night, so everyone sleeps late. But not me. I is up early, thinking about Gwynia, wondering if she is still being in Ostia or is returning back to Roma."

Gwyn scoffed. "I'm sure you had better things to think about." Several of the butterflies in her midsection tumbled in a zephyr of delight.

That beautiful white smile again, so vivid against his black skin. Even with the broken tooth on one side she thought it perfect in its imperfection. He took her hands in his, soft fingers tickling her palms. "I is knowing I would be seeing you again, because the gods must have decreed it. Too many coincidences is being divine work. Will you be coming in to see the home of Izem?" He drew her inwards, shutting the door with a click. "My master will be sleeping until afternoon. Slaves be lazy too, if they can. Quiet house."

It was. He showed her the public rooms—arranged for dining and entertaining, as well as business. The proprietorial air he displayed puzzled Gwyn. Izem had declaimed against being a slave, yet talked about his 'master'. The slaves at the door had deferred to him, though the bruiser had not hesitated to voice his low opinion of her friend. "Izem," she asked hesitantly, "what work do you do in this house? Are you the doorkeeper?" Wouldn't that be a slave's job? And would he get in trouble for having a lady-friend visit? She was a trespasser, not a guest.

Izem halted, and she feared she had upset him. *That's bollocks—it's a harmless enough question.*

"I is doing what the master needs me to do, but sometimes I is saying no," he grinned, then took pity on her. "The master is being my half-brother," he said. "His father was my father. His mother—our father's wife. My mother—a slave. But we is growing up together and we is being brothers. I will always be having a place in his house, though he freed me once he is becoming the master when our father died. I is older—I is looking after him." The genuine affection with which he spoke contained no jealously or resentment. Izem seemed to have accepted his lot, and enjoyed the freedoms that came from occupying a unique position in the household.

"That's why he bailed you out," Gwyn said slowly.

Izem's grin broadened. He led her down a gallery with frescos of nudes being chased by hairy men with goat feet. She didn't think much of the theme, but the painting itself was excellent. They emerged into a small courtyard garden, the centerpiece of which was a delicately bubbling fountain, topped by yet another nude. He sat by the fountain and flicked the tiniest splash at her. She blushed, remembering their flirtation in Ostia.

"He is getting annoyed when I fight," Izem said, "but he always comes for me. When he is getting very annoyed, he makes me stand in for Janus, or go to Ostia. But we is being brothers. He forgives." He reached out his dark hand and pulled Gwyn to sit on his lap. "And your family, Gwynia? Will the angry man who is not being your father come to fight me if I is kissing you?"

She shuddered at the thought of Gaius seeing her like this, let alone of him fighting the fit, tall and strong Izem. *What am I judging myself for? I don't belong to anyone but myself, and I can carry on with whoever I like!* With that defiance in her mind she smiled at Izem and leaned closer, tempting him to kiss her.

He scarcely needed the invitation. In a second the nervousness was gone as their kisses rekindled the passion she'd felt in Ostia. Fire tore through Gwyn's veins, awakening her muscles and skin as his mouth pressed firmly against hers. The desire to press her body against his took over and Izem's hands colluded, pulling her in tight and kneading her back and buttocks. The thrill of those hands exploring her made Gwyn breathless, and she was shocked at how quickly she'd gone from hesitant girl to wanton woman, and at how much she didn't care because it felt so good. It was a buzz, much greater and more confident than the hesitant longing she'd had with a younger Gaius, much, *much* more satisfying than the unrequited desire she'd felt for Alina.

"Is you wanting to see the part of the house where I sleep?" Izem broke off his kissing and asked, his eyes burning. She stroked the long scar that tore across his eyelid and gashed down his cheek, finding it taut yet softer than the skin around it.

"Yes," she squeaked, much to her mortification. Why couldn't she have nodded mysteriously or breathed a sultry, sexy 'yes'?

Izem didn't seem to care. He pulled her to her feet, towing her along in his wake as they followed a different corridor and up a stairwell to a locked door. He paused to kiss her again, hungrily, pressing her against the wall and for a terrifying moment Gwyn thought of Vlad, trying to rape her. Izem didn't notice her freeze up as he extracted a key from his belt purse and opened the door. He gestured for her to enter and she hesitated. Izem cocked his head. "You is wanting to be here, Gwynia?" He took her hand and traced shapes on her palm, then kissed it. "I is wanting you here."

This is not Vlad. You chose to be here. You can run away at any time. Could she though? Once she was in that room it'd be a whole lot harder to leave. Even from this corridor he could stop her easily.

Time stretched as her fears swirled and memories of all the aggressions she'd survived clamored in her brain. Her heart pounded and it took all her effort to let go a tight breath she hadn't even realized she'd been holding. She looked at Izem. He waited patiently, still tracing the lines in her palm, and the shivers were back in a good way. She pushed away her fears and smiled shyly, catching his hand in hers.

He smiled back at her, swung an arm around her waist, and pulled her into the room.

* * *

Sometime later, Gwyn lay in Izem's arms. She gazed up at the cool stone ceiling of his room and listened to the sounds of the household slaves going about the business of their day. It was hot outside, and she was grateful for the breeze that drifted through the window and cooled her sweaty skin.

So that was... pretty amazing. She couldn't prevent the smile from creeping back onto her face, even as she blushed to think about what she'd just done.

Izem hadn't rushed her, but he hadn't dawdled either. He had made it clear with his hands and his mouth and his eyes that he found her desirable. That alone thrilled her and made her feel sexy instead of awkward. She still hesitated, waiting for him to lead the way, but he had carried her forward and she dared to touch and kiss and allow him to kiss her in places that she would have been embarrassed to stop and think about. But it felt so good and she had shuddered with a high pitched half-gasp, half-scream. Izem had grinned with satisfaction and kissed his way out from between her legs, pausing over her to guide himself into the warm wetness that was sending shudders up and down her body.

Her little yip of pain slid into a groan of amazed astonishment. She had wrapped her legs around him and pulled him closer, deeper. He'd gripped her butt and tilted her up so he could thrust steadily, bending to kiss her deeply with a mouth that tasted warm and different. Her groans continued, muffled and staggered.

Just when Gwyn thought she could take no more her brain exploded in bliss and she dug her nails into his back, a wordless cry falling from her throat as Izem buried his head in her shoulder and bit—not too hard, but hard enough to juxtapose against the wave of pleasure she rode upon and make it all the more delightful.

"Oh my God." Gwyn almost cried, overwhelmed. Her head felt spaced out and it was all she could do to lie there and pant. She wanted to giggle and sleep and sob all at the same time. "Oh my God." Any other words seemed inept.

"Mmm." Izem rolled off her and lay with his head on his hand, elbow bent, and traced circles on her stomach with a lazy smile. "You are so beautiful, Gwynia." The hand traced lower. Butterflies in her stomach fluttered their wings again.

"Oh," said Gwyn. It was too much. She caught his hand but he simply pulled free of her grasp, leaning to kiss her again. Gwyn didn't know whether the sound she made was protest or anticipation but her hips rose to meet his hand as he swirled past her pubic hair and rubbed into the slipperiness below. It didn't take much before her brain exploded again and she sank back, still twitching, but well and truly spent.

Wow. Just wow.

"It is good?" Izem asked, knowing her answer but the gleam in his eye told her he wanted to hear it anyway.

"Mhmm." She was too relaxed to blush now. "I'd say a definite yes." She yawned. After the attack in the street and the assault by Secundus it had taken her forever to get to sleep the previous night. The sick fear had roiled through her body and mind, and every noise in the house had made her twitch. She'd only slept a few hours before creeping out of the villa, not wanting to talk to Stephanus. She'd needed to reassert control over her body, and had sought Izem to do that.

Another yawn and she covered her mouth with the back of her hand. "Sleep, Gwynia," Izem breathed in a low voice. "I is not going anywhere. No one will bother us."

She barely heard his last words as she drifted off.

* * *

Dreams of sex turned into the reality as she woke to hands caressing her skin. A lazy smile drifted onto her face and before she had time to be embarrassed about being naked in a man's bed she was turning to kiss

Izem. She dozed again after their lovemaking, then woke when the hunger in her stomach demanded to be heard. Her belly growled loudly, making Izem laugh and rub it. "I is hungry too but I is thinking you is going to be sleeping forever!"

"Actually, I kind of need to…" Gwyn sat up and crossed her arms over her breasts. *Dammit, how do I say I need to pee? I don't even know where the latrine is. Or is it just chamber pots?* The idea of urinating in front of someone she'd just had amazing sex with really killed the romance.

"Pot is under bed." Izem pointed, getting up. He saw Gwyn's hesitation and laughed as he pulled a tunic on over muscles that moved in clear definition. Her stomach flipped over, increasing her discomfort. "I is waiting for Gwynia outside. Tip pot out window—garden is being there." He sauntered out, all sleek and smooth, with hair too short to be mussed like hers, a confidence in his body that she'd never felt in hers, but wanted to.

Wasting no time once the door closed, Gwyn leaped out of bed and used the chamber pot with relief. She tipped the contents out the window onto the lemon tree below, checking first that nobody saw her. It was the same little courtyard they'd sat in earlier. Just as she finished she saw the female slave who had answered the door saunter out and pick some flowers from the garden. Gwyn retreated quickly, turning to look for her clothes. Her tunic was rumpled and needed a vigorous shake. She needed a clean one, not to mention a bath. The room smelled of sex and sweat, and while it wasn't unpleasant, she could taste it.

She dressed and peeped out the door. No one was in sight. Her heart thudded. Was she expected to wander through this house alone, searching for him? Relief flooded through her when her lover bounded up the stairs carrying a cup. "For you, Gwynia," Izem bowed as he proffered the cup.

It was water. She drank gratefully. Her stomach rejoiced for a second then realized that water was not what it wanted, and rumbled again. "I'm sorry," Gwyn said automatically.

"For being hungry? Gwynia, come—I cannot be having you faint from no food." He guided her back down to the courtyard where a tray rested on the edge of the fountain. Gwyn almost fell on the food, and was glad when Izem matched her bite for bite. She grinned when he lifted a fig to her lips, and enjoyed the sensation of being waited on as he poured water and wine for her and encouraged her to try various nibbles and treats on the tray.

"Is your master awake yet?" she wanted to know once food had taken the edge off her hunger. The length of the shadows in the courtyard told her it was mid-afternoon.

Izem nodded. "He is out of the house, so I know it is safe for you to be here."

Gwyn frowned. No sooner had she opened her mouth to ask why it would be unsafe than a man's voice bellowed, "Izemus! Where are you?"

Izem stiffened, then in one sinuous movement stood and strode to the open doorway to one side of the courtyard. He didn't reach it before a richly dressed, olive skinned man burst through it, almost colliding with the tall African. "What are you doing, brother?" the man steadied himself on Izem's arm. "They told me you were sleeping so I left without you but then I realized I needed you so I came back..." He trailed off and peered around Izem at Gwyn.

She coughed and pulled her scarf over her hair, becoming flustered when it kept sliding off. Izem tried to put an arm around the shoulders of the man to guide him out but was shaken off. "Who's this, Izemus?" The man's smile made Gwyn uncomfortable, as did the way his eyes lingered all over her. "Hello, I'm Lucanus, master of this household."

"She is being a friend," Izem answered shortly. "She is leaving."

Gwyn took the hint and jumped up. Her small bag was up in Izem's room, but fortunately the stairway to those quarters lay behind her, so she bowed quickly and walked away. She guessed the olive skinned man was Izem's half-brother and master—they shared some facial features. She resented his intrusion but was also embarrassed at being caught in his house, eating his food and canoodling with one of his staff.

As she retrieved her things from Izem's room, a noise behind her made her turn. Izem's brother stood in the doorway, Izem hovering behind him, an irritated look on his scarred face. "You is saying you wanted to go, Lucanus." Izem clearly wanted to pull his half-brother away but held back—for fear of reproach or punishment, Gwyn wasn't sure. The license he seemed to exercise must depend on his brother's goodwill. She paused, unsure how to handle the situation. It was a horrible realization of her earlier fear, she wanted to leave, and a man was blocking her way. Was this punishment for seeking out Izem? *Bullshit!*

Then Gwyn kicked herself mentally and straightened. So much of her use of the pocket-watch's powers had involved creeping about, being inconspicuous and blending in. Sometimes, however, boldness was called for. "I'm leaving now," she announced authoritatively to Lucanus and stepped forward, willing him to move aside.

To her intense relief he did. The look on Izem's face was one of astonishment, but she didn't break stride. She didn't run, nor did she look back, though she itched to do both. Down the stairs and back towards the kitchen. The muscle-bound slave she had seen that morning directed her to the servants' door and she was out of it and on the street before Izem caught up with her. "Gwynia!" She stopped and turned. He was alone.

"I figured it was best if I left quickly," she explained.

"You is being right, but how? My master never..." he bit off his next words.

"Never what?"

Hesitation. "He is never letting beautiful women just walk past. Always he is saying something, usually more than saying. I was being afraid. He is my brother, but he is also being my master." He looked extremely unhappy about the dichotomy. "He is letting me do as I wish, as long as I is not annoying him or stopping him do as he is wishing."

"Uh huh," Gwyn drawled. "And women are some of the things he wishes to do?" The close call she'd had shook her, but not as much as she would have expected. Perhaps knowing she could fight back mentally and physically reduced the helpless rage and humiliation that usually came with being harassed. Perhaps she was feeling more confident after having gone into Izem's arms so willingly. She'd chosen that—it hadn't been chosen for her. She would also choose when to leave.

"This is being true," Izem hung his head. His dejection at not having protected her was clear. She patted his arm.

"You tried to stop him," she said. "You should have warned me about him when I first came to see you, though."

"I is so happy you came!" he declared. "I did not want you to be leaving so soon. I was thinking you is being safe!"

She didn't reply that he had been selfish. Who was she to judge? Hadn't this whole visit been selfish? A fun, no-strings-attached thrill? She sighed. "Never mind. I have to go, Izem, thank you for today. It was… really lovely."

He looked bemused. "You is leaving?"

Guilt plagued her. She pushed it away. "This was just a bit of fun, Izem—I won't be staying in Rome so you probably won't be seeing me again."

He didn't protest but looked confused all the same. She stiffened and nodded briskly, wanting to get away from him now their interlude was over. She left and walked down the road. It was time to find Stephanus again and make sure the plot was on track.

Twenty-Three

1890 AD

The door had a simple bolt. Michelle slid it back as slowly as she could. As she opened the door it made the tiniest creak and Owen's head shot up. He was sitting at a table, tinkering with something metallic. Michelle put her fingers to her lips and closed the door behind her.

"Michelle?" Owen's voice was a breathy squeak. His dark hair was messy and long, but he looked well enough. "What are you doing here?"

"Rescuing you," she replied and stepped towards him. "Time to go. Is there anything amongst all this," she gestured at the crystals and holo-casters and screens strewn across the wooden workbench, "that you need?"

"No, no, I can't leave. I have work to do!"

Michelle frowned at him. Her aching body didn't want another fight, and the longer she tried to convince Owen to leave, the more likely one of his kidnappers would find them. "Get your stuff, Owen," she ordered.

Owen stood and moved behind his stool, putting it between him and Michelle. She took another step and his dark eyes widened. "No! My research! They brought me to this time so I could observe the stars—I haven't completed my calculations."

Michelle stared at him. "What the hell are you talking about, Owen. I'm here to rescue you. Are you telling me you came willingly? Have you defected from the Agency?" A speck of saliva flew from her mouth as she spoke.

Owen patted his pockets and produced a small crystal computer. "No, it's not what you think! They brought me here, but I didn't know why. They drugged me and jumped me but once we arrived they explained the importance of the research I must do. I'm the only one who can do it. No one else understands the time-space calculations like I do—the Shift is coming, you see!"

Michelle snarled. "I know the damn Shift is coming, why d'you think I'm saving your sorry arse? We need you back at the Agency! We're almost out of time! The Shanista are staving off the political bullshit as best they can but we need to show the Council evidence, and that means your calculations!" Her fists clenched and unclenched, the knife she'd stolen from Diego tantalizing on her hip. *I ought to just belt him over the head and carry his stupid butt out of here!*

"Michelle." Owen's voice was low and urgent. "There's more to it than we ever thought. What the Shanista told us—it's only half the truth. It's not the first time the Shift has come. It's about to happen in this time."

Michelle stared at him, hating his sallow face, his earnest expression. "What?" she demanded in a whisper.

Owen came around the front of the stool again, holding his hands out wide, the computer still in one. He bowed to her, and automatically she returned the social gesture. It went some way towards calming her. "You came all this way for me," he said. "That must not have been easy. You used my tracker?"

"Tell me what's going on." The edge was still in her voice.

He closed his eyes for a moment. "The Shift was engineered to change history, history of those who would one day threaten its maker. Humans managed to fight it off by the end of the twenty-first century, so they have generated it again, in our time."

She shook her head. "Bullshit, Owen. The Shift is a natural phenomenon. I learnt that when I joined the Agency. You learnt that! I've seen the calculations by the Shanista, by our Rilan and Nolii technicians. I've seen the predictions for our pattern of history if we don't set the past to rights!"

Owen mimicked her head-shake. "You haven't seen all of it. Maybe the other species have, but not humans. We are critical to the survival of the Allied Planets. We may be their youngest member, but we have proved we can fight the chaos the Shift brings."

"That doesn't even make sense. It's an energy wave that affects time travel wormholes. You can't fight it, you just have to make sure everything is secure before it hits and then survive it. Like a storm."

"No," he interrupted. "That's not true. It's an energy wave, yes, but it has... additional features. The one in this time seeks to disrupt humanity's progress, to increase conflict and war."

Michelle took a breath and smiled patiently. "Owen, humans have been at war for millennia. The next two centuries are nothing different; it's only the technology that has advanced."

"Then why didn't we self-destruct? Why did humans suddenly turn around and change? I'll tell you why. It's because the Shift passed and we survived it. We fought the hatred and the cruelty and we survived. The ones who sent it wanted us to wipe ourselves out, but we didn't. That's why we are critical to the Allied Planets."

Michelle rubbed her eyes and her temples and leant against the wall. "This doesn't make sense. Even if what you are saying is true, why wouldn't the Shanista tell us? Our knowledge makes no difference if the end result is the same. We know the Allied Planets need humans to fight what is coming. That has been the whole purpose of all my missions. If this... malevolent being really created the Shift, and isn't simply riding in on the back of it to take advantage of our weakened situation, why didn't it come to wipe out humans now?"

"They are too far away."

"What?"

Owen shook his head. "Look, I don't know enough about this entity except what I can extrapolate from their technology and their behaviour. They have the means to see through time, and to create the Shift to affect history, but they are operating from a phenomenal distance. That's why my astronomical observations in this time are so important. I need to map where it's coming from, and compare it to the readings in our time."

She clasped her hands. "Then why didn't the people who brought you here clear it with the Agency? This is the survival of the Allied Planets we're talking about!"

Her friend fidgeted and glanced to the side. He leant forward and whispered, "They're Earth First, Michelle. They want to bargain humans into a position of power in the government. They want Shanista secret technology and a deciding say in politics and trade. They want humans listed as primary Citizens and all other species secondary."

Michelle's lip curled. "And you are helping them?"

"I didn't have a choice! This research needs to be done! And the Shanista shouldn't have kept it all a secret!"

"Bullshit!" Michelle launched herself to her feet. "They are better than us, that is why they can be trusted to be in charge. I've crawled through some of the darkest pits of humanity; I know what humans are like. Being part of the Allied Planets makes us better—we need them."

Owen's dark eyes looked... almost sad, as well as frightened. "Look at what they've made you. You used to be so happy and fun at uni. You're violent now. You hurt people."

"I do it because I must. And you're coming with me back to the Shanista to explain how you've betrayed everything we've worked for. Get up!" She yanked him upright by the wrist. He fought and grabbed her arm, then froze.

"You have data space on those crystals?" His hand had found her wrist computer.

"What?"

He spoke urgently. "Data—is there space on your crystals? I can give you what I've learnt so far, to take back."

Michelle narrowed her eyes. "You're trying to trick me, to delay us."

"No." He shook his head. "For real. Look—I know what the Shanista have done to you isn't right, and they shouldn't have lied to us, but... you're also right. They are the best hope we have." He manipulated a crystal free from her bracelet and placed it onto the screen of the computer he was holding. He dragged across data with his finger and typed in codes to unencrypt it. Michelle watched suspiciously. She held out a hand for the crystal and Owen gave it back. About to fix it back into the bracelet, she paused. Heavy footsteps thudded in the passage outside the room.

"You bastard," she hissed at Owen and scanned the room for another way out.

"No!" He looked panicked. "I didn't delay you on purpose! They must have been listening on the monitor."

Her look was incredulous. She drew Diego's knife and slid it into her boot. "You knew they were listening?" *Unbelievable.*

"He couldn't know for sure," a new voice drawled outside the door. "We don't monitor him constantly, you see. We didn't really think he'd be receiving visitors."

The door swung wide and a man stood there smiling. He held a gun, and had it pointed at Michelle.

Twenty-Four

1890 AD

Twice in a day, was Michelle's first thought.

"Now this is a catch," the man continued, still smiling. "Agent Michelle herself. You are supposed to be dead."

Keep talking, you prick. If this man decided she should be dead and shot her straight away, she was screwed. She could only hope she was more valuable to him alive and that would get her closer to the cave entrance to make a jump.

"Now hand over that computer of yours—we can't have any data getting into those bugs' claws." He stretched a hand towards her and dipped the barrel of the gun to encourage her to comply. It wasn't a weapon from their time, she noted, but a pistol probably picked up here in Argentina. She scowled, stripped off the bracelet of crystals and handed it over.

"Don't call the Shanista 'bugs'," she said. "They're better citizens that you'll ever be."

"A cat-fucker like you would think that," the man replied, shoving the computer bracelet in his pocket and indicating she should step out of the room. "Continue with your research, Owen, we'll deal with you later."

"I had to delay!" Owen gabbled. "I knew you'd come—I delayed her!"

Michelle didn't even know whether to feel sorry for him or not, let alone whether to believe him. "I'll be back for you," she said as a parting shot—a promise or a threat; that would depend on him. "Where are you taking me?" she demanded of the man with the gun. He led her through the tunnel up to the main cave then took a left towards the smaller cave filled with light and the smell of food.

Her captor didn't answer, and she considered whether she was quick enough to overpower him. Maybe if she'd been fresh and not bruised, aching, tired and hungry. She also wanted more information about these Earth First nutjobs.

The circle of faces in the small cave was not a friendly one, despite the smiles. Michelle recognized one woman—a technician from the Agency. "More traitors," she said flatly.

"That depends on your point of view," the woman sniffed, running a hand through her auburn hair. "I'm loyal to my species, at least."

"What the hell do you hope to accomplish?" Michelle went on. "If the Shift comes and history isn't right, humans won't join the Allied Planets. We'll be vulnerable to whatever comes next."

"The Allied Planets will be vulnerable," a short, dark-skinned man answered. "Humans are the key, and as such deserve the most important role, and the power that comes with it. No more being subordinate to bugs and cats and slugs and rock-eating dinosaurs."

Michelle had heard this vitriol before but this went beyond. Earth First would risk every species' existence, including humans', to gain the chance at being in charge. She shook her head slowly, using the movement to observe everything in the cave.

"She get anything out of Owen?" a short, dark-skinned man wanted to know.

"Nothing important," Michelle's captor replied, jabbing her forward with the gun. "I got the crystals she was trying to steal data on." He tossed her computer bracelet to the dark-skinned man, who examined it briefly then passed it to the woman.

"See if there's anything useful on there," he ordered.

"You gonna question her?" The fourth member, a tall, heavy-set woman with dark olive skin eyed Michelle. There was malice in her gaze.

"How about I just shoot her?" Her gun-toting captor jabbed Michelle's back again. She suppressed a snarl. He seemed to be asking permission, which she hoped meant he didn't have the authority to kill her off his own bat.

"No." The short, dark-skinned man appeared to be the leader. "I want to know how she found us. I want her timepiece, and I want to know anything she knows about the Agency, the Shift and the Shanista."

That was her cue. She wasn't about to lose her timepiece. Michelle ducked and punched her captor as hard as she could in the belly. An 'oof' of expelled air was drowned out by the 'blam!' of the gunshot and one of the women screamed. Rather than fight to wrest the gun from the man and risk being overpowered by the others, Michelle dodged around him and ran.

Swearing chased her but she had a head start on the Earth First crew. Out the small cave and back through the big cavern. *Forget Owen, he'll have to wait.* She stumbled out the cave entrance and slid down the gully floor just as another shot rang out above her head. *Shit!*

She ran south, away from the rubbish heap and the latrine. She'd lose too much momentum if she scrambled up to opposite slope, not to mention present herself as a clear target. Crystal beams flashed up and down the gully, and while Michelle cursed the darkness that made it harder for her to run, she knew a light of her own would just give her position away.

"There she is!"

Too late. She ran faster, keeping her knees and ankles soft to flex with the uneven ground. It wasn't enough. She tripped and went flying, wrist jarring badly.

Shit! She breathed hard and staggered to her feet. Her momentum was gone. She would have to time-jump.

Breathe. Concentrate. Just a small jump, take yourself to morning.

The sound of time travel rose in her ears. *Flick!*

* * *

It was dawn. Michelle collapsed onto the ground. Time travelling when injured and exhausted was not a good idea. In the gully, she listened for sounds of pursuit.

Nothing.

She heaved a sigh and hauled herself to her feet. She needed to get some distance between her and the cave and then rest. She couldn't walk a whole day on no sleep, and there was barely a mouthful of food left in her backpack. She needed water too.

Michelle climbed up the eastern slope and stopped again to check her surroundings. The sun shot several rays over the horizon, but it was a thin, weak sunlight than provided no warmth. Michelle trudged on. Perhaps if she'd been more of an outdoors person, more attuned to wildlife and natural sounds, she would have noticed the odd silence.

The stream where she had left Diego's horse was just up ahead in another small gulch. She didn't expect to see the animal there, but she was a little surprised that not even a bird was in sight for a morning bath. She crouched by the stream and took a long drink. The splash of cold water on her face woke her up, and her senses screamed alarm.

Crouched as she was, the long knife she'd stolen from Diego was easy to reach. Michelle whipped it out and turned as the cougar leapt on her. The blade sliced the feline but wasn't fatal, so it was in a flurry of yowls and claws that they fell into the water. The rush of bubbles in her ears cut off the sound, but most of the air had been forced from her lungs so it was anything but peaceful as Michelle stabbed and stabbed at the great cat's side. Clouds of blood obscured her vision. Her chest screamed for air but the stabbing pain in her shoulders lessened. Bumping the bottom with her feet, Michelle heaved the cougar off her and broke the surface. The first breath was sharp and painful, mirrored by a final, jerking swipe of the animal's claw on her face as it thrashed, then was still.

Several more times she went under before her feet cooperated and got her upright. The stream ran quickly but was only waist-deep. It had saved her life, however—falling backwards onto rock would have killed or stunned her. The body of the cougar floated away and snagged on a rock before disappearing around a bend. Michelle hauled herself from the shallows and coughed until she threw up.

"Urgh." She flopped over and stared dizzily at the sky. *Not good. Cut up. Can't jump.* The clouds and sky spun crazily and her eyes closed in an effort to block out the faintness overcoming her.

"No!" She rolled back onto her stomach and crawled some more. Going to sleep now would be fatal. Another cougar, or the Earth First crew, or hypothermia would get her. She knew she was going into shock. She needed medical attention and the closest people for that wanted to torture her. She struggled out of her jacket and collapsed against a boulder half a dozen meters from the bank. *Just a minute...* Over the sound of her rasping breath, footsteps crunched.

Several figures came into view. They were men, and not the ones from Earth First. Broad brimmed hats topped tanned, mustachioed faces. They stalked up the bank from downstream. One of them spotted the blood staining the dirt and stones from where Michelle had crawled out of the water.

Michelle began to laugh, and didn't stop even when the men pointed their guns at her. One of them came towards her to investigate. "Here's your knife back," she chuckled. "It works well." She held out the blade, hilt first, then dropped it when the shivering took over.

Diego stooped and picked up the knife, not taking his eyes from her. "I told you there were mountain lions, Señora," he said.

* * *

In deference to the deep claw wounds in her shoulder, Diego and his men didn't handle her roughly. Diego checked her for weapons and tied her wrists, but obliged when she asked him to pull her medicine pouch out of her backpack.

"That, that one there," she indicated with a finger at a tiny capsule. "Break it open and jab me with the pointy bit."

Diego considered the capsule and exchanged suspicious looks with Miguelito and the other man, whose name Michelle didn't know. "What does it do? Will it not hurt you?"

Michelle bit her tongue and inhaled through her nose. "It will stop me going into shock, and t'will eradicate any infection that gets in my wounds. Please just jab me. I'm in a lot of pain and the chances of me dying out here are high."

"Let her die," the other man muttered. Michelle tried to glare but her vision was swimming.

A small struggle seemed to be taking place in Diego's conscience. Perhaps he wanted to keep her alive for questioning. He snapped the capsule in half and stared at the five-millimeter needle, then sank it into her arm. Michelle sighed as the numbing agent poured through her system, followed by the antiseptic and antibiotic, as well as other chemicals designed to promote fast healing and keep her in the land of the living. "Did you find your horse?" she slurred, head lolling to the side in relief.

"Sí, Señora." His face had become quite alarmed at her response to first aid.

"I'll be alright." Michelle dragged the words from her lips. "Just need sleep. 'Nless you need me t'ride. S'adrenalin there."

"No." Diego scooped her up and nodded to his men. "We shall tie her to a horse. Let us go."

That was the last thing she remembered before she passed out.

Twenty-Five

96 AD

Stephanus was sweating. Gwyn could see the beads of perspiration on his brow and hoped it would be attributed to the heat. "Practice again," she told him, and stood back.

He lunged forward, drawing his knife from his bandages in one swift move. Then he tripped. Gwyn skipped back. Stephanus flung the knife away as he hit the floor.

"Concentrate!" Gwyn scolded. "If you stab yourself you've got no chance!"

Stephanus glared and retrieved his knife. He sat on the chair again and held his left arm out for her to re-wrap. Gwyn went to the table first and poured two cups of well-watered wine. She drank hers then offered the other to Stephanus, exchanging it for the knife. "Stay calm," she said quietly as she rolled the cloth strips. "I'm going to be with you all the way into the palace. There's no reason why anyone would suspect you." She hoped that was true, that Parthenius or any of his cronies hadn't sold them out. She hid that thought, though, and kept her voice reassuring.

"No." He shuddered and rested his empty cup on his knee. His skin was more sallow than usual, his dark eyes bloodshot. "No one but Domitian. He suspects everyone. But he knows I... I have been loyal in the past."

Gwyn frowned as she balanced the knife carefully on Stephanus' forearm. It was eight inches including the hilt, and wickedly sharp. "What do you mean?"

The sneer re-established itself on Stephanus' face. "You Christians.

You've weaseled your way into Rome like a plague from the east, but the true Roman gods will strike you down. Domitian is no god, but at least he doesn't pretend the gods are false. I stand for what is true."

Gwyn stopped winding the bandage. "You betrayed Flavius Clemens to the Emperor." She had wondered as much, but to have it confirmed so blatantly shocked her. "You sent him to his death."

The man in front of her shrugged. "His time was up. He and his wife were part of the Christian infestation. I did Rome a service."

The urge to snatch the knife and stab him with it was so strong that for a second Gwyn twitched. *Unbelievable.* She breathed through her nose. "Well," she said slowly, "you certainly are the right person to save Rome from Domitian."

Stephanus eyed her suspiciously, but she met his gaze with a somber look. He looked away.

"Come on," Gwyn finished wrapping and stepped away. "Let's try again."

Several more practices and Gwyn pronounced herself satisfied. Her thoughts were churning and she just wanted to get the whole thing over with. "Let's go," she said, tapping her foot. "We don't want to be late."

"We don't want to be early," Stephanus sniped. "The prophecy is for the fifth hour. Domitian is going to be jumpy as a virginal whore until he thinks that time has passed."

Gwyn pursed her lips in disgust as she thought that through. "Let's just go now." *Will he argue every little thing?*

The walk to the palace seemed to take forever and Gwyn felt sick with nerves at one point. She disguised herself as a male slave again; brown tunic and dusty sandals. They trudged along the Via Sacra and turned up the Clivus Palantinus. *Why is it either stinking hot or pouring with rain everywhere I go?* The air pressed down with the beating sun, so it was with extreme relief they were shown into a cool marble waiting room up on the Palatine Hill. She recognized the beautiful, multi-colored marble. It was the room she'd appeared in on the first day. Semi-circular alcoves made the room seem both larger and more cozy at the same time. Light floated in through high windows, but left out the heat of the sun. If she'd been less agitated, Gwyn would have appreciated the elegance.

"Refreshments," a slave intoned, flicking judgmental eyes at Gwyn's sweaty appearance. The slave's own white tunic was crisp and fresh. Gwyn tensed defensively before reminding herself that she needed to be calm, not pretty. She swallowed the juice that had been brought before offering the cup to her companion. Stephanus waved her away, looking disgusted. There was only one cup. *Oops. Probably wasn't meant for me. And he doesn't want to catch my Christian germs, or queer germs, or whatever other stupid germs he thinks I have!*

Time passed. Gwyn scuffed her foot on the greenish-grey marble floor. Several other petitioners came and went. Gwyn used the reflective walls to tuck escaping wisps of hair under her cap. She wished she could ditch the thing—it made her head hot and itchy. "How is your arm, Domine?" she asked when Stephanus fidgeted too much. He subsided and cradled it, shooting her a glare for the reminder.

Finally Parthenius appeared. He led them across a colonnade and past the fountain in the center of the courtyard. They walked down a long corridor and past another courtyard, identical in size to the previous one but with a pool and miniature island in the middle. Gwyn thought it was the same one she'd run across the first day but there were so many courtyards and pools and fountains in Roman palaces it was easy to mix them up.

Parthenius ushered them through a smaller entrance hall. "We are now in the Domus Augusta, the private wing. Our Master and God has retired to his bed chamber for his lunchtime rest. I will tell him that you have requested to see him urgently, to tell him details of a plot."

Stephanus nodded, his jaw tight. As much as she loathed the man, Gwyn reached out and rested a hand on his shoulder, projecting all the calming vibes she could muster. She felt him relax at first, then shrug her off when he realized who it was.

"Just don't fuck up," she muttered. *Don't let him get to you. Just focus. It's almost over.* Rooms, halls, antechambers—nothing was direct and nothing was simple. The ceilings were all different heights, capturing the sunlight through arched and rectangular windows and reflecting it across mosaics and multi-colored marble surfaces. Some walls shimmered, while others absorbed the light with a quiet glow. Was it real? *Concentrate, Gwyn!* She was here to murder a man. *It's not murder—you're fixing a broken timeline!*

They tramped down a stone staircase, passed yet another courtyard and turned into a small antechamber. Parthenius signaled them to halt. He disappeared through a doorway but returned shortly and beckoned Stephanus. The sweating assassin gulped, then went in.

Three men entered the chamber from the opposite door. Gwyn tried to make herself invisible as they nodded to one another. Parthenius returned and murmured, "Clodianus, Maximus, Satur. I have told him Stephanus brings news of great importance that he should not delay in hearing. He sees him now."

One of the men nodded. "There is but a hilt under his pillow, no knife."

Everyone listened as muffled voices were heard on the other side of the closed doors. Gwyn felt a great welling of pressure in her skull and she gasped and squeezed her eyes shut.

"Treachery!" A man's scream battered through the rushing noise in her ears. "Guards!" It choked off, then following deep, desperate grunts that made Gwyn think of gorillas wrestling. She opened her eyes to spots of light and blinked them away. The men in the chamber, Parthenius, Clodianus, Maximus and Satur stood frozen, staring at the door to Domitian's bed chamber.

A child screamed. That galvanized Gwyn. She lunged for the doors and dragged them open.

The screaming child was a curly haired boy slave who clutched an empty knife hilt. He stood by the bed, terrified. The grunts and roars came from Domitian and Stephanus, scrabbling at each other with vicious intent by the end of the bed.

"Kill him!" The Emperor screamed. Stephanus made no reply, just grunted again as he wrested his knife free from the other man's grip and punched it repeatedly into Domitian's gut. Stephanus' arm dripped crimson. Gwyn's stomach churned and she tasted bile. Domitian must have gouged his assassin's eye—it was a sickening mess. Both men were covered in blood.

The Emperor sagged to his knees, vomiting blood. Only then did the other conspirators leap into action. Clodianus pulled a dagger free from his tunic and stabbed Stephanus in the back of the neck. Gwyn screamed as the man's remaining eye bulged and he choked. *Oh shit!* Maximus gripped what little there was of Domitian's hair and tilted the

Emperor's head back, plunging his knife into his throat. Satur lunged for Gwyn.

"No!" She darted back and hit the bed. Rolling across to its other side, she grabbed the screaming boy slave to steady herself. She almost thrust him forward at her attacker then stopped herself. "Come on!" she yelled and dragged the boy out the opposite door. They fetched up in another antechamber as guards poured past them into the room, drawn by the screams.

Gwyn surveyed her options. They weren't good. If she jumped back to the future she'd land underground, not to mention she'd be abandoning a child to his death. Running wasn't an option—more guards were spilling in from all sides. They couldn't escape across the courtyard behind them and entry back into the room was blocked by Satur. "Assassins!" the man screamed, pointing for the benefit of the guards. "They killed the Emperor!"

And then Gwyn had it. She knew what to do. Gripping the slave tightly, she breathed deeply. *You've done this before, you can do it again.* She ignored the slave, ignored Satur and the advancing guards. Her eyes lost focus as her brain felt back in time.

An arm rose. A knife fell. Gwyn blinked as a blue haze rose.

Flick.

Twenty-Six

96 AD

Gwyn clapped a hand over the mouth of the slave boy before he could yelp. She felt his body quiver—he only came up to her chest. "Ssh!" she breathed in his ear, and looked around. She widened her eyes to see better in the dark. She had jumped them half a day back in time and it was the middle of the night. They stood outside Domitian's bedroom still, but a cool breeze tickled its way under the door from the courtyard outside. "Are you going to scream?" she asked the boy.

He shook his head, trembling. She hoped he wasn't going to be sick. She'd seen time travel affect others that way.

"Okay." She relaxed her grip. Whispering still, she said, "We need to sneak out without waking the Emperor."

The shadow of his head nodded. "But... that man stabbed..."

"That hasn't happened yet. It's confusing, I know, but right now the Emperor is alive and asleep in that room, and we need to get out without anyone seeing us. Otherwise they'll torture us both to find out why we are here at this time of night."

The darkness hid the boy's expression but with her hand still gripping his shoulder, Gwyn felt how tense he was. "I'm scared," he whispered.

And I'm not? Gwyn took a deep breath. "I know you are. What's your name?"

"Jyri, Domina."

"I'm no Domina," Gwyn told him. "Call me Gwynia. Can we get out this door, Jyri?"

"It's a servants' door. There are guards outside it."

Gwyn ground her teeth. "What time did the guards come on duty?" Gwyn asked.

"In the evening. They change at midnight."

She closed her eyes and felt for the timepiece mentally. It was after midnight. *We've got one shot at this.* "Okay, stand still. In a minute we're going to step out of that door and you must tell the guards to be quiet because the Emperor is sleeping. Tell them he is done with me. I will pretend to be a... a whore." She didn't like saying the word.

"But... you don't look anything like Earinus!" the slave squeaked and she shushed him.

"Who?"

"His eunuch," he whispered.

Gwyn paused. She hadn't known Domitian liked men or boys, even castrated ones. "What about a female whore? Will they believe that?"

"Yes, but... how?"

"I'm not really a boy." She shook her hair out of its cloth cap. "It's a disguise."

The belt she had worn loose she now cinched tight to accentuate her hips and waist. She twisted some of her hair up and left the rest loose, then donned the earrings and necklace that had been in her belt purse since she'd left her waitressing job. *Deep breath. Will have to tell Gaius that I'm constantly dressing up as a prostitute to get past Roman guards.* That thought almost shook her out of her composure, but she centered herself with a determined breath. Light snores punctuated the air from the room next door. Gwyn tried not to think of the man she helped murder sleeping peacefully. "Ready?" she asked the boy, putting a hand back on his shoulder. He didn't move.

"Come on, Jyri. Once we're out of here we can find somewhere quiet to have a rest."

She felt him nod slowly. She gave him a nudge and he moved. Glad he couldn't see the tension on her face, she followed him as they crept over to the servants' door that hid behind a wooden screen. Gwyn caught the edge of the screen with her shoulder and froze. Nothing happened—it was too sturdy to knock over. She released her breath slowly. "Be calm," she whispered. "If you are relaxed they are less likely to suspect."

He opened the door and light spilled in. Gwyn tensed, peeping back at Domitian's bedchamber. The screen blocked most of the light but what if even the slightest glimmer was enough to wake him? She was desperate to push through and run. That would be fatal.

Jyri stuck his head through the door and murmured to the guards. Soon he tugged on Gwyn's arm. She emerged, blinking, and wrapped her arms protectively around herself, projecting coyness. *I'm harmless, inconsequential. Just look me over and wave me on my way.*

The guards chuckled and nudged each other. Gwyn cast her eyes down so she wouldn't roll them. The boy gestured for quiet and tugged her away. Gwyn could feel the eyes of the guards on her—she resisted the urge to run. Both she and the boy sagged in relief once they rounded the corner at the end of the hallway but they didn't stop walking. The walls lost their ornamentation and sheen of cleanliness. The rooms they ghosted through seemed to be for slaves, not Emperors.

"Is there a way to leave the palace, Jyri? We need to be gone by morning."

Jyri halted and shrank back. "Leave? Domina, Gwynia, I've no wish to be a runaway. They'll punish me ever so badly and I'll lose my place."

Gwyn faced him and squatted down so she was looking up at him. Jyri's small, frightened face was unmarked by scars or bruises, his brown curls soft and well-brushed. He was a well-kept slave, one of the few who served the upper echelon and were fed, clothed and treated well. As much as she hated slavery, Gwyn knew that to take him away from the life he knew would be cruel.

But to leave him here would mean death, not to mention the possibility he would warn the Emperor. Even if he avoided the earlier version of himself until after the Emperor was assassinated, Parthenius and his cronies would hunt for him.

"Jyri." She looked into his wide eyes. "Those men were going to kill you. If they find you in the palace, they *will* kill you. Even if you hid for a few days, eventually someone will notice you."

He looked about to cry.

"I'm sorry." Gwyn wanted to cry herself.

Jyri flung himself on her and sobbed. *He can't be more than seven.* She wondered how much affection he'd had in his life, to throw himself at a stranger. "It's alright," she shushed him, rocking back and forth. She looked around. The flickering light of a wall torch showed doors. "Where were you taking us, Jyri? Is there a quiet corner somewhere we can sit and have a rest?"

The boy snuffled and nodded, pointing to the third door down even as he tucked his head into her shoulder. Gwyn led him into a little office, taking a candle from the basket and lighting it from the torch. She melted a little wax into a dish and stuck the candle in firmly before shutting the door. "Let's have a sit down and catch our breaths."

She sat on the floor and leant against the wall. The boy snuggled into her and promptly fell asleep. Gwyn shook her head, astonished. Despite being exhausted, her brain kept racing. She was grateful for Jyri's warmth but wished someone was there to hold her. All she could think about was how she'd arranged the murder of the Emperor of Rome, and in doing so led Stephanus straight to his death.

* * *

Gwyn woke with a start. She heard voices on the other side of the door. The candle had long since burnt out and she was stiff and sore and astounded at herself for falling asleep. She tried to move her legs and panicked when they didn't respond.

"Huh?" The weight on Gwyn shifted and her legs were free.

"Oh!" She remembered Jyri. "I'm sorry, but shh!" She listened hard, holding her breath and stilling herself in order to pick up every sound she could..

The voices got louder and both Gwyn and Jyri tensed. Then they passed and faded down the hall.

"We need to go," Gwyn told her companion. "Is there a safe way out?"

He shook his head frantically. "I can't run away, Domina!"

Gwyn took a deep breath, biting her tongue. "Jyri," she coaxed. "It's not running away. We're just going somewhere safe while all the fuss dies down. We can't stay hiding here because they'll find us."

Her conscience twinged at lying but her heart raced at the thought of being trapped in the palace. She didn't want to abandon a child but if he didn't move soon she would.

Jyri squeezed his eyes shut and shook his head. "They'll torture me," he whimpered. "They always torture slaves. They'll crucify me and feed me to the lions."

Gwyn opened her mouth then stopped. "Yes," she said, hating herself for being cruel. "They'll torture you and feed you to the lions *if they find you!* We have to go *now.*"

Wide-eyed, the trembling boy took Gwyn's hand and led her to the door. The torches smoldered in the windowless hallway. They backtracked up the hall then through a number of storerooms, past a kitchen and across several courtyards bathed in morning light. Gwyn was hopelessly lost. Jyri hesitated several times, even wavering as if queasy once, then led her on. They climbed a wooden staircase up to ground level and reached a guarded gate. The guards jeered and one of them groped Gwyn on the backside, but let them pass.

More worried about people trying to get in, no doubt. Jyri was at a loss now, that much was obvious, so Gwyn steered him down the street. What to do with him? She needed to stay away from Flavia Domitilla's house. It was mid-morning judging by the sun so the past version of her was still there. Proximity sickness would affect her if she got too close.

Junilla's apartment? She doubted she'd be welcome there, even if she could remember the way. Vibia's caupona? She dismissed that too. Adi and Gaius' home seemed the safest option—could she prevail on them to look after Jyri while she collected her things from Domitilla's house? Then what?

Gwyn was so preoccupied she didn't see the figure approach her until dark-skinned hands arrested her progress. "Gwynia!" Izem's voice was pleased.

Jyri looked ready to bolt so Gwyn grabbed his shoulder and said, "It's alright, he's a friend." She looked at Izem. Of course—he frequented these streets so much she wasn't surprised to run into him again. "Izem, I need your help."

She steered both boy and man to the opening of an alleyway and explained that Jyri needed to be kept safe and away from the palace. "I'd be grateful," she promised, letting him read into that as he wished. Sex with him wouldn't be a hardship, and if it meant saving a child who'd never deserved to get mixed up in plots and murder, then she was winning.

Izem furrowed his eyebrows, drawing his scar inwards across his face. He took them to his home and they slipped in through the servants' door. They sat in the courtyard. Gwyn looked about anxiously.

"He is asleep," Izem reassured her, speaking of his half-brother master. "Now, you is telling me what is going on."

Gwyn kept it short and simple, looking Izem in the eye. "Something will happen in the palace just before midday today that will endanger the life of young Jyri here. I need to fetch some things from where I have been staying and work out where he can go. Can you keep him here, and let nobody bother him? No one needs to know where he's come from. I'll return for him later."

She was asking a lot from someone she hardly knew but had little choice. *What was it Michelle said? Good use of the resources at hand.*

Izem's lips went tight and his nostrils flared. "Gwynia," he whispered. "What are you saying? You cannot be bringing an imperial slave here; you will be bringing our Master and God's eye on this house!"

Gwyn met his eyes squarely. "After midday that won't be a problem. Now will you help?"

Izem refused. "No," he said. "You must be going, Gwynia, and take this slave with you!"

Um… This was not supposed to happen. She was meant to be able to persuade him to help her. "Izem," she began, but he cut her off.

"Go, please, Gwynia, you must be going!" His voice was low, urgent, and fearful.

Well, shit. She attempted several more times but Izem hustled them out the door, shutting it firmly in her face. Disgusted, Gwyn dragged Jyri away, stopping only when she noticed the poor boy limping. His dainty palace sandals were disintegrating on the Roman streets. *Another thing to stop slaves from running away.* Gwyn scowled. Jyri quailed.

"I'm sorry, Jyri—I'm not annoyed at you." She was, a little. Why couldn't she have just left him to die? That's what Michelle would have done, no doubt. Then she was ashamed. "Here, climb on my back."

She needed to get him into cover before too many people noticed the odd picture they made. It occurred to her that the streets would be chaotic once news of the Emperor's death spread. The Praetorians, as well as the Urban Cohorts, were likely to be dispatched to maintain order. That meant violence.

If that were the case, she had to get them to safety soon.

* * *

Gwyn hammered on the door. Jyri weighed heavily on her back but if she put him down she'd never pick him up again. Thumping sounds stopped inside and Adi opened the door, holding an armful of cushions.

"I'm sorry, Adi," Gwyn burst in, panting. "This is the last time you'll have to help me, I promise. It's almost over."

"Gwynia!" Adi threw her hands up. Cushions went flying. "What are you doing here? I told you it is dangerous for you to be in this house."

"Adi, I swear, this is the last time." Gwyn stumbled past and put the boy down. "Sit down here, Jyri." She faced Adi. Her eyes were bloodshot and her face smeared with dry blood. "One last time, Adi. That's it, I swear."

Adi's lips pursed and she turned away. She went out into the courtyard to draw a bucket of water from the well. She poured it into a pitcher and offered the water to Gwyn with a cloth and a sour look.

"Thank you." Gwyn offered an apologetic smile. She dipped the cloth and used it to wipe Jyri's face, neck and arms, removing the boy's broken sandals and bathing his blistered feet. "You need a proper bath," she told him, "but this is better than nothing."

"I'm hungry," Jyri piped up, then cringed as if he expected to be struck.

"I have some date cakes," Adi said, maternal instincts kicking in. "Gwyn, bring him into the kitchen. I'll bring a basin so he can wash. You too. What have you been doing?" Her voice tremored as if she didn't really want to know.

Gwyn replied as they went into the kitchen. "The thing I set out to do. It'll be over by midday, but I imagine the next few days might be a bit... unsettled. Where is Gaius? And your daughters?"

Adi went white. "You mean... you...?"

"Not yet," Gwyn stripped Jyri's tunic off and made him stand by the basin. She washed him all over with the cloth while he crammed a date cake into his mouth. "What is the hour?"

"The third or the fourth." Adi closed her eyes, trembling. "Maria and Antonia have gone to the market. Gaius walked with them to talk business with someone he knows. I must go find them." She looked faint.

Gwyn put out a hand to forestall her. "I can go. I need to retrieve some things from where I was staying." Amongst other things, she had hidden the rest of the money that Domitilla had given her at the lady's house. The money wasn't hers but Gwyn felt no guilt over taking it for Adi and Gaius. It was the least she could do.

Adi gave her directions, biting her lips.

"Will you look after Jyri, please?" Gwyn asked. "He was in the wrong place at the wrong time and I couldn't leave him. They would have killed him," she whispered the last part and beseeched Adi with her eyes.

Adi hesitated then nodded. "Come on, boy; pop your tunic back on. I'll find you something else to eat."

Gwyn walked briskly through the street and found Antonia and Maria buying bread at the nearest market, the house slave behind them with the baskets. Gwyn went straight up to them.

"Go away," Antonia said rudely.

"Antonia, Maria—where is your father? Your mother sent me to fetch you all home. It is urgent."

Maria, hands on her swollen belly, exclaimed as she realized who Gwyn was. Gwyn repeated herself.

"How do we know mother sent you?" Antonia asked.

Gwyn huffed impatiently.

"Gwynia?"

All three women turned.

"Gaius!" Gwyn's relief was palpable. "Gaius, you have to take Maria and Antonia home now. Adi sent me to find you all."

"What?"

Her temper flared. The longer she spent explaining the less time she would have to retrieve the money from Domitilla's house. She took a deep breath. "You must go home. Now." She had no idea what would happen after Domitian was killed, but there were bound to be frightened people in the streets. It would be best to stay home until law and order established itself again.

Her message must have sunk in. Gaius paled and pulled his daughters away from the baker's stall. "It has happened?" he whispered.

"Soon," Gwyn whispered in return. "I can tell you about it later, just take the girls home."

Antonia was frowning but Maria rocked from side to side, hand on her belly. She stared at Gwyn as though she had only just seen her. Flashes of nightmarish memories could be seen in her eyes. "Father?" she said tremulously.

Gwyn noticed the house slave standing close enough to eavesdrop. *Fair enough.* It would affect him too. She beckoned him over. He looked startled, then joined them, gripping the shopping baskets firmly.

Gaius glanced at him and nodded. "We will buy more bread, a sack of chick peas and green lentils, and some large sausages. Vegetables too."

Even Antonia nodded reluctantly. "Right," Gwyn said. "I have to go fetch something, then I'll join you. Make your purchases and get home." She turned to go.

"Wait, where are you going?" Gaius put out a hand. "Gwynia, it's not safe."

She frowned. After all she'd done, he still wanted to coddle her? "I'll be fine!"

"Please, Gwyn."

She clenched her jaw. "Fine!"

Gaius turned to Maria. "You know what to buy?" She nodded. "Be quick about it then, and do not stop to talk. Antonia," he addressed the younger girl, "help your sister and get home quickly. Bolgios, can you carry everything and see them home safe?"

"Aye, Domine," the slave assented. "I is getting everyone back to Domina Adi very soon-like." His pale skin showed him to be of Celtic heritage, but his manner of speaking was like that of Izem. Gwyn's ears burned at the thought of her one-time lover. *It's probably best I didn't stay with him. He's lovely, but I don't know if I can trust him.* She hoped she hadn't made a mistake telling him about the Emperor's assassination.

There was no time to dwell further. She and Gaius set off briskly through the marketplace. Gwyn told Gaius the street they had to go to, he directed them to a short cut across the Caelian Hill. "It's not as steep as the Aventine," he puffed, "and less crowded than going down past the Flavian Amphitheatre." The unspoken desire to stay away from the palace hung in the air between them.

Two streets away from Domitilla's house, Gwyn experienced a gut-wrenching wave of nausea. She doubled over, hands on her knees.

"Gwynia, what's wrong?" Gaius grabbed her by the shoulders and steadied her.

She retched but nothing came out. Then it passed and she gasped in relief.

"Are you alright?" Gaius demanded.

She waved him away and straightened, wiping sweat from her forehead. "I think… I think I must have just passed close by." She and Stephanus had left the villa at about this time.

Gaius pressed his lips together. Gwyn noticed. "I'll explain everything once we get back to Adi. Please, let's just hurry. I know it's confusing."

He said nothing more as she badgered the door slave to let them in. He was perplexed by her seemingly swift return—he'd only just seen her leave with Stephanus—but she bamboozled him with a lie about getting knocked into the dirt and being sent back here to clean up and change. Throwing his hands up, the doorkeeper let them both in.

"Whose house is this?" Gaius asked quietly as he trailed after her through empty rooms and deserted halls. Gwyn strode quickly, locating the room where she'd slept and digging out the bag of coins she'd concealed under a heavy stone chair. "Money?" Gaius exclaimed shocked as she handed it to him. "Gwynia where did you get all that?" The bag was of a decent weight.

"Flavia Domitilla gave it to me," she replied, sweeping her meagre possessions into her travel bag. "It's yours now. For helping me. You made it possible for me to get to her—this is her house."

"Gwynia, I—"

"Take it, and let's go. I don't know how much time we have left."

He dropped the bag and swept her into a tight hug. "You still are the bravest girl… woman, I know."

Her eyes blurred and her chest tightened, and she buried her head in his chest. She could smell the light sweat he'd acquired from racing over here with her, but his odor was reassuring; warm, male and solid. "I'm sorry," she whispered. She didn't know exactly what she was apologizing for: leaving him at Masada, or coming back and wreaking havoc in his life.

He lifted her face in his hands and smiled. "You were my first love, Gwyn." He kissed her gently and hugged her again, then stepped back. "Now let us go from here."

Mind a tumble, Gwyn let him lead the way back across the Caelian to his apartment building at the base of the Aventine. All around them Romans carried on with their everyday lives, unaware of the political upheaval that was about to take place.

The atmosphere inside Gaius' and Adi's ground floor apartment was anything but tranquil. Maria screamed when Gwyn and Gaius walked inside, and a tear-streaked Antonia flung herself into her father's arms. "Papa!" she cried. "They took Mama. They took her!"

"What?" Gaius demanded. "What happened?"

Gwyn's heart almost stopped when she heard Maria explain. It seemed the same Praetorians who had chased Gwyn that very first day had been dispatched to find a slave who had been seen leaving the palace that morning. Normally runaway slaves were the province of the vigiles, but this slave happened to be the young boy who tended the shrine to the Lares in the Emperor's own bedchamber. Gwyn thought numbly that whoever had sent these two to investigate obviously hadn't checked to see if Jyri was still in the palace.

The Praetorians had bullied and intimidated their way to Adi's front door, asking those in the street if they'd seen a young palace slave. Upon discovering Maria and Adi in the house with Jyri, the guards recalled another fugitive and became angry that Maria still appeared to be pregnant. While they didn't take her into custody, they wasted no time searching the house, upending furniture and knocking Bolgios to the floor when he tried to stand between them and Adi.

"They took your mother," Gaius repeated, dumbfounded.

"And the slave boy," Antonia sobbed. "Where have they taken her, Papa? What will happen to her?"

Gwyn's stomach sank through the floor. Her ears roared. This was all her fault. She'd interfered with history, and now Adi was gone.

Twenty-Seven

96 AD

Reality snapped back to Gwyn with a clarity that hurt. "Where would they have taken her?" she asked.

"Papa, what is *she* doing here?" Venom laced Antonia's voice. "It's her fault the Praetorians came! They were chasing that slave and Mama said that *she* brought him here!"

Gwyn couldn't argue with that. "You're right, it's my fault. But I need to know where they might have taken her so I can try get her back!"

"How can that be? You're just some woman who showed up out of nowhere and brought trouble to us!" Antonia radiated fury. Gaius hugged his daughter, staring at Gwyn. She read guilt in his eyes—guilt that he'd accompanied her instead of going home to his wife.

She would have done anything in that moment to erase that look.

"Antonia, stop." It was Maria, grimacing as she rose from a couch, cradling her belly. "What are you, Gwynia? Or is it... Ruth?" The eyes of a small girl looked out from the woman's face. Gwyn remembered seeing that girl perched high on the edge of an underground water cistern, hiding from her suicidal kin and invading Romans.

Gwyn straightened her shoulders. "It's Gwyn. But yes, you knew me as Ruth at Masada. I warned Eleazar about the Roman attack. I'm here now. And I can rescue your mother." She forced herself to believe her own words. She couldn't afford to doubt now.

"They will have taken them back to the palace," Gaius said. He looked like he needed to sit down. Gwyn pushed a chair towards him and sat on the floor.

"Everyone be quiet, I need to think." She closed her eyes and ran through the possibilities.

One: she could sneak in to where Adi and Jyri were being kept and try to sneak them out.

Guards. Locked doors. Stupid idea.

Two: she could time-jump in and out of the prison somehow, the way she had done in Wallachia.

Still got the problem of guards and locked doors! Not to mention time travel burnout!

Three: she could dress Gaius up as someone important and demand Adi and Jyri's release.

You need to do the talking—you're the one with the pocket-watch. Gaius won't convince anyone.

Four: she could try to bribe the guards.

Risky. You don't know how much you'll need. They might also just take the money and laugh in your face.

She growled silently. There were too many variables. She wished she could just march on in and demand Adi's release, and sweep up Jyri at the same time. They would question him, and evidence from a slave was only admissible if obtained under torture. He didn't deserve that. But Gwyn wasn't anyone important. All the people she knew who had influence were in on the plot to murder Domitian, except for Flavia Domitilla, still sitting on her island in exile.

Flavia Domitilla. Gwyn turned the name over in her mind. *They certainly like reusing names. Domitilla. Domitian. Domitia.*

Domitia. The Empress.

The idea was so tenuous that Gwyn dared not look at it directly. She was vaguely aware of the others in the room. Antonia was straightening furniture and tidying the mess the Praetorians had made. Gaius and Maria were staring at her. Gwyn let her mind relax, like it did when she connected to the timepiece. Excitement bubbled as the idea bloomed in her mind. She reached slowly into her belt purse and drew out a gold coin. The words DOMITIA AVGVSTA IMP DOMIT encircled the likeness of a woman Gwyn had never met.

"I need writing things," she said, looking straight at Gaius. "And some sort of hard vegetable—a carrot or similar. And a knife. I'll need you to accompany me, but dress as a palace slave." She looked at Maria and Antonia. "I'll need a dress, and jewelry too. We need to hurry. We don't have much time."

* * *

She could have made time, Gwyn reflected, but she was already doubled up in this timeline and she didn't think she could manage another jump. To burn out now would remove her last chance of escape if all else should go wrong.

"Just let me talk," she murmured to Gaius. They were in the bowels of the palace. Her friend walked beside her, fists clenched and jaw working. "It'll be okay." She brushed her hand against his, trying to project reassurance.

"Shoulda picked a gladiator," a strapping Praetorian advised her with a lewd look as they passed. "Or me and the boys can show ye what yer missing."

Gwyn was about to sneer disdainfully before remembering that a noble lady wouldn't sneer at lowly guards. She raised her nose haughtily instead and stalked on. Her destination lay only yards away. She took the last few steps. "I have an order from Her Imperial Highness, most beloved wife of our divine Master and God, to bring to her the female and boy currently in your custody. She has questions for them." She behaved as if this errand was beneath her.

"What?"

Gwyn tried again. "Read it!" She waved the scroll, adorned with red wax bearing what looked very much like the seal of the Empress. She hoped the picture she'd carved into the end of the carrot would trick the guards. "I've been sent to take the woman and the boy to my most honored mistress. If you have questions, you may ask her!" She loaded authority into her tone. She had to tilt her head back to stare up at the guard who had questioned her.

The guard snatched the scroll from her hand. He examined the seal briefly then said, "My tribune will have to approve this."

"Who do you think I've just come from?" Gwyn hissed. "Do you see fit to question imperial authority when your tribune doesn't?"

A long look from the guard. He glanced at his partner. He then cracked the seal and scanned the contents, lips moving silently. Gwyn breathed through her nose, fighting her internal terror.

"The woman is prisoner," the second guard grunted, his accent revealing his plebian origins.

Gwyn forced her gaze across and pinpointed the wall just to the left of his ear. "You think my slave can't handle a woman and a child? They'll be bound."

Gwyn pushed with all her willpower. "Fine," she snapped. "I'll tell the Empress you saw fit to ignore her orders. What are your names?"

A grunt and the first guard rolled up the scroll. "You can take the woman. The boy stays. He's a palace slave, the boy for our Master and God."

Gwyn's glare could have frozen flames. "Why do you think her Imperial Highness wishes to... question him? She wishes to know why he abandoned his duties. Give him to me, or I'll take neither."

The second guard heaved a glacial nod. He hefted a ring with iron keys and turned one in the lock. The door swung in and Gwyn shoved all her fear and nervousness into a tight ball and stalked in, terrified they'd shut the door behind her. "Come with me!" she ordered. "Her Imperial Highness wishes to see you both. Quickly now!"

She could have cried at the bruises on Adi's fearful face, visible even through the gloom. Jyri was a squeak in Adi's skirts. Gwyn trembled and thought it best that the light from the doorway cast her own face into shadow. A cry of recognition or relief could be fatal.

When both prisoners shuffled forward Gwyn turned and swept out of the cell, ignoring both guards. A warning glance at Gaius had him play his part correctly when Adi emerged—her exclamation was cut short by a rough shove and binding of her wrists. Jyri was tied behind her and another shove set them all walking.

"A good cock up her would sort that stuck up bitch out," the first guard muttered to his partner.

"I shove ut in her mouth, so she shuts up," was the reply. Gwyn shuddered in rage. *Some things never change—men are so unoriginal in their threats.* She quelled her fury and stalked onwards and upwards, taking them towards the light.

Out of sight of the guards she stopped and quickly stripped the tunic off Jyri. "Be quiet and follow," she murmured to the boy, hating herself for causing this indignity. Without his white tunic he was a nameless slave, not palace property. Adi's ropes she cut and whispered, "Follow me."

Silently, eyes down, Adi, Jyri and Gaius tailed Gwyn as she led them from a lower gate in the palace, down the hill and through the streets near the Forum. They needed to change, to throw any witnesses off the scent, and Gwyn knew just the place.

The sixth hour was approaching and the lunchtime rush would soon begin. Scaurus idly straightened tables as Gwyn barged past him and into the caupona. "What's your pleasure, Domina!" the old waiter leapt to attention.

"Scaurus, it's me, Gwynia. Keep watch on the door and make sure no one comes in. Is Vibia about?" Gwyn hoped not. The proprietress or her husband would be a lot harder to deal with.

"Gwynia?" Astonishment was plain on Scaurus' face, then familiarity as a silver coin made its way into his hands.

"Quickly, put this over your hair," Gwyn passed her palla to Adi. Gaius stripped his tunic and donned another. He produced an oversized garment for the shivering Jyri. The boy stared until Adi took pity on him and tugged it over his head to hide his nakedness.

Gwyn wrenched her hair from its pins and hitched the long dress with a belt, making it more practical and plebeian in appearance.

"What's going on, Gwynia?" Scaurus loitered near the door, keeping an eye on the street. "You're lucky Vibia isn't here—she'd throttle you if she saw you."

"Stuff her," Gwyn said.

"Scaurus, I've left your patched tunic..." the speaker trailed off as he entered the caupona from the door at the rear. Gwyn gaped. It was the mystery man, the one she'd followed then been arrested for her pains.

He was too busy blushing to recognize her. Gwyn flipped a scarf over her face and said nothing as the man spluttered then beat a hasty retreat.

"Scaurus," Gwyn demanded in a whisper. "Who is *he*?"

Scaurus mumbled something incomprehensible.

"What?"

"Ahem, special friend," Scaurus turned beet red and shuffled his feet. Gwyn stifled a laugh. "Is he political?"

"Don't ask that, Gwynia!"

She shrugged. "It doesn't matter now," she told him. "But the last night I worked here I heard him ask two men to deliver a letter. I saw him the next day when he'd said he had to go to the Campagna, and I thought it was odd."

"Oh that," Scaurus waved a hand. "Some evidence against the steward of poor old Flavius Clemens. It's all done now. The steward's finished—our Master and God won't put up with embezzlement against members of his own family, even the ones who aren't in favor."

Gaius, Adi and Jyri stared at Gwyn with anxious eyes as she absorbed this information. "Right. Thanks, Scaurus. I'd keep inside for the next day or so if I were you."

Before he had time to ask her what she meant, Gwyn hustled her companions out the door. "What's the hour?" she asked Gaius.

"Almost the sixth." They increased their pace. Jyri stumbled and Gwyn stopped to kneel so he could ride on her back. "Gwynia…" Gaius stared up a small side street. They were half way home, skirting back near the river through a poorer district.

"We have to hurry, Gaius!"

"Please, my love." Adi was distraught. "If they come for us again…"

"They are going to be very distracted soon, aren't they, Gwynia?" Gaius patted his wife's shoulder. "This will only take a minute. I am the head of my household and I must protect *all* my family."

Before Gwyn could work out what he meant Gaius strode up the side street and into a dingy apartment building. She frowned. It looked familiar.

Ten minutes later a harassed but stubborn looking Gaius returned with an extremely disgruntled Junilla. His sister shot a cursory scowl at Adi, reserving an even fouler look for Gwyn, but when she opened her mouth Gaius ordered, "Don't start. Just walk."

Gaius elbowed his way through growing crowds as they crossed the Aventine. Adi and Junilla followed, with Gwyn and Jyri bringing up the rear. Gwyn was grateful when their path turned downhill—it meant they were almost there. The streets were busy despite the heat—full of Romans finishing their morning business before lunch. Clusters of people formed on street corners; Gwyn heard gasps and saw children shoot off in different directions, eager to gain tips for spreading the news.

"It's happened," she called to Gaius.

"And we are home. Everyone inside." He held the door and barred it firmly once they were all inside. Gwyn heaved a tremendous sigh of relief.

"Oh mama, thank Juno and Ceres you are home!" Antonia burst into the living area. Groans could be heard from the bedroom behind her. "Maria is having her baby!"

Twenty-Eight

96 AD

Gwyn admired Adi so much in that moment. Bruised, frightened and exhausted from being marched to the Palatine and back, Adi shed all that and straightened. "Gwynia, come with me," she ordered. "Antonia, you cannot go for the midwife. We must all stay indoors."

"But, Mama!"

"My love, make sure Bolgios guards the door," Adi ordered Gaius. He nodded and dug out a cudgel from the kitchen. Adi locked eyes with Junilla.

"I will prepare soup for everyone," Junilla declared. "If her labor is long, she will need something for strength, as will we all."

Adi nodded. She swept from the room, Antonia and Gwyn in tow. "I don't know anything about having babies," Gwyn protested. Maria's screams and groans alternated between high pitched keening to a lowing bellow that would put a water buffalo to shame.

"Then it's time to learn. I'm here now, my dear." Adi entered the room and sat on the bed beside Maria, who was on her hands and knees, shuddering as the contraction released her.

"Mama," she cried, her white-knuckled grip transferred in a flash from the blanket to her mother's hand.

"You're doing very well," Adi crooned. "How long have you been having the pains?" She felt gently around her daughter's abdomen. "Antonia, fetch cloths to soak. Gwyn—a bucket of water from the courtyard well. Go!"

They scrambled to obey. Over the next few hours, she bathed Maria's sweating body with damp cloths. Gwyn took turns supporting the woman as she hobbled about the room and almost had her hand wrenched off as Maria's contractions intensified. Adi stripped Maria down to nothing and had her stand in the hip bath while they poured water all over her.

I never want to have a baby. Gwyn felt faint when Maria finally hunched over a chair, screaming as a small bloodied head emerged between her legs. Gwyn wanted to cross her own legs in horror but was using her full body weight to balance the chair and couldn't move. A scream that turned into a groan then a gasp then a sob marked the arrival of a squalling baby boy, caught by Adi's deft hands and presented to a smiling, crying, Maria. Antonia supported her sister back to the bed and Gwyn wondered if anyone would notice if she collapsed.

"Well done, my darling!" Adi hugged her daughter and grandson tightly. "You have a beautiful boy. That's it, put him on the breast. Take a breath. You still have a bit left to go."

If Gwyn had thought she would faint before, she felt nausea overtake her at the arrival of the afterbirth. She ducked out just in time and retched in the garden.

"Tsk, tsk." Junilla leant on the doorway. "Not much of a stomach? As bad as a man."

"It's disgusting!" Gwyn moaned, staggering to the well and rinsing her mouth.

"It's very natural and a miracle besides," Junilla admonished. "However do you manage at the butcher's stalls? It's just blood."

Gwyn wanted to argue that the meaty wobble of the placenta in a chamber pot was very much not just blood, but she closed her eyes instead. *Think I'm gonna faint.*

"Come back in and make yourself useful," she heard Junilla say. She sighed and obeyed.

* * *

A week later, the family sat in the main room of the apartment.

"He's gorgeous, Maria," Gwyn said as she stroked the squished up pink wrinkly thing. Maria's baby was a lot cuter when asleep, though she'd never admit this to the adoring mother or aunt or grandparents.

Would she feel that way if she ever had a baby? She doubted it. *One more reason not to ever have one!* The pocket-watch had messed with her periods—would it also prevent her from becoming pregnant? She resolved to do a test when she got back to her time just in case.

And when will you go back, Gwyn? While the official succession of Nerva had been declared on the same day Domitian had been assassinated, the streets remained unsettled and both the Praetorian Guards and the Urban Cohorts patrolled Rome to keep the peace.

Gwyn, Gaius, Adi and their family stayed inside. Gwyn learnt about the sleep deprivation that came with a newborn. Junilla and Adi came to a wary truce, with the former commanding the kitchen with Jyri as her shadow and the latter doting on her exhausted daughter and grandson. Gaius opened the door to Maria's husband who had risked the streets to be with his wife, while Antonia tolerated the extra guests with some grace.

"I'll be going home tomorrow," Junilla announced one morning, "and I'll take the boy with me."

Gwyn stared at her, bleary-eyed, from her position on the couch next to Maria. She'd done a stint rocking the baby to sleep in the night. She'd cursed his cries even as she hummed nonsense rhymes and was relieved when the squalling turned into snuffling, then into peaceful, open-mouthed breathing as his eyes fell shut.

"Tomorrow?" Gaius sat up straight, putting down his beaker of muslum.

"Yes. After you name the babe. I've been away long enough. No doubt thieves have taken anything of value but I cannot impose on you any longer." She drew herself up stiffly, casting sour eyes on her brother's family. "And you have enough mouths to feed. I've grown fond of Jyri. He can come with me."

Gwyn wouldn't have thought that 'fond' was the right word, but she supposed in her own brusque way, Junilla showed affection to the ex-Palace slave, serving him second helpings at meals and sewing his tunic for a better fit.

"I'll adopt him." Junilla shocked them all still further. Gaius' jaw dropped, though Gwyn spotted Adi hiding a smile. "You offered me money for a dowry once, brother. I do not want that, but if you could arrange the papers and give me some money for his education I'd be grateful."

Jyri gave a little yip and hugged Junilla around the waist. She stroked his hair and stared at them all as if daring them to comment. No one said a thing until Adi spoke. "Congratulations, sister, it is a kind deed."

"Thank you... sister," Junilla replied. Everyone else hastened to wish her well. Maria's son woke with a yell and was silenced by a nipple to the mouth.

Gwyn thought she would use the conversation to declare, "I have to get home too."

Everyone's gaze turned to her. "Home, Gwynia?" Adi asked, gently.

"You're leaving us?" Gaius asked. Dismay flashed in his eyes.

"Where is your home, anyway?" Antonia's suspicion of Gwyn had allayed somewhat, but her curiosity remained. "Maria said you were at Masada."

Gwyn sighed and fixed her gaze on the baby, who was suckling in his sleep. "I don't know if it would help for you to know. No one would believe you."

"It shall never leave this room," Adi said matter-of-factly. "Antonia, I met Gwyn when I was but your age. I was a Jew then, and had fled Jerusalem to Masada after Titus sacked it. Gwyn had... a prophecy about our fall."

Gaius carried on. "She escaped the fortress and tried to convince Silva, who commanded the forces at the time, to forget the siege and leave the Jews inside alone."

"I failed," whispered Gwyn. "The fortress fell. Everyone inside committed suicide."

"Except for me, and Maria, and Sarah, and the boys," Adi reminded her. "You told us where to hide, and sent Gaius to find and protect us. You saved me." Gwyn met her eyes gratefully, brushing tears from her own.

Antonia looked between her parents and Gwyn in consternation. Junilla's expression was similar. Gwyn was glad that Maria's husband had left to keep his carpentry shop open. "But... how old are you?" Antonia demanded.

Gwyn sighed again. "Nineteen. Mind you I'm probably getting close to twenty with all the time I've been away. I travelled through time. It's only been a few months since Masada for me. That's why I'm not much older."

"You have grown up, though," Gaius went and stood by his wife. "Hasn't she, my dear?"

Adi smiled. "Yes. And I hope you will visit us again, Gwynia, but... just don't bring so much trouble next time."

Gwyn blushed as the baby woke again and cried.

Twenty-Nine

96 AD

It had been a big day. They had celebrated the naming of Maria's son: Gaius Flavius Gwynius. Maria had insisted and Gwyn was too stunned to argue. She was glad she'd arranged with Adi to buy a gold-foiled *bulla* to gift to the boy, using some of the money she'd kept back from Domitilla's funds.

Junilla and Jyri had departed earlier. Antonia, Maria and the baby were fast asleep, as was Bolgios the slave. Maria's husband had promised to return the next day to collect his wife and child now that Rome was calm again. Quiet relief permeated the household, though everyone spoke quietly and stopped to listen momentarily anytime there was a shout on the street.

One thing still worried Gwyn. It was the reason she hadn't skipped out of this time, aside from the fact that she wanted to see things settle down for Adi and Gaius.

"The guards," she explained to Adi and Gaius late that night. "The Praetorians who recognized Adi and Maria. What if they return again? I... I thought about trying to find them and... taking care of it, but I have no idea where to start and I don't know if I could..." She bit her lip as her eyes pricked with tears.

"You're not a killer, Gwynia," Gaius put a fatherly hand over hers as she clutched her wine cup. She favored the watered down beverage now, but tonight could have drunk it straight.

"I am," she burst out. "I came here to arrange a man's death. Because of me, Stephanus is dead! Sure they were horrible people but... I killed them!"

"You didn't strike the blow," Adi consoled, holding her other hand. The tale of Gwyn's efforts to bring about the plot for Domitian's death had left Adi and Gaius appalled, but they comforted her all the same.

"No, but they're both dead because of me," Gwyn sniffed. "And in Wallachia I killed a man with an axe. And at Masada…"

"You saved my life from Joshua." Adi lifted Gwyn's chin. "You've done some brave and terrible things, Gwynia, but no worse than many do to survive. I do not know if God or the Gods will judge you harshly. You have saved more lives than you have taken."

"You brought us together," Gaius smiled at his wife. "I'll be forever grateful to you for that."

Gwyn sagged. She was tired. Part of her longed for the comforts of the modern world and to see her family again, but part of her clamored to stay just a little longer in this oasis of domesticity. She didn't want to face the questions her parents would have, didn't want to have to explain to her brother and sister. And when would Michelle show up again? How long would she be carrying this pocket-watch in her hand? It was so much a part of her body now that she scarcely noticed it, but the burden it had placed on her soul reminded her every day that her life was no longer normal.

"Thank you." She squeezed both Adi's and Gaius' hands and smiled. "But the guards…"

"Do not worry about the guards," Gaius said. "Nerva is old and unpopular with the Praetorians. I think they'll be occupied with trying to control him over chasing stray women on the street. You cannot protect us from everything, Gwynia."

She supposed he was right. She half-laughed. "I spent the whole time at Masada trying to get back home, then half the time in Wallachia trying to rescue someone and bring them with me. Now I've spent longer here than in either of those places and times and I don't really want to leave. What if I never get back to see you again?"

Gaius patted her hand once more. "There is a life after this one, Gwynia. You will see us again."

* * *

Gwyn hugged both her friends farewell that night and went to the small storeroom where she slept. *I'll go now before I start another day and chicken out. I can't stay here forever.*

She stood in the center of the room and took several deep breaths. She was dressed in her own clothes, with her belt purse tied on. Several tokens of this time would stay with her as mementos. Her knife, her strigil, several coins. Maybe she could donate them to a museum one day.

Think. She opened her mind to the timepiece, sorting through the flow of moments around her and reaching forward into the timeline. Slow at first, then picking up speed, her mind whirled through weeks, months, years and centuries. She was three-quarters of the way there when she came to a screeching halt.

Another zig-zag. Another rock in the stream of history—diverting the flow and sending rivulets off every which way. It felt wrong, looked wrong in her mind's eye. But she couldn't pinpoint the moment or the place. It wasn't the same as when she'd searched for the turning point surrounding Domitian's assassination—at least there she'd known what year to look for.

"Shit! What am I going to do?" She opened her eyes and looked around at the storeroom. Maria's dress and the boy's tunic were folded neatly for Adi to find in the morning. She stared at them and thought.

She closed her eyes and reached forward again in the timeline. There it was, somewhere in the late fifteenth century to the north of Rome. She tentatively pushed past the zig-zag and found...

Uncertainty. No one timeline felt right to her. They intertwined and separated and disappeared through multiple dimensions. The further she stretched the worse it was. She had no way of finding her own time, the one where everything was normal, the one where she belonged.

"No!" a choked cry accompanied her fall to the floor. Gwyn's face crumpled with dry, silent sobs and she stared despairingly at the floor. *What am I going to do?*

Slowly her breathing calmed and Gwyn's back straightened. There was only one thing to do.

She rose, changed into Maria's dress and tucked her own clothes and the boy's tunic into her bag, along with the sandals she'd worn. The knife she tucked into her belt, making sure it was accessible. A scarf covered her hair.

Steeling herself, Gwyn stood in the center of the tiny room. She closed her eyes once more and concentrated on the earliest year she could feel the zig-zag begin. It was 1492. She breathed in deep.

Flick!

Thirty

1890 AD

Michelle woke in more pain than she had ever been in before, and that included the time she had been tortured. Blearily she realized that the effect of the first aid capsule had worn off and all her aches, bruises, cuts, scrapes and wounds had sent her body the bill. She cursed in Mayash, some choice phrases she'd learnt from Brrrys, which attracted the attention of the man guarding her door.

Miguelito regarded her sourly, his pistol and knife within easy reach. He tapped the door and it opened a crack. "She is awake," he reported and shut the door.

"Not taking any chances, hey?" Michelle tried to feel amused. They considered her dangerous. While she liked the respect, she preferred staying under the scanner. Being underestimated was a big help when it came to escaping.

Miguelito just glared at her, so Michelle sighed and fell back on the bed. At least she wasn't chained to a post in the stable. Someone had bandaged her wounds and bathed her. She wondered if it was Diego then decided not. He didn't seem like the type to wait on anyone, and she doubted he had forgiven her for knocking him out and stealing his horse. Michelle was proven right when a sturdy woman entered with a bowl of soup for her, first checking the bandages and raising her eyebrows at the scabbing over that had already taken place. She made the sign of the cross and left, so Michelle was left to eat her soup under the glowering gaze of her guard.

She slept. When she woke a priest was sitting in the small wooden chair beside her bed. He was reading his Bible but marked his place with a finger and looked at her when she stirred.

"What can I do for you, Father?" Michelle struggled to sit up. She didn't like being lower than someone she was talking to. She managed, despite the pain from the gouges in her shoulders, and eyed the priest.

"Perhaps I am here because God can do something for you, child?" The priest's voice was higher than she expected from a heavily bearded face. "I am Father Pedro. Do you wish to ask God for forgiveness for anything?"

Michelle almost choked. Everything she did, she did for a reason and for the greater good. She knew that was a dangerous line to take but she had the advantage of knowing how history should turn out. She wasn't a dictator who acted out of fanaticism and greed. "There are probably a lot of things I need forgiveness for, Father," she said, "but if there is anything after death I'll have to wait until then and hope that my good deeds outweigh my bad."

She expected to shock Father Pedro, but he returned her gaze levelly and responded, "It is too late by then. You must ask God for forgiveness in this lifetime and try to make amends."

"If you say so." Michelle closed her eyes. "I am grateful to Diego for saving my life, though if they hadn't attacked the train none of this would have happened."

Father Pedro's lips curled down. "Only God knows what will and will not happen." She sensed disapproval of the train heist, or perhaps it was disapproval of her killing two men.

"I'm tired, Father." This was the truth. She was in no condition for moral arguments. She needed to rest and recover, then jump into her time as soon as she was physically up to the trip. The priest took the hint and left.

He was back the next evening after her bandages were changed. "I'm lucky to be alive," she commented as he took a seat, Bible in hand.

He smiled. "God's will is not luck, my child."

She smiled insincerely in return. He read aloud from the Bible and Michelle let her mind drift.

In her dream, she stood before Citizen Colsa of the Shanista. The scientist twitched antennae as its dragonfly wings fluttered. "Why didn't you tell us the Shift had come before?" Michelle demanded of the alien.

Click, click. "It was not your place to know, human." That wasn't right. Colsa was never disrespectful when speaking to her. Or was that how it really thought? Were Owen's words true and humans were just pawns in the Allied Planets' game?

"Tell me!" Michelle's arms were held by two Mayash; Brrrys and Grrrel.

"Shut up, human." A Rilan spewed slime from her mouth over Michelle as she screamed and choked. A Nolii rolled her around on the floor until the slime hardened and she was encased in a solid, amber shell.

She couldn't breathe. The Nolii swung her knobbed tail and cracked the shell. Michelle tumbled out and gasped. Blue claws scrabbled on the floor as she steadied herself with her hands. She stared at the claws— they were on the ends of her blue furry fingers. A weight pressed down on her back. She swiveled her head to see heavy armored plates on her body, and an oozing amphibious tail below them. "What have you done to me?" She tried not to panic but her vision was splitting and multiplying. Her eyes were becoming faceted.

"You don't want to be a human, Michelle." Colsa bent over her and clicked. "You know how weak and inferior they are. "Now you are like us, like all of us."

That she was. A nightmarish blend of all the other species of the Allied Planets. "No!" she tried to protest. "I just want what's best for humanity!" But her voice was a burble of a click and a growl and a roar and a gargle until all that came out was a monstrous scream.

She woke up. It was dark. Father Pedro had left. Michelle lay awake for a long time, thinking.

* * *

Michelle recovered gradually. A week passed before she could walk and care for herself. The clothes they'd given her were the travelling dress, petticoat, stockings and blouse she'd bought in England. Not the trousers and shirt and jacket from her own time. They'd hidden her boots too.

"Where are my things, Father?" she asked that evening.

Father Pedro looked surprised. "I will have to ask Diego, my child. I do not know."

She accepted that. She could jump without most of it but she preferred not to leave anything futuristic behind. She understood they were limiting her potential to escape, which she respected, but she did need her boots. Also, her all-weather jacket had been expensive.

Father Pedro came in the next day with a smile. "He did not want you to have them, but I said what harm could it do? You should not wear trousers though—it is not modest for a woman."

Michelle smiled back, letting the modesty comment slide. She had what she wanted. Also, the priest was the friendliest person there. Miguelito and the other man who guarded her door—outside the room now—glared at her with disgust while the woman who brought food and emptied the chamber pot seemed frightened. Normally she wouldn't care, but her forced inactivity made her determined to be pleasant and gain the goodwill of these people. She remembered with embarrassment her antisocial behaviour amongst her rescuers in Aotearoa. Yes, Diego and his men had attacked the train but they were farmers forced to steal to survive and she'd killed two of them for the crime of being desperate. They had kidnapped her but she escaped. Now they had saved her life. She had lain there thinking a lot in between dozes, and had taken the time to meditate. It had calmed her.

Before she disappeared though, there was something she wanted to do. "Father, the men I... killed on the train. What were they like?"

The priest gave her a hard look, then frowned. "Guillermo and Manuel were... hard-working men. Manuel loved his wife, and they came to Mass regularly." He struggled to find the next words. "They did their best to provide for their families."

Interesting. Michelle was not sure if this was a good recommendation or not. Were they selfish? Did they beat their wives and children? She took a deep breath. "Do you think... their wives would permit me to apologize to them? For taking their husbands away. Would they hear me?" She sat stiffly on the edge of the bed, hands clutching her skirt.

"They might be too upset," Father Pedro answered cautiously. Michelle nodded, relieved.

"Then I would trust you to do something for them please, Father."

She picked up one boot and slid a tiny fabric pouch from a sleeve in the ankle. Opening it, she tipped two tiny gold bars onto her palm. "It's a poor recompense, but I hope a little money will help."

The priest's eyes widened. "I can trade these in Mendoza for a substantial sum. This will help the widows, indeed it will! How did you come by these? They are not nuggets."

Michelle shrugged. "They're just currency for me. I trade them for money to buy food and clothes." *I won't need them soon*, she almost said.

Father Pedro didn't press her further, but he folded the gold bars carefully into his handkerchief and tucked them into a breast pocket. Michelle hoped her faith in him wasn't misplaced.

Thirty-One

1890 AD

"Do you feel able to ride, Señora?" It was Father Pedro, knocking at her door. Michelle intended to have one last meal to fortify her for the time-jumps, so the priest coming in with her breakfast was timely.

"Ride?" she queried, spooning up porridge.

"To Mendoza. I have convinced Diego and the others we would be best to return you to your people and trust no more will be said. If you can ride we will leave today."

Michelle set down her spoon. She didn't need to return to Mendoza to jump back to her time. On the other hand, once she arrived in her time she needed some way of arranging communication and transport with the Time-Space Agency on Earth, or at least those elements of it who knew she was on a mission. Western South America in her time hadn't fared well with environmental disasters—earthquakes, landslides and desertification. Maybe she'd be safer organizing transport back to Buenos Aires.

"I can ride," she said at last. "Diego… they believed you when you said that?" She understood the deal offered to her. They would take her back to civilization, in return for her silence about the train heist.

"Yes," Father Pedro replied, giving her a long, steady look. "I have faith that you will do the right thing."

Michelle grinned. "As I do in you, with regards to looking after those widows. When do we leave?"

* * *

Traffic increased as they neared Mendoza. Mostly this wasn't a problem, but one party approaching Michelle's group refused to give way. Diego was riding point and a flurry of swearing in Spanish and English arose when the other group tried to force him off the road.

"Make way for your betters, you grubby mestizo!"

"Get out of my country, you thieving English dogs!"

"Oh for fuck's sake." Michelle kneed her mare forward. Two snappily dressed Englishmen, backed up by a posse of grooms and footmen, had started the drama. Michelle would have simply moved and made a rude gesture at their backs, but Diego was too proud to do anything other than hold his ground. "Can we just let them pass and get on with it?"

"Taking advice from a woman are you, mestizo?" This appeared to be the funniest joke, as both gentlemen laughed uproariously.

"It is his wife, or his whore?" One wanted to know.

"How can you tell?" More laughter. Diego's hand moved to his pistol. He didn't understand all of what was said in English, but some words he knew quite well.

Michelle wasn't bothered by the insult, just irritated at what was degenerating into a fight. Someone else took issue with the name-calling, however.

"That's Lady Stucely! How dare you say such awful things about her?" A small blonde lady riding side-saddle trotted to the fore.

"Well, I'll be damned," Michelle said in English. "Hello, Miss Morton."

"Please," Penelope Morton blushed. "It is Penelope to you, my dear friend."

"You know this woman?" The rude English gentlemen were astonished.

"You said you weren't English!" Diego stared at Michelle in fury.

"I'm not!" Michelle turned to Father Pedro, looking uncomfortable on his gelding. "Father, I swear to you I'm not English. Miss Morton and I made acquaintance on the ship over."

The standoff was blocking the road, but no one else was in sight. "If they are acquaintances, perhaps the Señora should go with them," Diego advised stiffly.

Father Pedro looked concerned, but Michelle translated for Penelope's benefit. "My dear, I don't know if you heard that a train was attacked some weeks ago, but I fell from it and was rescued by these men. They have brought me to Mendoza but I wondered if I might prevail upon your earlier offer of hospitality as all my things have been lost…" She leant her willpower into the words.

"Oh of course! Papa will be so pleased to see you!"

"I can go with them," Michelle said in Spanish to Diego and Father Pedro. "I'll trouble you no longer."

Diego looked surly, then astonished when Penelope rode up to him and bobbed an odd curtsey in the saddle. "Fear not, Señor," she said in badly accented Spanish. "I shall take good care of her. I thank you for rescuing her and bringing her back to safety."

Diego leant forward and kissed her hand. "It was nothing, Señorita, for the chance to see so beautiful and gracious a lady as you." Michelle hid a grin at the chagrin of the English gentlemen. Penelope blushed.

"Would you escort us back to my father's estate?" the young lady asked of the Englishmen. Michelle deduced they must be the same two men she'd overhead on the ship talking of Mr Morton's silver prospects and of possible marriage to Penelope. As the parties split and Michelle waved to Father Pedro, she wondered if the chance meeting had dashed the hopes of Penelope's suitors. Certainly the young lady seemed enamored of Diego, though it was likely her romantic nature at play.

Michelle shrugged. She'd have a few quiet words with Penelope, but the girl would have to make her own future.

* * *

It was several days later, as the train steamed into the main station in Buenos Aires, that Michelle finally heaved a sigh of relief. Tension left her shoulders, then she squared them again and pushed through the crowds to find the ladies room. Privacy was always best when time-jumping from daylight, except in emergencies.

Flick. Flick. Flick. She switched to night jumping and kept going. She wasn't fully recovered from the cougar attack but pushed through. The sooner she reached her own time and decent medical facilities, the better. The years blurred into decades until she ground to a halt, exhausted. Seventy years had passed. She cursed her weakness. Nineteen-sixties Argentina wasn't the best place to take a nap, but she had no choice. It was pitch black, wherever she was, so she took a deep breath and half-reached for the next time-jump. The blue glow that arose showed Michelle she stood in a toilet no longer, but a dusty storage closet.

Perfect. She let go of the glow and slumped to the floor, shivering with cold sweat. Pulling her all-weather jacket tightly around her, her eyes thudded shut.

The next morning she began another series of jumps. She reached 2010 AD before she collapsed. The storage room had been demolished and the new platform she landed on was hard concrete. Her head smacked it and she felt a trickle of blood. Lying there for several minutes, Michelle fought unconsciousness.

"Dios! Señora, are you alright?" For a second she thought it was Diego, but it was a deep-voiced woman who spoke instead.

"Leave her be, Mama, she's probably drunk or on drugs." A younger voice, a man, spoke.

"Cesar, shame on you! I think she's been robbed. Here, help me roll her over."

Light hurt Michelle's eyes. She clenched them shut, but not before seeing a square, matronly face with dark curls framing an expression of concern. Concern of a different kind was on the face of the woman's son. "Mama, Julio's train is arriving. He's expecting us." The whine of a locomotive's brakes accompanied the rumble that drew near. Even if she'd been lying on the tracks Michelle could scarcely have dragged herself to one side.

"Then go find your brother. We need to take this lady to the hospital. You two can carry her."

Michelle was vaguely aware of another man joining them, then the sensation of being lifted and eased into a vehicle. A taxi, she decided. Tense mutterings irritated the edge of her hearing. She stayed awake until a different voice pronounced her not concussed. She felt a sting in her arm before blackness swamped her.

Thirty-Two

2010 AD

Murmurs intruded on Michelle's sleep. She twitched. It was painful. When she opened her eyes white assailed her from every direction. She blinked and her brain struggled to catch up. *I…burnt out from jumping?* Or was it just that her body couldn't cope with the demand of time travel on top of healing severe injuries? Either way, she realized that despite it being only 2010, she was in a hospital, and that was the best place for her.

Resistance as she moved alerted her to the drip in her hand. Bandages swathed her forehead, and there were fresh dressings on the claw wounds in her shoulders. At least they knew about basic antibiotics in this time. "Nurse?" she croaked, then coughed. Her fingers fumbled and found a button on the side of the bed.

The curtain surrounding the bed slid back with a metallic scrape. An Argentinian nurse inspected Michelle, peering at her chart over half spectacles. "Do you have pain?"

"Uh, yes, but where am I?"

"How strong is the pain? Ten? Five?"

"Um, six?" It was true she ached all over, and her shoulders burned when she moved, but it was much improved on her state in Diego's village. Besides, she had a high pain threshold.

"Hmph," the nurse said, and disappeared. She was back in less than a minute with a plastic cup of pills and bottle of water.

"Where am I?" Michelle repeated. The nurse ignored her, checking her bandages and scribbling notes on a chart. "Excuse me? Can you please tell me where I am?"

Brown eyes flicked over glasses. "Hospital Alemán."

That meant little to Michelle. Without her computer bracelet she couldn't research the place or time. She cursed its loss, but nodded stiff thanks to the nurse, who sniffed and backed away from the bed, sweeping the curtain shut.

There was a low shelf nearby. On it were Michelle's boots, clothes and bag. She breathed a sigh of relief and assessed her options. Two year jumps all the way to her time was going to be agonizing. She risked burnout, collapse, or landing in a situation where she needed to fight her way out.

Alternatively, she could jump one year into the future, locate Gwyn and get the girl to take her back to her time. Gwyn had been to Michelle's time before, so with the right coaching would be able to avoid timeline uncertainty.

The problem with that idea was that she had no way of finding Gwyn, much less obtaining a passport and flying to Europe. Michelle growled and dismissed that plan.

The curtains around her bed swept back again. A tall man wearing a white lab coat and stethoscope scanned Michelle's chart and ran his eyes over her body too, skipping her face. "Do you wish to make a police report?" He sounded bored.

"No."

He raised his eyebrows at that. "You were attacked."

"I fainted. No one else was involved."

"Do you know your attackers?" His tone was condescending now. "Is it something you wish kept from the police?"

Michelle raised her eyes slowly to his. "No. Please excuse me, I think I'm about to vomit."

The doctor leapt back and called, "Nurse!" Michelle faked retching noises until he retreated, then apologized to the nurse for a false alarm. The nurse looked suspiciously at Michelle and then at the direction the doctor had gone, and knitted her eyebrows together in a heavyset frown.

"Could I have some more water, please?" Michelle asked meekly. "And use the toilet?" She was helped to the shared bathroom at the end of the ward, then returned to her bed. The nurse twitched the curtains shut.

Michelle checked her things. Everything was there, little as it was. One of the travel dresses she bought in London. Her first aid kit. The data crystal Owen had given her, hidden in her boot.

She lay back. When the doctor looked in on her again, she feigned sleep. That turned into real sleep and when she woke she was hungry. The hospital food was poor but she ate it all, then read her chart and decided her own medicines would not interfere with the antibiotics and painkillers given to her by the nurse.

Time to go. It was evening now. Other patients farewelled their visitors or ate their dinners. The nurse offered Michelle a magazine but she declined. The curtains were shut. The rounds had been done.

She swung her legs out of the bed and shed the hospital gown, yanking the drip out and dressing quickly. She snapped open a capsule from her first aid kit and jabbed it into her arm. Adrenaline flooded her system; her brain began to buzz.

She was out of the ward and past the nurses' station before they could leap up to stop her. Fire stairs, ground floor, hospital entrance and onto the street. Dodging taxis, around a corner. The temptation to break into a run burned through her, but Michelle forced her body to a stop and focused.

Flick. Flick. Fli-Fli-Fli-Fl-Fl-Fl-Fl-Fl-Fl-Fl-Fl-Fl-Fl-Fl-Fl-Fl-Fl!

She soared into the future.

2623 AD

A couple were out on a date, strolling along the recently redeveloped boulevard. Buenos Aires looked nothing like it had six hundred years previously—sea level rises had seen to that—but the reconstructed canal city enjoyed a second life. The couple stopped to admire the lights of ships and hovercraft on the water of Canal de 9 de Julio, then shrieked in alarm as a blue cloud appeared in front of them and a woman fell out of it and into the water.

"Shit, honey, do something!" One woman yelled and her partner staunchly kicked off her heels and leapt into the inky canal.

The other woman sent an 'ambulance-required' alert on her wrist com, then unwound her scarf and tied it to her belt. She threw the makeshift rope to her partner, who caught it with her free hand, clutching Michelle tightly with the other arm. Pulled to safety, Michelle coughed, twitched and spewed water onto the grass. Her rescuers stayed with her until the ambulance arrived, lights flashing and siren blaring as it hovered just above the ground.

A crowd had gathered—this walk was popular in the evening—and the two women who had rescued Michelle enjoyed the excitement of being heroes.

Michelle woke in a half-shell medical pod some time later. A robot nurse appeared as soon as the monitor registered that she was awake. The robot whirred and scanned her, and asked her how she felt.

"Terrible," she whispered. "I need to access a com straight away, please. Can you arrange that?"

The robot replied in smooth tones that it would check with its superiors.

"It's an emergency." Michelle forced strength into her voice but it was a pitiful effort. "It relates to a top secret police investigation. I need to report immediately."

The robot whirred and scooted away on small treads. Michelle slumped back. While she had been on the road to recovery from her cougar attack, the time jumping, the head injury and the adrenaline-fueled leaps through time had undone any healing she'd achieved.

I'm in my time, now. They'll fix me up. She was asleep again in a moment.

A doctor stood over her when she woke. "Agent Michelle," ze said blandly. Ze was neither male nor female, as far as Michelle could see, so she reverted to the non-binary pronoun in her head.

"How do you know my name?" Alarm bells chimed in her brain.

The doctor smiled. "Facial recognition program. Such a dramatic appearance had us running you through the scanners. How are you feeling? You've been unconscious for a few days."

"How long?" Alarm gripped Michelle. She sat up. Nausea welled but she forced it down. She realized her chronokinetor was gone. They had extracted it from her left hand. "How many days?" she repeated.

"Almost three days since they brought you in. I understand you need to com someone urgently? I can arrange that for you."

Michelle had to stop herself from snatching the small com unit.

"Thank you," she gasped, holding her hand out. The doctor passed it to her with a look of concern on zis hairless face; Michelle's monitors beeped as her blood pressure went up. "I'm fine, just relieved," she said, then keyed in the com address she needed.

Official Agency channels wouldn't do. If the political furor was still dragging on, not to mention the court investigation, she wanted no one to know she had been time travelling. How Colsa and Director Dirk were explaining her absence when she was supposed to be sending in twenty-four hour blood reports was not her problem, but she didn't want to expose them if they had managed to cover up.

"This had better be good, whoever this is," Brrrys' warm voice yawned at the other end of the com. "I was sleeping."

Michelle wished with her whole heart she was curled up next to him, instead of being on the other side of the planet. If she was the sort of human who cried, the sound of her friend, colleague and occasional lover's voice would have set her to tears. "Brrrys, it's Michelle. Get Colsa and Dirk immediately."

There was a muffled bump and growl. Relief and anxiety swirled through Brrrys' tone. "Where are you? Are you ok?"

"Can't say. Injured but stable and recovering. Need a secure line." She glanced at the doctor, whose eyebrows would have been on the roof if ze had any. "I'm potentially in danger here, doctor. Is there a secure com address I can give my superiors to reach me here?"

If she hadn't been identified, the doctor may have simply humored her and done a mental health assessment for paranoia. Being a Time-Space Agent—as controversial as the Agency was these days—had some perks. Ze tapped in a series of numbers for the hospital's secure line and handed the com back to Michelle.

"Listen Brrrys, I hope I'll see you soon, but if I don't, I need to know: did you know *it* has happened before on Earth?"

She could almost hear her furry friend thinking as he worked out what she meant. "It? You mean the—"

"Don't say it!"

The confusion in his silence was palpable, then Brrrys said cautiously, "No. I didn't know. I'm guessing you can't tell me how you found out."

"Not over the com. Hopefully, I'll be back in Berlin soon." She paused. "I've missed you. I hope you're recovering." The guilt of how she'd walked him into a trap and torture still twisted her gut.

This time the silence was full of surprise. "I've missed you too." The warmth in his voice sounded genuine. "Maybe they'll put us convalescents together and we can have some proper downtime."

"That'd be nice," she whispered.

"I've messaged Dirk and Colsa. Expect a com soon. Take care of yourself, Michelle."

"You too." She closed the link.

The doctor took back the com. "Should we put you in a secure ward, Agent?" ze asked quietly.

Michelle nodded. "Might be best." Normally she would have scoffed at extra protection but the information she held was more important than her pride.

The nurse robot returned and Michelle's half-pod clicked from its moorings. She floated along behind the doctor up corridors and to a different level. No sooner than she entered her new room, the doctor's wrist com buzzed. "Your call, I believe. I'll get it patched through." Ze caught her look. "This ward is secure, Agent. I'll raise forcefields and have a robot nurse on guard."

Michelle had to accept that. The doctor disappeared into an office and returned with a different com unit—much more solid and requiring retinal scans and vocal authorization before it was handed to her. "Michelle here," she said.

A tiny hologram of Citizen Colsa's face appeared. The Shanista's multi-faceted eyes flickered with rainbow colors. "Agent Michelle, good to hear from you. I have bad news though."

"What?"

"You are under arrest."

Thirty-Three

2623 AD

"Under arrest?" Michelle repeated stupidly. She glanced up hurriedly. The doctor had disappeared once ze had raised the forcefield around her pod, but the energy field wasn't sound proof. There were several other pods in the ward—only one down the end had a forcefield around it, the rest were empty. Michelle lowered her voice nonetheless. "What the hell for?"

"Jaysen Fitz has pressed charges against you for assault, disruption to a private conference, theft and failing to pay for accommodation."

"That slimy, cretinous, chauvinistic, xenophobic jerk! What about him torturing Brrrys? What about trying to murder us by having our hovercraft crash in the middle of the ocean?"

"Agreed," Colsa interrupted calmly. "But due process must be followed now formal charges have been laid. Your failure to check in with blood tests have allowed the Fitzes to smear your character and that of the Agency further, but now you have resurfaced a formal arrest will be made."

Michelle spluttered then clamped down on her emotions. She had gone to rescue Owen, knowing she breached the freeze on all Agent activity. If she hadn't done that she wouldn't now know that Earth First wanted to blackmail the Allied Planets. Jay Fitz trying to make her look bad was insignificant in comparison. "How long do I have? I have data from Owen I must give you." But was handing over the crystal's information the right thing to do? Could she really trust Colsa, or any of the Shanista? They were the ones who had hidden the information in the first place.

"Police will be there in the morning. I requested of your doctor to report that you are in a secure ward, and thus cannot escape. Can you transmit the data over this line?"

Trapped! The protective green light of the forcefield had become a cell. Michelle choked back her rage. "I can, stand by." She held the data crystal over the com's input receptacle and hesitated. "Citizen Colsa, I have to ask…" This was it. Would Colsa come clean about manipulating humans? She'd known from the time she was made full Agent that the directive of the Time-Space Agency was to prepare for all attacks on the Allied Planets. Without unity they would be picked apart planet by planet by an unknown force. A force that appeared to have overwhelming military superiority in all projected timelines. The war against the Clarish had shown humans to be valuable fighters, but more than that, she'd learnt that humanity had thrown off the confusion and chaos of the Shift before. No wonder the enemy, whoever they were, wanted to eliminate humans from the equation. But were the Shanista, and possibly other species, just using them?

The hologram of Colsa flickered above the com. "Yes, Agent Michelle?"

She shut her mouth. "Here's the data. So am I rogue or not?" She pushed the crystal into the slot and watched the lights indicate loading and transfer.

"Technician Schlössen has identified a turning point in Ancient Rome that has resolved itself, however another one has presented itself approximately one thousand, four hundred years later. It begins in a similar area but spreads in a most bizarre way."

"Who?" Michelle remembered the Rilan technician who'd given her the tracking computer. "And what do you mean, resolved itself?" Her brain clicked. "You mean Gwyn interfered?"

"From our observations it appeared she identified and corrected a deviating turning point. That shows great ability and initiative."

Michelle's temper boiled. "Unbelievable!"

Colsa's image wavered for a moment. "Agent Michelle, your data transmission is complete. It will need to be analyzed but at a glance it appears to confirm our suspicions that the Shift has come to Earth before, and it is not a natural phenomenon. It also appears someone is trying to hack this com line, so I will disconnect. All I will say is that while young Gwyn may have rectified one aberration in history, she will not be able to do so again. Not alone, that is. Colsa out."

The com was silent, Colsa's hologram vanished. Michelle stared at the unit as if willing her superior to call back, to state that it had been a miscommunication, that Michelle's world wasn't crumbling down around her.

Nothing. "Doctor?" she called, looking about. The forcefield glowed around and over her in a pale green glow. She knew better than to touch it. "Nurse!" She pressed the call button on her pod. The robot nurse trundled into view. "Nurse, I need to see the doctor night away."

"I'm afraid the doctor is unable to see you, Patient Michelle. Is there anything I can do?"

"Please lower the forcefield, Nurse."

"I am not authorized to do that, Patient. You are to remain contained until police come to remove you and the doctor authorizes your release."

Dammit! The doctor must have known about her arrest status. But why hadn't ze put her into this ward while she was unconscious? It would have made her suspicious, that's why, and she wouldn't have called Brrrys. Perhaps they had eavesdropped and tried to learn what she knew. She dressed herself while she waited. The police might not arrive until morning and it was still before midnight, so she could sleep, brood or plot her escape, but damned if she was going to do it in a hospital gown.

She couldn't sleep. The injustice of it all infuriated her. She was pissed off at Colsa, at Gwyn, at Jaysen bloody Fitz and everyone in between. She didn't know how to bring down the forcefield, and even if she escaped, the hospital had many more safeguards for containment.

Voices and boot steps alerted her to company shortly after midnight. *Couldn't even wait till morning,* she thought bitterly. The Director for Time-Space Agency affairs on Earth, Dirk Tokoyashi, approached with Michelle's traitorous doctor in tow. She glowered at them both.

"It is the middle of the night," the doctor protested.

"Better she is gone before the media get ahold of the fact she has been here," Dirk responded, looking about the ward. He was a tall, black man with very short, curly black hair and a calm demeanor. His measured gaze matched his deep, steady voice. "I have a pod to transport her. Is she medically well enough to travel?"

The doctor assured Dirk that Patient... Prisoner Michelle was physically well, healing from injuries at an excellent rate and up to any form of transport. Michelle sneered at zim.

"Michelle, I am bringing up a transport pod. I will raise the forcefield then ask the doctor to lower the medical pod field. Please place yourself inside the transport pod and allow yourself to be restrained." Dirk ordered. Michelle clenched her teeth. The Director was an extremely competent, capable Citizen. He'd supported Michelle and other Agents through many missions, and she had liked and trusted him.

She obeyed the directive. There was nothing else she could do, short of self-harm. Soft straps leapt over her body and bound her to the transport pod when she lay down. "I'll have any of her tech too, please," Dirk asked the doctor. "It is evidence."

A small round case was handed over and Dirk led the hovering pod out and up to the roof level. A ship was waiting. Despite her prone position Michelle recognized it as the same ship that had collected her and Brrrys from Aotearoa. Even the Nolii pilot was the same—he helped load the pod into the main cabin, secured the ship, then took off. Once aboard, the pod's forcefield was lowered.

Dirk leant forward and snapped the restraints off Michelle. She sat up. "I used to respect you," she spat.

Dirk held up a hand. "I still respect you, Agent Michelle. You are the best, the only Agent we have. The other four are dead or missing—two we suspect have defected. We need you to go back in time and save us."

"What? But I'm under arrest!"

"And the police are going to be very annoyed when they arrive at the hospital in Buenos Aires in the morning to find you gone. All I ask is next time, try to arrive a little closer to the time you leave. We have less than a week of our time before the Shift arrives."

"You're... I'm... You're ordering me to go rogue? Completely?"

Dirk smiled and Michelle saw grey at his temples, grey that hadn't been there several weeks ago. "You were always something of a rogue, now we need you to save us. Find the girl Gwyn. Hopefully the two of you together can repair this last turning point, or series of points as it appears to be."

Michelle stared at him, then lay back. "I need data. I need my timepiece. I need a computer that can locate her and I need resources to survive in different times."

"All here and more," Dirk said. "Let me give you a full briefing."

* * *

They flew through the night. Dirk insisted both he and Michelle get some rest. She coaxed her mind into a meditative sleep—only years of practice kept her from being so excited she buzzed. No more political bullshit. No more second guessing friends and allies. Just the mission.

She resented the thought of having to work with Gwyn. Yes, the girl had done well at Masada and on Vivaldis, but her teenage attitude had asserted itself when Michelle had given her the mission in Transylvania. "She'll just slow me down," she muttered as she rolled over in her pod.

When she woke, they were flying over the Swiss Alps. She was so glad to enjoy a thorough cleanse in the ship's hygiene facility that a smile broke over her face when she emerged for her briefing with Dirk.

"The timelines start going awry in the late fifteenth century," the Director said, bringing up a hologram map of southern Europe in the main cabin. "This isn't like anything we've seen before—it's not a single turning point that's been knocked askew. It's like the Shift has thrown everything it's got because we're almost out of time."

"But… it's not sentient. Is it?"

Dirk shook his head. "We never thought it was, but the data you transmitted to Colsa firms up our suspicions that the time-space energy wave is being controlled. Whoever or whatever the entity is, they must have the technology to view through time and send pulses of energy through time. This also explains why our technicians can scan the same period without result and then suddenly come across a turning point. It's in a constant state of flux."

Michelle absorbed this. "And do you believe the Shanista should have told us that humans are critical to the defense of the Allied Planets? That the Shift has come to Earth before?"

Dirk sighed. "Michelle, they didn't know. They had theories. I was in the room when the theory was proposed and again when some of the initial research came in. They were just as surprised as us. I think... I think they also thought humanity might not want the burden of being the savior species."

Michelle chewed on a knuckle. "Humans are not who I would have chosen as a savior species."

Dirk grinned. His white teeth contrasted beautifully with his dark face. "Me neither, but we have to step up. Maybe 'savior' is the wrong word. The Allied Planets are only strong if we work together. We can't have any one member thinking they are more important than the other."

Michelle nodded, returning his grin. She started to reply that Earth First was proof of that when an explosion sounded and the ship rocked.

"Hanli! Report!" Dirk barked at the pilot.

"Under attack, Director. Unknown assailant. Not responding to hails."

"Shields up!"

"On it." The Nolii pilot was calm. Michelle scrambled to grab her gear. Another explosion rocked the ship.

"Evasive manoeuvers, Director. Strap in."

The ship banked, throwing Michelle hard against a wall panel. An emergency harness activated. She and Dirk hung on grimly as Hanli drove the ship upwards, relying on the shields to fend off the laser fire. Michelle didn't know much about aerial combat but she suspected the attackers wanted them to crash into the snow-capped mountains, or to destroy them mid-air.

"How the hell can this happen?" Michelle yelled. "This is Earth!"

Dirk was on his wrist com. "Someone's blocking us. I can't reach the local authorities or even Berlin. It's probably only temporary but that's all it'll take to blast us into pieces."

The pressure in the cabin altered, then normalized. The ship slowed. "We're in the ionosphere," Hanli reported from the pilot's cabin. "It appears they were an atmospheric ship. We should be safe for now."

"Bullshit." Michelle thrust aside her harness. "If they can block our coms they can source more ships. We don't have long." She grabbed the timepiece Dirk had returned to her and jammed it into her left palm.

Her eyes rolled back a second as the technology fused. With a shuddering breath she refocused. "You've got to drop me somehow and get out of here."

Dirk joined her. He looped a crystal computer bracelet on her right wrist. "I forgot to say, I worked on the chronokinetor while you were asleep. You should be able to do fifty year jumps now."

Michelle stared at him. He grinned. "I started as a technician. Schlössen commed me instructions. It's not as good as the model you lost to Gwyn, but I re-configured the crystals and links to give you more range."

Michelle looked at the timepiece in her hand. "Shit, yeah," she grinned. "That helps me a lot! Alright, what else?"

Dirk handed her the plain woven backpack. "Food, metals, jewels, clothes. Miniature forcefield—don't overuse that, the battery has no way of recharging outside of this time. Data on your computer, plus a tracking algorithm for the girl."

"Almost a normal mission," Michelle replied.

"Incoming," Hanli spoke from the pilot's cabin.

Dirk grabbed something from an overhead compartment. He slammed it onto Michelle's back, and spidery links shot out and around her chest from it. "Hanli, dive to one thousand meters and then open the main cabin door. Agent Michelle is going to drop from there."

"Affirmative. Secure yourselves. Diving in five, four, three…"

Dirk leapt backwards and harnessed himself in. Michelle grabbed hers and double looped the straps around her wrists.

The ship plummeted.

* * *

Explosions from laser fire blasted in her ears and acceleration pressed her body against the wall. Michelle held on tightly and tried to stay calm. She'd been under pressure doing time-jumps before, but this was something else.

"Fifty thousand meters!" Hanli called.

Without the dampening field inside the cabin, Michelle and Dirk would have passed out from the acceleration. As it was, this kind of maneuver wasn't ideal. Dirk was green in the face. Michelle was grateful for her strong stomach, but her nerves weren't helping.

"Thirty thousand meters!"

By the explosions Michelle knew the attacking ships were still in pursuit. *Fuckers.* She steeled herself and thought about the jump she was about to make.

"Ten thousand meters!"

"I'm ready!" Michelle shouted. "I'll time-jump from inside the cabin, just slow us down enough!"

Dirk looked alarmed. "Don't take the ship with you!"

A reckless grin spread across Michelle's face. "Wouldn't dream of it, Director. Hanli! Call it!"

"Five thousand meters, levelling out. You're somewhere south of the mountains. On my mark. Three, two, one, mark!"

Michelle let go of the straps and leapt into the air. Before motion could return her to contact with the ship, she disappeared in a haze of blue.

"She's gone!" Dirk yelled.

"Copy!" Hanli engaged the ship's subspace thrusters and the ship blasted forward. Their attackers were left in an astonished clutter. They were halfway across the Mediterranean when an official military cruiser hailed them from space and ordered them to stop. There was no escape.

"We only broached atmospheric flight restrictions because we were under attack!" Hanli argued.

"This is Earth, not a war zone," the official on the other end of the com retorted.

Dirk joined Hanli in the pilot's cabin. "This is Director Dirk Tokoyashi of the Time-Space Agency. Can you confirm that there are no ships in pursuit of us? We were attacked over the Italian Alps, several hundred kilometers north of here."

The official didn't seem impressed by Dirk's title. "That is restricted information. Please proceed to the coordinates being issued to you for impoundment and investigation. If you do not comply we will fire."

Dirk patted Hanli on his shell, which quivered in anger. "We did what we had to, Hanli. Let's just follow orders and hope the right people are watching."

The Nolii pilot wrinkled his leathery face. "Bet you ten credits Earth First is behind this."

Dirk strapped himself into the co-pilot's seat. "I don't doubt it."

* * *

Michelle fell.

Flick. Flick. Flick. As the air roared in her ears she jumped fifty, a hundred, two hundred years. She wanted to be clear of any time where air travel was a possibility. She narrowly missed hitting a plane as she fell through the twenty-second century. She tumbled in the slipstream, throwing her concentration. The sky and earth spun as the ground rushed towards her.

Stay calm! She closed her eyes. The drop vest Dirk had slapped onto her would deploy automatically if she hit a certain altitude. She whirled uncontrollably but managed to reconnect to the timepiece and make the next jump.

The stabilizing component of the timepiece stopped her tumble. She still fell. Mountains grew snow as global warming rolled back. Rivers meandered back and forth and coastlines swept in and out.

Almost there. Bam! The drop vest opened and wings extended. Fall became glide, and Michelle flashed through the remaining centuries. She hit 1492. Fields and forests stretched out below. A town could be seen to the southwest. Villages dotted the greenery underneath her—she aimed for one. Landing unseen on the outskirts would be ideal. She could talk or trade her way into food and shelter, as well as transport to the town. From there she'd concentrate on fixing the timeline and finding Gwyn.

The fields rushed close. Michelle put out her feet and hit the ground at a run. A stray rock caught her foot and she crashed in a heap.

"Fuck!" She put her head up and looked around. There was no one in sight. She breathed a sigh of relief. Standing, she stretched and cracked her back and neck.

"Right," she said. "Let's get to work."

Read on for a sneak peek at Gwyn and Michelle's
next time-travel adventure:

Renaissance Woman.

One

"Stop her!"

"Demon!"

"Whore!"

Michelle bolted down the muddy alley, chickens squawking in her wake. The villagers were close behind. If they caught her she would be tried as a witch. She couldn't afford to time travel away—so many jumps had worn her out, muddling her wits. She needed food and rest—not an enraged mob screaming at her heels, determined to burn her.

If she hadn't been so tired she never would have walked directly into the main piazza where a crowd listened avidly to a preacher. She would have loitered around the edges, stolen a dress or begged a bite to eat. Instead she had strolled into the view of the ugly Dominican friar who fixed on her and cried indignation at her uncovered hair, her masculine attire.

"Sin!" He had pointed and the crowd had followed his enraged gaze. "Not only wanton with her hair uncovered, unbound, but flaunting her body in God's eyes. Such sin!"

Michelle had frozen in the face of his fury. Like a pack of beasts, the crowd roared and surged towards her. Michelle did the only thing she could think of doing.

She ran.

"She's getting away!"

She hoped so. Fit as she was, this unexpected sprint was unwelcome, and the fields around the Italian village provided no cover. A sideways lunge into a stable and a dash between stalls. She kicked open the back door then scrambled up a ladder into the hayloft. She flung herself behind some bales and hoped her hiding place was good enough.

"That way!" Angry men flooded the stable below, sending horses into panicked whinnies. Michelle forced her breath to slow and projected an aura of nothingness.

"Out here!"

Feet thundered on the flagstones below and out the door. Quiet returned. Michelle peeked out as a middle-aged man with a straggling beard emerged from a stall and petted his charges, calming them one by one. The groom circled the horses twice then stopped at the bottom of the ladder.

"I see you run up there, maybe you is agone now, but I don't think so." The musicality of his voice made him sound whimsical. "They is gone, they who is chasing you."

Michelle raised her head cautiously. "Thank you. I'm afraid the preacher in the piazza took against me."

The groom leant on a stall, stroking the head of the gelding that whickered over his shoulder. "That Savonarola. Don' take much to get 'im all a-riled up. I'll be glad when 'e goes to Florence."

Savonarola. *Just my luck.*

"You're not a fan of his?" Michelle slid down the ladder.

The groom shrugged. "I prefer looking after the horses—they is simpler." He patted the gelding affectionately, feeding it an apple from his pocket.

"Sensible of you." Michelle brushed stalks of hay from her trousers. "Now is there any chance you could tell me where I might purchase a dress, a place to sleep and some food?" She pulled out a small silver ring, one of those she'd been issued with for this perilous trip into the past.

The groom eyed the ring speculatively. "Si. Climb back up into the 'ayloft and I is bringing a dress and the food. You can sleep there—there is no rats."

Michelle smiled. "Thank you, signor."

* * *

Kind as the groom seemed to be, Michelle still took precautions. She activated her tiny force field dome and stretched before she went to sleep. Footsteps below woke her and she deactivated the field seconds before the groom's head emerged at the top of the ladder. He brought her an old, moth-eaten brown dress and a pail containing lukewarm pottage.

"I'll be off and away at first light," Michelle said, managing not to pull a face at the taste of the pottage. "Thank you for your help."

"Si," The groom watched her eat, to her annoyance. She would wait until he was gone before she changed into the dress. "Where is you a-going?"

"France," she lied.

"Si. For another of those rings I could give you the direction?" he added hopefully.

"No thank you, I know the way." She didn't, but she wasn't about to burn through her funds when she could use the chronokinetor to guide her.

"Hmph." The groom didn't leave. "It was not easy, getting the dress and the food up 'ere. Folk in the village still a-riled up. Might be you need 'elp leaving without a fuss."

"I'll be fine." Michelle put steel into her tone. She ate faster, trying not to gag, and handed the pail back to the groom. "Thank you. You'd best get back to your duties."

"Hmph." He rubbed his beard and retreated down the ladder. Michelle waited until it was fully dark, snuck down and relieved herself just outside the door, then climbed back up the loft and set the force field before lying down in her bed of hay.

She rose well before dawn, knowing a groom's day would start early. With her own clothes stashed in her backpack, she concentrated on being inconspicuous in her shabby dress as she crept down the ladder.

"Folk still be a-looking," the groom's hoarse voice sounded by her ear.

Michelle whirled and stopped herself from hitting him. "I don't have any more money for you!" She strode to the main stable door, conscious that he was a step behind her. When she reached for the bar his bony hand grasped her wrist. Michelle dug her fingernails into his skin and twisted her arm free. She yanked his own arm up behind his back and pushed him against the stable door. "I said, I don't have any more money for you."

"I was just trying to 'elp!" he wheezed.

"Whatever you say, my friend. Now unless you want a broken wrist I suggested you stay in this stable while I leave. And don't think about telling anyone I'm heading to France, or I'll come back and break both your arms."

She waited until he grunted affirmation and let go, lifting the bar on the door and slipping out before he could say anything more. She hurried along the back laneways of the town in the black early morning. By the time the grey light of dawn crept into the sky, she was well on the road to Milan.

AUTHOR'S NOTE

Ancient Rome. It's the source of countless stories, fiction and otherwise, simply because it is well-documented and has left so many physical monuments. Centred on the Mediterranean, the Roman Empire traded, conquered and merged with a plethora of other societies, leaving legacies in culture and in stone.

I was never actually that interested in Ancient Rome when I was younger. It was too mainstream for me. But then came my university years and my friend, Rosemary Morel, introduced me to Marcus Didius Falco, and my love of Rome began. Author Lindsey Davis—I owe you so much for bringing this world alive to me, which made me unafraid to tackle Colleen McCullough's *First Man in Rome* series.

Domitian's assassination was something of a no-brainer for me as a turning point in history. Dramatic event, conspiracy theories, not to mention… it was only twenty-odd years after Masada so it was too good an opportunity to miss, since it let me bring my beloved Gaius and Adi back into Gwyn's life.

Beyond that, I made Gwyn work for this turning point. She's grown a lot since the first book, and I hope that shows as she takes risks and perseveres to make history turn true, even as she stumbles and makes mistakes.

Michelle, on the other hand, is slowly softening. The capable, fearless fighter has depth that I'm endeavouring to draw out as the story goes on. She doesn't like to open up, however, so I look forward to working on her in books four and five to see what we might learn.

ABOUT THE AUTHOR

Jodie Lane is an avid amateur historian, combining her love of travel and adventure with fascinating stories from the past. Brisbane based, she studied a variety of modern history at the University of Queensland, and loves to read a wide range of historical and science fiction.

Her travels have taken her all over the world: she has lived and taught English in China and Romania, backpacked through Europe and South America, and holidayed in the Middle East, Central and North America, South East Asia, New Zealand and South Africa. She speaks basic Spanish as a second language and her sport of choice is wing chun (kung fu).

To Kill An Emperor is the third book in "Turning Points"—a time travel adventures series visiting pivotal historical events and exploring an exciting new future for humanity. You can find out more via www.jodielane.com.

BIBLIOGRAPHY

Boyle, A.J. and Dominik, W.J. Flavian Rome: culture, image, text. Boston: Brill. 2003.

Earinus the Eunuch: Martial (from Book 9) and Statius (Silvae 3.4). http://www.stoa.org/diotima/anthology/earinus.shtml. Translation and notes copyright © 2002 John T. Quinn.

Jones, Brian W. Domitian and the Senatorial Order: a prosopographical study of Domitian's relationship with the senate, A.D. 81-96. Philadelphia: The American Philosophical Society. 1979.

Jones, Brian W. The Emperor Domitian. London: Routledge. 1992.

Jones, Brian and Milns, Robert. Suetonius: The Flavian Emperors. A Historical Commentary with Translation and Introduction. London: Bristol Classical Press. 2002.

Muzzy, Walter. Domitian's Assassination. http://www.jeffbondono.com/TouristInRome/WaltersTours/DomitiansAssassination.html. 2005.

Roman Clothing: Women. http://www.vroma.org/~bmcmanus/clothing2.html.

Southern, Pat. Domitian: tragic tyrant. London: Routledge. 1997.

The Magic of the Andes: Climbing Through the Clouds in South America. http://mikes.railhistory.railfan.net/r022.html.

Viscusi, Peter L. Studies on Domitian. Michigan: University Microfilms International. 1982.